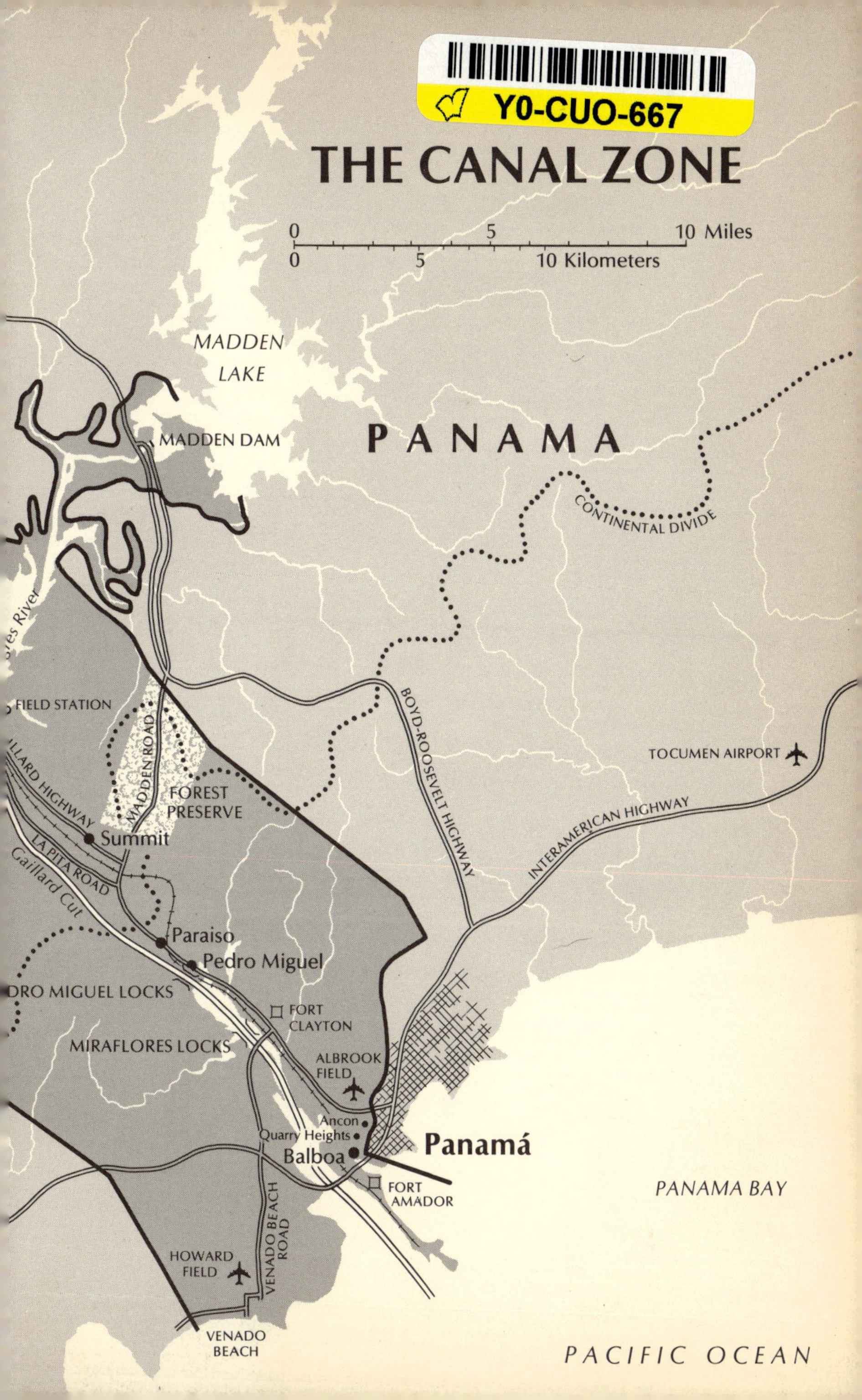
THE CANAL ZONE
0 5 10 Miles
0 5 10 Kilometers
MADDEN LAKE
MADDEN DAM
PANAMA
CONTINENTAL DIVIDE
FIELD STATION
MADDEN ROAD
FOREST PRESERVE
BOYD-ROOSEVELT HIGHWAY
TOCUMEN AIRPORT
INTERAMERICAN HIGHWAY
Summit
LA PITA ROAD
Gaillard Cut
Paraiso
Pedro Miguel
MIRAFLORES LOCKS
FORT CLAYTON
ALBROOK FIELD
Ancon
Quarry Heights
Balboa
Panamá
FORT AMADOR
PANAMA BAY
VENADO BEACH ROAD
HOWARD FIELD
VENADO BEACH
PACIFIC OCEAN

THE PANAMA PARADOX

A JOAN KAHN BOOK

Books by Michael Wolfe

THE PANAMA PARADOX
THE CHINESE FIRE DRILL
THE TWO-STAR PIGEON
MAN ON A STRING

THE PANAMA PARADOX

Michael Wolfe

Harper & Row, Publishers
New York, Hagerstown, San Francisco
London

A HARPER NOVEL OF SUSPENSE

For information address Harper & Row, Publishers, Inc., 10 East 53rd Street, New York, N.Y. 10022. Published simultaneously in Canada by Fitzhenry & Whiteside Limited, Toronto.

FIRST EDITION

Designed by Sidney Feinberg

Library of Congress Cataloging in Publication Data

Wolfe, Michael.
The Panama paradox.
I. Title.
PZ4.W85625Pan3 (PS3573.0525) 813'.5'4 77-3808
ISBN 0-06-014717-2

77 78 79 80 10 9 8 7 6 5 4 3 2 1

For J. K.
who took a chance

Author's Note

The Panama Paradox is a work of fiction. The characters and situations come from the author's imagination. On the other hand, there is a Panama Canal, a Canal Zone and a Republic of Panama, and the situation in which the United States is currently involved there is fact. So far the nations concerned have behaved with admirable restraint. This does not bar the very real possibility that an extremist group, as in many other troubled areas, could not enter the picture at any time. *The Panama Paradox* depicts one form such intervention might take.

The author wishes to thank Captain Alvin Gallin, U.S.N., ret., Captain William T. Lyons, Sergeant First Class David Laracuente, U.S.A., ret., all of the Panama Canal Company, and many others who rendered valuable advice and assistance.

All locales and institutions depicted are real with the exception of the Columbian Institution and its field station.

M. W.

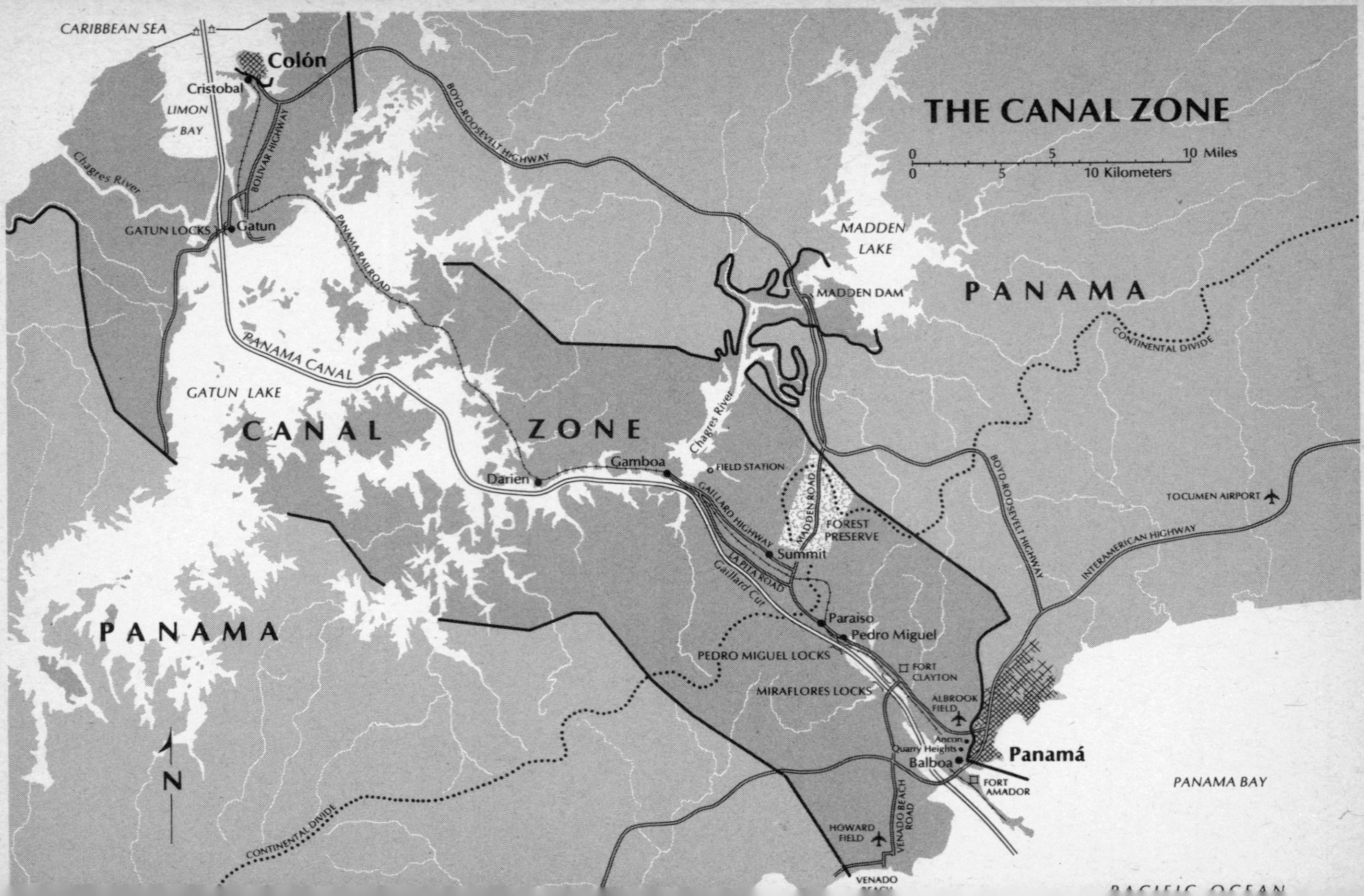
THE CANAL ZONE
0 5 10 Miles
0 5 10 Kilometers
CARIBBEAN SEA
Colón
Cristobal
LIMON BAY
Chagres River
BOLIVAR HIGHWAY
BOYD-ROOSEVELT HIGHWAY
GATUN LOCKS
Gatun
PANAMA RAILROAD
PANAMA CANAL
GATUN LAKE
CANAL ZONE
MADDEN LAKE
MADDEN DAM
PANAMA
CONTINENTAL DIVIDE
Chagres River
FIELD STATION
Gamboa
Darien
GAILLARD HIGHWAY
MADDEN ROAD
FOREST PRESERVE
Summit
LA PITA ROAD
Gaillard Cut
Paraiso
Pedro Miguel
PEDRO MIGUEL LOCKS
FORT CLAYTON
MIRAFLORES LOCKS
ALBROOK FIELD
Ancon
Quarry Heights
Balboa
Panamá
FORT AMADOR
VENADO BEACH ROAD
HOWARD FIELD
VENADO
TOCUMEN AIRPORT
INTERAMERICAN HIGHWAY
PANAMA BAY
PANAMA
N

• • •

1

We knew it was morning because the meal that was wheeled in was scrambled eggs, sausage and a covered platter of French toast. I went over and poured myself a glass of canned orange juice, then stepped away to drink it while the others gathered around to help themselves. No one seemed to have much more appetite than I had, looking on the meal more for its value as a break in the routine than for any real nourishment it might provide. The food itself didn't do much to attract you to it. It was warm enough, but it must have come quite a way for the eggs to have acquired that gelatinous look and the French toast to have reached such an advanced state of sogginess. The steward who had brought it in took a last look to make sure that nothing had vanished during his trip and then, without a word, turned and knocked on the door. It was opened from the outside by someone unseen and the man left us. If he followed his regular routine, he would be back in exactly thirty minutes to wheel the cart away, and again he would do it without a word.

While I drank the juice I watched the others get plates and begin to help themselves. From the way each one did it you could tell a lot.

Doc Nagy, a small, plump, balding man, was making his regular sandwich—two slices of buttered toast larded with scrambled eggs. He'd eat that first and then come back for more toast and some jelly to have with his second cup of coffee. After he'd finished, we could expect him to go to the washroom and shave before he'd be ready to get down to anything serious.

Behind Nagy came Captain Murfree, the Navy's contribution to our group. He'd already done his calisthenics, showered and shaved, and dressed in a fresh white uniform shirt and slacks. There was a marked odor of some expensive kind of after-shave lotion that mixed with the smell of sausage and coffee. He chose the French toast and one sausage to take back to his place.

It wasn't until the captain stepped away that Master Sergeant Ralph Hutto began to load his plate. He had the sausage, a full portion of eggs and two slices of toast, all neatly arranged on his platter so that no item actually made contact with any other. Someone had once taught Sergeant Hutto that neatness counts and he'd learned his lesson well.

Sidney Fox held himself to an orange, which he peeled and chewed up stolidly.

I served myself next, taking the minimum amount of everything. I already knew precisely how everything would taste, but as I said, it might help pass the time. I carried my plate and cup to my place and watched to see what the last member of the group might do.

Herbert Klingman was still sitting with his back to the wall, his long legs crossed and bearing the weight of a heavy book. The frequency with which Herbert turned its pages might have led one to believe that he was merely looking at the illustrations, but I already knew that he was getting every word, weighing and assessing it and filing in his memory such facts as he deemed worthy of attention. When he did get up and come to the cart, it was only to make himself a jelly sandwich and take a glass of milk before returning to his reading.

I poked around with my fork and tried to eat, but the idea of actually picking anything up to put in my mouth was too much to consider. There was nothing wrong with the food on the plate. It was as good as what I've eaten in military messes for a good part of my adult life and better than lots, but either the surroundings or the lack of exercise or the company took away what little appetite I usually have in the morning. I even tried to think of all the times when I've been ravenously hungry; that didn't work either. Finally I finished my coffee and returned the china to the food cart. I helped myself to an apple just in case I might want something later, and took it back to my place.

The thin lieutenant colonel at the end of the room watched me sourly, his look giving a precise reading on his opinion of me and of the whole deal; he kept his peace, though, sitting almost motionless with his hands on his desk as he did each time he came on duty. Even the knowledge that the arrival of our breakfast signaled the imminent end of his tour didn't seem to do a thing for his disposition. Every time I looked at him I felt like an old lady in Salem facing a well-known witch-burner.

By the time the cart was picked up we had all finished. Captain Murfree had fired up his pipe and settled back to read. Sergeant Hutto was in a deep study of an elaborate diagram he had drawn the day before and Nagy and Herbert were playing chess. There was no board and no chessmen—both had been forbidden—but the two of them managed to play on a scrap of paper, listing the moves as they passed it back and forth. Most of the time it was in Nagy's possession; he bent over it, his lips moving as he muttered to himself. When he'd make a move and return the paper to his opponent, it took Herbert only a quick look and a moment to note his move and pass the game back.

There was no longer a clock in the room and all our watches had been confiscated, but there was no doubt about the arrival of eight o'clock. The door swung open and our new watchdog, his round face beaming, came in to begin his shift. The witch-burner yielded his place at the desk, shaking his head in response to the new man's question. Then, without a backward glance, he went to the door and sixteen hours' freedom from his duty.

The new guardian was a major, a short, stubby General Staff type and the least objectionable of our three warders. We'd named him Dumbo among ourselves, and I have to admit that he had earned it with his all too obvious eagerness to be loved. He settled himself at the desk and used a minute or two to reorganize it to his own system. He laid out a fresh foolscap tablet, a battery of ballpoint and felt-tip pens in a tasteful selection of colors and an assortment of Life Savers, which would be gone by the time his relief arrived. Finally, when everything had been arranged to his satisfaction, he beamed around at us and proceeded to the first order of business. He called the roll.

That's right. There were only the six of us and that's all there ever had been since we were first locked up together. None of us was allowed out of the place and we weren't permitted any visitors, but Dumbo still called the roll. He'd done it the day we'd arrived and then, because it was part of his routine, he did it again each time he came on duty. Mixed as our bunch was, he'd had some trouble in organizing it by rank, but finally he'd decided to do it alphabetically. It was as close as Dumbo could get to a regular reveille formation and it did serve to start off the day's work, assuming that there was to be any work.

Dumbo cleared his throat and began the ceremony.

"Dr. Sidney Fox?"

Fox grunted and then, as he had every morning at that moment, headed for the washroom, where he would remain until the next event on our daily schedule. If his diet was working, I hadn't been able to detect it. Dr. Fox was the walking embodiment of the word "professorial," complete with paunch, graying hair, rimless glasses and an impressive set of jowls.

"Master Sergeant Ralph M. Hutto?"

"Here, sir."

Sergeant Hutto was in Class A uniform, the creases knife-sharp, the brass gleaming like old gold. His three rows of ribbons were surmounted by the silver insigne of the EOD, Explosive Ordnance Disposal, the Army's version of the bomb squad. Despite the rows of service ribbons, Hutto had been uneasy at first, trying to sort out just where he belonged in the pecking order of the group. He was a quiet man at best and while he settled in like any good soldier on a bum detail, he was clearly anxious to attract as little notice as possible and sweat out the job in almost complete silence. He spoke when spoken to and left it at that.

"Captain Michael Keefe?"

That's me. U.S. Army Signal Corps. Military Occupational Specialty, Motion Picture Production Specialist. Present assignment, Defense Photo Operations Executive—DPOE. That's what you get if you ask the question and aren't entitled to know any more. If you are, you'll find I have "additional duties and assignments," and maybe you'll learn a little more.

"Mr. Herbert Klingman?"

Herbert was sitting with his eyes closed, doing his breathing. He raised his left hand in response and kept right on inhaling and exhaling with a measured cadence. The exact purpose of this ritual had never been explained, but if the idea was to build himself up, it wasn't working. For all his five ten, I don't think the kid weighed an ounce over a hundred and twenty. In motion he looked like a badly assembled marionette, all arms and legs that seemed to be operating each on its own without any central control. He'd had little to say, and so far that hadn't been much help to the rest of us.

"Captain Patterson Murfree, U.S. Navy?"

"Present."

Murfree was the ranking man in the crowd, but he was locked in just the same. Navy captain is the same as Army colonel and every so often that makes for some confusion on an interservice operation, but you didn't need to be told that Murfree was a hell of a lot senior to me. Above the four wide stripes on his shoulder boards he had one of those mishmashes of gold leaves and acorns that the Navy uses to distinguish a specialist like a dentist or a supply officer from the regular line officer. They all look alike to me, but they seem to mean something to the Navy. Murfree, to my eye, appeared pretty young for his rank considering that Navy promotion is supposed to be a lot slower than ours. He was big enough to play fullback on anybody's team and that was what he'd been doing that day in Philadelphia when a cadet tackle had broken his nose as he crossed Army's goal line.

"Dr. Stanley Nagy?"

Nagy didn't bother to look up either. He just nodded at the sound of his own name and went right on studying the material in front of him. He was really concentrating, his chin thrust into his palm while the fingers tugged at his bluish cheeks. His eyebrows were drawn together, accentuating the sweep up to the top of his bald head. I already knew that Nagy was a Nobel laureate for the work he was doing on animal behavior at the Columbian Institution. He must have been pretty young when his family had made it out of Hungary, but there were still traces of accent in his speech and a kind of inverted word order in his sentences. Of the group, he was taking the confinement worst, prodding the rest of us to get to work in hopes that we might all return to the outside world a little sooner.

Once Dumbo had called the roll, he moved to the next item on his agenda. He circled the room, picking up stray crumpled pieces of paper that we'd thrown away in disgust, straightening the maps and charts on the walls, returning books to their proper places on the shelves. He checked over the coffee maker and the stock of tea bags that had been supplied for Sidney Fox. Later the steward assigned to us would wheel the whole thing out to be cleaned and refilled before it was returned to its place by the washroom door.

All this fidgeting took only a few minutes, but Dumbo made the most of it. I'd hate like hell to be in any outfit where Dumbo pulls an inspection. Though he may not have been as warlike as your average working Army officer, he had an eye like an eagle for dust or lint. Finally even he was satisfied and he marched back to his desk and took his seat facing us, ready for whatever might happen next.

Probably he looked like a schoolmaster presiding over a very peculiar class. His desk was set at the exact mathematical center of the long wall facing the line of six identical desks assigned to us. Behind each was a standard Army cot, a small chest of drawers, a straight chair and a clothes tree. A laundry bag was hung in regulation manner from the foot of each cot, waiting for the time when it would be passed out the locked door, its contents to be washed and returned.

The worst thing about the place was the quiet. No sound penetrated the walls or the heavy outer door and only the small noises we made ourselves broke the utter stillness. The thick carpeting and the drapes muffled those even further; the effect must have been the reason we all spoke in lowered voices, even in anger.

For the next few minutes only the scratching of pencils and the rustling of papers were heard. If I'd had even a stupid idea I'd have brought it up just to get something started, but nothing came. Dumbo sat, his hand ready to switch on the tape recorder, and we sat. Nothing.

We were still hard at doing nothing when our regular daily caller arrived. Now, if there was any real justice, that visitor and I would have been thousands of miles away, beyond the reach of official telephone calls, enjoying a long, lovely month of total privacy, white sand, green water, moonlit nights, gourmet food, tropical drinks and all that goes with them. We'd searched long and hard through stacks of travel brochures to find the one absolutely perfect place to spend our first long leave together. Before you get the wrong idea, I'd better say that the visitor was my boss, Margaret Eriksen, Lieutenant Colonel, U.S. Army. To those who know her well enough she's "Tiny."

Of course, tiny she's not. Just under six foot in her uniform heels plus a bit more for the mass of rich auburn hair she piles on top of her head, she tends to kind of stand out in a crowd. When you meet her you've got to remember that there are three items about Tiny that are classified Top Secret: first, her age; second, her weight; and finally, the exact nature of her duties. The first two are her own personal policy and the last is by Army Regulation. The answer generally given to those who ask without a "need to know" is that Tiny is in charge of WAC recruiting in the Aleutian Islands. For all I know she may be, but it leaves her plenty of time for other duties, mostly relating to the security of the Army itself.

Tiny is a dish, a big one but with everything up to specification and shown to the best advantage, like her skin, which needs only a touch of makeup, and that spectacular superstructure. As if that weren't enough, she's whip smart and a bear for work. If they ever go for a female Army Chief of Staff, Tiny is a shoo-in for the job. Had it not been for her passion for doing her duty, we never would have been there at all. We'd have been off on our own, sampling a variety of sports, outdoor and indoor, and doing our best to forget the rest of the world, instead of sitting in the heart of that goddamned mountain.

She came into the room and perched herself on the edge of Dumbo's desk. She wasn't in uniform for the occasion. Instead she wore a soft gray wool suit that she'd told me was a real Chanel; she'd bought it when she made captain. It had cost over a month's pay but she figured to be wearing it even after she'd done her thirty years and retired. She fished a crumpled pack of cigarettes and her lighter out of a jacket pocket and lit up, giving the six of us a good look at those long, slim legs. Finally she blew out a cloud of smoke and looked around.

"Well, gentlemen, what have you got to report?"

I knew I didn't have anything to say and I didn't have much hope that there would be anything forthcoming from the others. Tiny looked at each man in turn without drawing any response until she got to Stanley Nagy.

"You have something, Dr. Nagy?"

He nodded. "Yes; something that is guaranteed to do the job. All you need is a shipload of Jell-O. When you reach the right spot you simply open the seacocks and let the water into the ship. The ship sinks, the Jell-O dissolves and flows out, and then it sets. Nothing will be able to move until the Jell-O is all eaten up—with, or without, whipped cream."

Deadpan, Tiny looked directly at him. "Sorry, Doctor. You're going to have to do a lot better if you really want to blockade the Panama Canal."

2

Some people in service spend their leave days a couple at a time. They use a day or two now and then, hooking them onto other days off to make a three- or four-day weekend. Some try to save up enough to take a couple of weeks off twice a year, usually winter and summer. Ever since I went on the payroll I've tried to save it up in big chunks, a month or more, and then I can really get away from the routine long enough to forget what it is I do for a living.

Regulations say that unless you're doing something so important that it would hurt your job, you've got to be given your leave when you ask for it. Tiny and I had picked the date months before. She had plenty saved up that she was going to lose anyway and we planned to be gone for a month or more. We put in our requests and the Headshed approved them. The tickets were bought, the bungalow reserved and the deposit receipted, the boat was ready, the maid engaged and, as far as I was concerned, all systems were go.

Where were we going?

None of your damn business. Someday we're finally going to take that trip and maybe we'll tell after we get back. Let's just say that it involved the purchase of two complete outfits for scuba diving, deep-sea fishing, golf, tennis and some more intimate equipment, all in all a couple of thousand bucks' worth of good, clean recreation for a boy and a girl.

I'd been on a routine job in Korea. Our cover was our regular one—a film team covering maneuvers—but the real object of the exercise was to check out a cathouse up near the DMZ that was a shade too anxious to attract a GI clientele. It didn't take long to establish that the cathouse was just a cathouse, with a well-developed system of promoting brand loyalty by means of some extra goodies served up to their parishioners. It was the kind of undercover job some people like, but all I wanted to do was get back to Hawaii in time to start our leave.

We signed in at the DPOE detachment and I shagged on over to see how Tiny was getting along with our preparations. I went up the stairs on cloud nine and turned in at her office, then almost hit the floor when I saw that the cloud had been yanked out from under me. Tiny didn't have to say a word. She stopped clearing out her files just long enough to toss me a teletype carbon stamped "Immediate Action."

The first line canceled my leave, the second canceled hers. By the time I got to the third line I already knew what it was going to say. We were "relieved of assignment and directed to proceed without delay via first available civilian air transportation" to so-and-so and such-and-such—that was, to our own headquarters, stateside, from which we would be reassigned. The ominous thing was that piece about the transportation. The Army is always on the lookout to save a buck on things like travel. Usually you wait for space on a military flight or for a vacant seat that the airline will sell the Army at a big discount. Our orders meant that the Transportation Officer was going to have to pay full price to get us back. Somebody wanted us real bad.

There was only one bright spot in the picture. Sam Wynn, chief cameraman, and John Potter, the still photographer on my team, were on the same order. I had Tiny to thank for that much. We'd all travel together and that seemed to mean that we'd be moving right out for some kind of operation.

We just barely made our flight. Once we boarded and took off, I expected Tiny to let me in on what the hell it was all about, but all she did was glower and stare out the window. She placed a call or two from San Francisco while I tried to find something for the cold I was catching and then we were on our way again. We got some breakfast over Kentucky and landed at Dulles before lunch. I felt like hell and all I could think about was hitting the sack at The Farms until my fever went down. It wasn't until we'd claimed our baggage that I discovered I wasn't even going to get to do that.

There were two cars waiting with drivers, one to take Sam and Potter out to The Farms while the other took us elsewhere. Tiny still wasn't doing much except curl her lip each time I sneezed or sniffled. She never did give me a look at the Top Secret annex to the orders and it wasn't until we reached the first outpost that I suddenly realized that we were headed for The Rock.

We got out of the sedan and went into the guard's kiosk. Tiny had to show our orders and our IDs before we could even get a call into the place. Everyone was very pleasant, but it was clear that we weren't going to go a step closer until the MPs were sure we were clear to proceed.

The place has an official name, of course, but everyone I've ever heard speak of it has simply called it The Rock, and saved the extra breath. Without going into a lot of detail, most of which is classified anyway, let's just say that The Rock is about the safest place you can be in the event of a full nuclear attack. When the missiles take off from wherever they live and head for Washington, the early warning system is supposed to give the top level of government enough time to get to The Rock, crawl inside the mountain and slam the doors behind them. There's room enough for the White House, the top cabinet officers and the upper echelons of the Pentagon to take refuge while the rest of us stay out in the fresh air and enjoy the radiation.

Inside they'll have plenty of stored food to eat, stored water to drink and even stored air to breathe. There's enough to hold out for quite a while, until they have to come out and take their chances with whoever is left. I asked Tiny what would happen to them when they ran out of air. Her answer wasn't the kind of thing you like to think about.

"If they have to stay long enough to use up their air, then there won't be anything to come out to anyway."

It makes you think.

Even with our orders, we didn't just get to waltz in and report. It was way past two before we were admitted through the last barrier and were actually inside. Now, I've got a thing about being in closed-in places. I wouldn't go so far as to call it claustrophobia, but there's still a real queasy feeling I get when I can't see a clear way out to fresh air. With any luck we wouldn't have to stay long, because I was sure that the longer I had to be there, the more I was going to want out.

We were met as we came through the doors by the major we were going to know better as Dumbo. Tiny was familiar with the place and she took off in one direction while I tagged along behind Dumbo. He was as proud of The Rock as if he'd designed and built it himself. As we made our way through a series of corridors, he gave me the full guided tour, acting for all the world like a chamber of commerce man showing the town to the visiting head of a big corporation. We went past doors marked for the lucky officials and officers who would occupy them when and if they were needed. Most of the people we passed, men and women, were in the uniform of one service or another and they all appeared relaxed and happy in their work. It looked like any other high headquarters I'd ever seen, with just one exception. Nowhere did I see any of the familiar "Restricted Area" notices. When I asked Dumbo if there were places I was supposed to stay out of, he shook his head.

"There's no place like that here. If you've gotten this far you have to be cleared for everything. It's up to you to keep your nose out of what doesn't concern you."

I kept looking for my old familiar closed-in feeling to start working on my stomach, but nothing happened. Instead I began to think about the lunch I'd missed and how hungry I was. I didn't know what was going to be next on the agenda and it seemed like a good time to get something to tide me over. I put it to Dumbo and he changed course and steered me to a small snack bar.

While I ate my sandwich and took a pill, he had a Coke and I got a little chance to look around. Whoever had designed the whole establishment must have been a student of psychology as well as engineering. In spite of the fact that we were deep in the heart of a mountain, there was an open, almost airy feeling. In the snack bar, for instance, one wall had a wide rectangular opening with a kind of window box filled with artificial greenery, and the blank wall beyond had been painted a light blue that contrasted with the bright colors of the rest of the place and fooled you into thinking it was the sky. There was plenty of room to move around easily, the tables spaced well apart to provide lots of elbow room. By the time I finished eating I'd almost forgotten where I was and was giving all my attention to Dumbo.

We left the snack bar and went down a level to a corridor whose widely spaced doors showed that the offices there were the jumbo, executive size. For the first time I saw one with a seated MP guard outside and that's where Dumbo stopped. The guard checked our IDs against a list and then unlocked the door. If I'd known what I was getting into, I'd never have walked in.

It had taken a little while to find out. By that time all six of us had arrived and each one was looking the others over and wondering what could bring together an animal behaviorist, a geophysicist, a naval architect, a philosopher, a demolitions expert and a military cameraman. Each man had taken the space assigned to him, desk, cot and the works. Sidney Fox tested the softness of his cot, Hutto unpacked his suitcase and then tightened up the blanket on his cot. He didn't toss a half dollar on it to test the tension, but I knew it would pass if he did. Herbert stretched himself out on his cot and closed his eyes. Nagy discovered the bookcase and began to look over some of the titles. Captain Murfree hung his uniform cap on his clothes tree and then sat at his desk, probably waiting for a steward to unpack his bag. I went to the washroom and brushed my teeth. Then I returned to my desk and sat down. If there was a way in the world to get myself off the detail, I'd be out of there before I was in too deep to pull out. Maybe Tiny wanted to get into this fandango, but that was up to her. I wanted out. I sat for a minute thinking up all the good reasons I could cite in support of my position, and then the door opened and I heard Tiny's voice ordering us to attention. The three of us in uniform snapped to and the civilians stood up as a little procession came into the room.

The first one in had a row of four stars on each collar and a couple of quarts of fruit salad on his chest. Right behind came Tiny, followed by Dumbo and a pair of light colonels. The bossman, taking the seat behind the desk that faced ours, put us at ease and gave the word to sit or smoke. Tiny placed a file in front of him and he took only a few seconds to look at the top sheet before he turned his attention back to us.

"Good afternoon, gentlemen, and welcome to The Rock. First, let me tell those of you in the military that this is not a voluntary operation. You are here under orders and no request for relief from this assignment will be received. The other gentlemen have been retained as special consultants to the operation by agreement with their superiors. I am told that you all know something of the manner in which this exercise will be conducted and have agreed to serve as long as you might be required. The name of this operation is Paradox. Its purpose, to develop, as rapidly as possible, a plan to blockade the Panama Canal."

Now, that's the kind of statement that doesn't have to be made in a loud voice to get your full attention. In fact, when you hear something like that you look around for people in white coats closing in on the man who makes it. I guess it was easy enough to get that idea from the expression on my face and probably the others', because for the first time the general permitted himself a tiny smile.

"Okay, it sounds crazy. Why would the United States want to stop the free flow of traffic through the world's most important waterway? Well, of course we don't. But"—and he paused to let his next statement sink in—"there are people who do. We have had clear-cut proof that there is a group with the means and the motive for achieving that purpose. Your job is to use your collective talent and training to test the canal defenses by working out ways in which that purpose—to render the canal impassable for a significant length of time—might be achieved. You work them out so that we can then take steps to neutralize your scheme or schemes."

He looked at Murfree, who had twisted slightly in his seat. "You have a comment, Captain?"

"Yes, sir. With all due respect to you, sir, and to the Army, which is supposed to defend the Canal Zone, what you are speaking of is, in the most literal sense, impossible. You cannot merely damage the canal. There is a possibility that, if you could evade the defenses, you might destroy one terminal or the other with a direct nuclear hit, but nothing less would suffice. The nature of the attack, the radioactivity produced, would make the whole area, including the adjacent parts of the Republic of Panama, uninhabitable for years. There would be no way to reenter the Zone for repairs. It would be necessary to build a new canal in another location.

"The present canal took ten years in construction, even with the use of a great deal of work that was done earlier by the French. Time-frame projections were made by the commission that reported recently on the construction of a new, sea-level canal and I'm sure that we're talking in terms of years—five to ten at a minimum—before a new canal could begin to carry traffic."

He settled back in his chair and waited for an answer. He got it right away.

"That's what we have been assured by our own study. There is no *known* way to stop the canal. Your job is to come up with one that has never been thought of before and against which we do not have an adequate defensive posture. I think the first thing we'd better do is to set some parameters. The damage created must be sufficient to halt all traffic for a period of six months to a year. It must be repairable damage so that the present canal complex can be reopened to traffic as soon as the work is completed. It must be accomplished overtly so that it will be impossible to explain away the stoppage by some cover story. We can assume that wide publicity is one of the aims of the project."

Murfree was right back at him. "Then I submit that what you are asking for is an impossibility. From the very first, American planning has given first priority to the security of the canal and the integrity of all its mechanisms. Ever since 1904 those measures have been restudied on a continuing basis, refined and expanded to cover every eventuality that the engineers could possibly conceive. The Panama Canal, sir, is as invulnerable as the mind of man can make it. Anyway," he went on, "who in the world would want to block it? It's not just a national asset of the United States. It's vital to every nation on earth in one way or another."

The general didn't answer him directly. He looked through his file for a moment and then extracted a sheet, which he passed to Tiny. She looked at it for a moment and then spoke.

"This document is Top Secret. I'll skip the first part and get down to the part that interests us here.

" 'At exactly 1200 an explosion was heard from the direction of the mechanism mentioned above and a dense cloud of smoke filled the area. Canal security police responded and were the first on the scene. A team volunteered to enter the area wearing gas masks but withdrew when they found the smoke too dense to proceed more than a few feet inside. When the smoke thinned they entered the site once more and found the device, which, when it had cooled sufficiently to be handled, was examined by our EOD team. It proved to be a smoke generator with a timer and activating mechanism.

" 'The device was, of course, activated without damaging the nearby lock mechanism, but in the opinion of qualified experts, had it been loaded with high explosive, it is likely that the lock in question would have required a shutdown and considerable repairs.

" 'An immediate investigation was launched to determine how the device, a cylinder approximately two feet long and eight inches in diameter, was introduced into the area, emplaced without detection and remained in place until the timer detonated it.

" 'All persons authorized to enter the area in connection with their duties have been screened without result. No evidence has been found to indicate the presence of any unauthorized person at the point in question or elsewhere in the neighborhood of the locks. Analysis of traffic records show no vessel in transit from which an unauthorized person might have effected an entry.

" 'We are forced to concede that the device was introduced by a person or persons unknown in a manner also unknown at the present time. At this time we are reexamining our security measures while still continuing the investigation. A number of theoretical studies are under way, and should they prove out, we will restructure our security with such possibilities in mind.

" 'The enclosed Attachment No. 1 was received by the Canal Zone governor on the morning following the incident and is being studied by our intelligence personnel.' "

Tiny flipped the page and went on reading.

" 'Señor Gobernador:

" 'The demonstration at the canal lock yesterday at noon was not intended as a theatrical entertainment. Its purpose was to convince you and your colleagues that we are capable of doing extensive damage to the canal at times and places of our own choosing, damage that will cause you to close the canal for an extended period. It is our purpose to show the world that your claim that only the United States is capable of adequately defending the canal and its zone, which slashes across our Republic, is false.

" 'If you wish to avoid the consequences of our main attack, you must take immediate steps to evacuate the Canal Zone within ninety days of all but those directly involved in the operation of the canal itself, leaving all other matters to the duly constituted authorities of the Republic of Panama. Unless such steps are begun immediately, we will be forced to provide you with still further demonstrations to convince you of our ability and our resolve.

" 'If you fail to comply, we will be forced to take the final step. Be warned that if we do, no vessel will move through the canal and the United States will be powerless to restore it to service for an indefinite period of months or years.'

"That's it. It was typewritten and the signature is a rubber stamp consisting of an outline map of Panama which does not show the Zone border, as is customary, and the words 'Frente Liberación de Panama.' "

She looked at the paper in her hand and then turned the page.

"This is the crime lab analysis of the letter. Nothing usable in the paper of the letter or envelope. Mailed at the central post office in Panama, the letter enclosed in an inner envelope marked, 'For the Governor Only.' It was typed on a cheap machine made in mainland China and sold widely in Latin America by an agency in Havana.

"I have also a report from our own agency detachment in the field, which has been confirmed by other sources. We have not one scrap of evidence on this Frente Liberación. Its name has never appeared on any roster of extremist groups known to any intelligence-gathering organization. I might add that our net in Panama, because of the sensitivity of the Zone, is one of our more extensive and well established."

She closed the file and replaced it in front of the general. He looked up at Murfree and said, quietly, "So you see, Captain, perhaps the canal isn't quite as invulnerable as you have believed. This FLP crowd has shown pretty clearly that they know what they're doing. So far all they've done is provide us with a sample of their work, but I think even you will have to concede that they're capable of doing what they threaten."

"But why, sir, why? Why would they want to destroy the most valuable thing in their little country? Half of Panama or more lives off the canal, one way or another. Why would they want to kill the golden goose?"

"They don't. They don't even want to ruffle its feathers. Still, they're closer now to their ultimate aims than ever before. In three months there will be a joint meeting of the Organization of American States and representatives of the world's biggest shipping nations. They will call on the United States to submit the Canal Zone situation to them for binding arbitration. As usual we'll advance the claim that we are the only nation which can guarantee the defense of the canal and allow it to remain open to all comers. That's been the keystone of our policy ever since 1903.

"Believe me, gentlemen, if the meeting convenes and the canal has been blocked to traffic, we're not going to have much to brag about. This FLP knows that as well as anyone, hence their timing. They are determined to block the canal. We're determined to keep it open. We've had our orders. The United States will negotiate as far as the national interest is consistent with the rights of others. We will not be blackmailed or intimidated.

"That's why you're in this room. We're taking every possible step on the scene to maintain the security level at maximum effort against known hazards. It's up to this group, with your special mix of talents, to come up with the unknowns, the weak spots the FLP will try to penetrate and exploit. You find them and we'll take what steps we must to protect the waterway. Problem: How do you block an unblockable canal? That's Operation Paradox.

"Colonel Eriksen will brief you and be responsible for keeping me informed of your progress. Her access to me is direct and she will have available the full weight of my authority over all the services for any support you may need."

He got to his feet, waving to us to remain seated, and left. Tiny waited until the door had closed behind him before taking the seat he'd just left.

"Gentlemen, some of you may wish to make some last-minute purchases before we begin. One of these officers will show you to the PX. Please limit yourself to personal needs. No reading matter, games, cards or anything else of that nature will be permitted in this room once you begin work.

"It will take a few minutes to complete our preparations and when you return you will not leave until there is no possible reason left for you to remain."

We filed out after Dumbo while another man brought up the rear. If we weren't prisoners, we were the next thing to it.

• • •

3

We weren't gone more than fifteen minutes, but somebody had been busy as hell while we were out. The drapes that had covered the walls had been drawn back, exposing a long line of maps and aerial photos that even at a distance I could see covered the whole of the Canal Zone and its approaches. There was one six-inch-to-the-mile of the whole width of the isthmus and even bigger-scale charts of the locks and dams and the military installations, each in both plan and cross section. On a long table was a ten-foot-long scale model of the whole Canal Zone, and on another, a working model of the lock mechanisms. To the books already in the room another couple of cases had been added, filled with heavy tomes and paper-bound pamphlets and reports.

On a separate table were piles of paper of all kinds, boxes of pencils and crayons and a small electric calculator. At the ends of the room were easels with blackboards and a pointer for each. The wall clock had vanished.

We milled around a bit, getting ourselves organized while the man I would come to think of as the witch-burner went from one of us to the next, collecting the contraband that might take our minds away from the central problem. Nagy gave up his traveling chess set, Captain Murfree his brace of Western novels. Herbert and Hutto had nothing, but I had to pass over the copy of *Penthouse* I'd bought in Honolulu and hadn't yet opened.

Finally we all got settled at our desks and Tiny called us to order. Operation Paradox was off and running.

"I don't want you to get the idea that we're going to tell you how to work, gentlemen. That's strictly up to you to arrange as you like, but perhaps if I explain why each one of you was chosen it might be useful. There's no special significance to it, but the way it works out, you three civilians were selected because of your high degree of intelligence and your reputations as original and innovative thinkers.

"Dr. Fox is our expert in earth sciences, geophysics, seismology, geodetics and the other disciplines that are involved with large masses of earth and water. I expect that anyone with that kind of background would have some ideas about causing gross damage to the canal.

"Dr. Nagy you've probably heard of for his work in the life sciences, with his Nobel in animal behavior and his talent for conceiving and carrying out all kinds of intricate experimental situations of a kind never before attempted.

"Mr. Klingman is our philosopher."

Out of the corner of my eye I saw Murfree stir in his chair. The idea that a philosopher might be of some use in our situation wasn't one that he shared.

"Just to fill you in on Mr. Klingman a bit more, I should tell you that he completed his B.A. at seventeen, his master's six months later and he'll get his Ph.D. if he ever takes the trouble to go around to pick it up. In addition to his rather astounding I.Q., which is well above the level where it can be determined by present test methods, Mr. Klingman has total recall, a photographic memory and absolute pitch. It was his breakthrough in the field of pure logic that is leading to a new approach in the application of Aristotelian methods." She took a moment to smile. "It was his paper on the paradoxes of Zeno that gave someone the idea for your operational code name."

I turned to look at Klingman to see what his reaction to all this had been, but he was just sitting quietly, his face composed and with nothing on it to show either pride or embarrassment.

"Now, over on the military side we have our devil's advocates. Their background is in the field. Captain Murfree, for example, has just completed a tour in the Canal Zone with duties directly related to the operation and maintenance of the canal. He was also on the sea-level canal inquiry and he knows that terrain as well.

"Sergeant Hutto is our explosives expert. His last tour was on the U.S. team engaged in the clearing of obstacles in the Suez Canal. If you need to blow up a pyramid or an anthill, he's your man.

"Captain Keefe is our expert in covert operations."

Even I was surprised at the sound of my own voice when I blurted out, "I am?"

It didn't bother Tiny, though. She went right on. "I won't bore you with a recital of his exploits except to say that none of them were done by the book."

Well, she was right about that part. She'd spent enough time smoothing feathers I'd ruffled here and there.

"What the panel which selected you gentlemen has in mind is that the first three experts mentioned will most likely be the ones with concepts, while the others do what they can to shoot them down. That doesn't mean you have to use that plan. Work any way you like to get the job done.

"We've tried to assemble here in this room everything you might need to help in your thinking. The maps are the best the Army has been able to find and if you want more detailed coverage it will take the Air Force only a few hours to make aerial surveys and get the data here from Panama. The books and reports were sent over last night from the Library of Congress. The Smithsonian has lent us the scale models from their collection and their data bank is also at your disposal. The Rock has its own computer and it will be manned night and day, with first priority on its use to Operation Paradox.

"Now a little on your living arrangements. Meals will be served at the regular hours unless you decide to change them. The snack bar stays open twenty-four hours a day and you can order from there. The same thing goes for any personal needs you may want brought from the PX. Fresh linen will be issued daily and laundry collected each morning and returned that night. You are authorized to make one five-minute personal phone call each day.

"There is just one thing I must impress on you. You will not leave this room."

Nagy waved his hand to get her attention. "What happens if one of us gets ill?"

"The Rock has a fully staffed hospital equipped for everything including major surgery. As long as the medics say a man is not too sick to function, he will remain."

Dr. Fox boomed out, "I have a seminar I must address next week in Cleveland. I've been preparing for it for almost a year. I can't possibly miss that."

Tiny nodded. "I've already gotten word on that, Doctor. Your dean at the Institute has agreed to appear in your place. He has your paper and will read it for you."

She took a moment to light a cigarette and then stood and paced down the line of desks before she spoke again.

"I realize that we may look pretty formidable with all the resources we've got to call on, but don't let that fool you. Everybody in on Paradox—and that means right out of this place and on up to the top—is scared as all hell. If it was only a matter of defending the canal against an armed invader, the military would know just what to do. The services have plans for that kind of thing to cover any possible contingency, just as they always have. They've got air power, land power and sea power, and not one of them is a bit of use in the situation we're up against now. What we're up against is brainpower, and the top-drawer stuff at that. If we're going to get anywhere, we've got to match their brainpower with ours and hope to God that ours is the better."

She pointed to the place where the general had sat. "That desk will be manned twenty-four hours a day by a field grade officer to help you in any way he can. They have orders to call me the moment it looks like you may have something that might work. Don't worry about my being a woman," she added, "because it doesn't bother me. If one of you gets a brain wave when I've got my hair up on rollers, you'll be in for a sight when I come charging in with them."

She would, too, and I'm the one who can tell you it wouldn't be the first time.

She went to the door, but before she rapped on it to be let out, she turned back and looked at us.

"Everything that we could think of has been done to make this think tank work. If you need expert scientific or engineering advice, we'll get it. If there is a book or document or chart that you think might help, it will be found and delivered. Some of you may think we ought to give the canal to the Panamanians or the UN or the OAS. Maybe you've got a point, but it's not up to me to decide. The law entrusts the safety and the defense of the canal to the Army and that's what it's trying like hell to do."

When the door closed behind her, there wasn't a sound in that room deep inside the mountain.

It had taken a while to really get started. I guess nobody wanted to look stupid after the big build-up Tiny had given each of them. I didn't have any reputation for smarts to lose, so finally I took a deep breath and broke the ice.

"I like simple things. Suppose you just took a ship and got up to full speed and rammed right into the locks? You ought to be able to do a hell of a lot of damage that would take months, maybe, to fix."

Murfree swung around in his seat, shaking his head.

"Sorry, Keefe, but that possibility was one of the first things the designers took steps to protect against. Remember, when the canal was designed the Spanish-American War had just ended. Navies still had battleships and heavy cruisers and each one was built with a giant ram in the bow. Even if a hostile ship could get up to full speed in the approach channel and crash head-on into the first gate, it wouldn't accomplish very much. Just about everything in the canal has been installed in duplicate and that goes for every pair of gates. The average gate leaf weighs over seven hundred tons and is built like a vault door of heavy steel plates over massive steel beams. They're strong enough to take the shock of any vessel that can transit the canal, and that includes icebreakers.

"Just for the sake of argument, let's say you got the biggest icebreaker ever made and you did, somehow, cripple both pairs of gates. What happens then? While the police are hauling you and your crew off to jail, traffic is diverted into the other lane of the canal—the one you didn't damage. It's done every year when first one lane and then the other is closed to overhaul the locks. Your ship is hauled out of the way and the damaged gates are removed and replaced with spares. A few days later it's back to business as usual."

That idea had been shot down neatly, but Murfree wasn't done yet.

"I've been talking about the lower gates, the ones a ship passes at sea level. How about the upper gates? Actually they're a lot more important since they hold back the water up in Gatun Lake, about eighty-five feet above sea level."

Nagy looked up. "That's right. If you crashed through them,

all the water in the lake would drain out. It would probably take months to fix things and fill it up again."

Murfree nodded. "Our people thought of that, too. At the locks at each end of the high level, the entrance to the chambers is protected with a massive steel chain. When a ship approaches and everything is okay, the control house operators lower that chain before they open the gates."

Nagy said, "That chain could be broken, couldn't it?"

"Theoretically I suppose it could. It's made of links three inches thick made to withstand a load of over two hundred and fifty tons. Even if you could generate that kind of thrust, the chain wouldn't break though. The whole thing is mounted on a special hydraulic mechanism designed to yield and slow a ship before a link can break. Even then the ship would still have to have enough speed left to breach the first pair of guard gates."

Sidney Fox held up his hand for attention. "Everything is operated from the control house, correct?"

Murfree nodded. "There's one operator on duty for each lane in service, plus a supervisor and several clerks. Each operator has had many years of training."

"Well, then, you send in a team of men like Keefe here and seize the controls. They open up all the gates and valves and then wreck the place. The water drains out and you couldn't do a thing about it until you'd repaired and replaced everything. That would fit the general's time frame, wouldn't it?"

"Sorry, but that was planned for, too. The mechanism just doesn't work that way. Every step must be done in the correct sequence. For instance, you can't let the water into or out of the locks if the gates are open at either end. If you tried, the handles just wouldn't turn. You'd have to spend years with the system before you even knew how the mechanical and electrical controls work and could rearrange them to do what you suggest in time. The probability factor would be up in the thousands. As a practical matter, the system is tamper-proof."

Since my first venture, I'd sat silently. The only other way I'd thought of to do anything to the canal was to drop a nuclear bomb on it. Not the big H-bomb, but something more modest, like a kitchen-table A-bomb. I didn't bother to ask about it; I'd already answered it myself.

If you tried to deliver it by air, the canal radar would pick you up far enough away to challenge you and then, if you didn't have the right answers, there would still be plenty of time to get the Air Force scrambling and the ground defenses alerted. Maybe you could hide one on a ship, but you'd still make the area radioactive for years. Just for a clincher was the thought that you'd have to get a guy to deliver the thing who didn't mind losing his life along with the rest of his crew.

While I was working all this out, Nagy had popped out of his chair and gone over to study the big scale model of the Canal Zone. Suddenly his finger stabbed at a point on the isthmus.

"Right here," he said, "the Gaillard Cut, is the narrowest part of the canal, where they had to dig through the mountains. Correct?"

"Yes. Minimum width through there is five hundred feet."

"And many modern ships are much longer than that?"

"Most of them are. The canal locks will hold ships up to almost one thousand feet."

"Then it should be possible to suddenly swing a big ship across the channel and then blow it up." He went back to his chair to wait for the answer.

Murfree allowed himself a little smile. "Nothing like direct action, eh? A few problems might hold you up a bit. First, every vessel from a twenty-foot sail boat to the biggest thing that fits the locks must have a Panama Canal pilot aboard. The bigger ships need up to four men to make sure they clear the chamber walls. Still, they can be overpowered and the ship could be destroyed. Minimum depth in the Cut is about forty feet, so you would still have a lot of ship above water, enough to be able to move her out of the way. In a few hours traffic would be moving past while you took your time refloating the ship and towing it out to sea. That's what they did a few years ago when a vessel sank in the Cut by accident."

He stood up and walked over to the blackboard at one end of the room. For the next few minutes he gave us a short but concise briefing on the canal. It was just what we needed to clear the air. I'll skip the details and just hit the high spots.

The real heart of the canal is Gatun Lake, made by damming the wild Chagres River, which had defeated de Lesseps and the French builders. He tried to dig all the way down to sea level and that's what licked him. By the time he figured out the mistake, his company was bankrupt and the Americans came into the act. They made an artificial lake eighty-five feet up and then built the locks to get ships up to it from one ocean and back down to the other. From where they saw the future, they built the locks big enough to take any ship that might ever be expected to drive up for a transit, 110 feet wide and a thousand feet long. That was big enough for almost half a century, before aircraft carriers and supertankers got too big to fit. Still, it's big enough for most of the ships afloat today.

They built the biggest earth dam the world had ever seen at Gatun beside the three-level locks there and created the biggest man-made lake seen up to that time. That was on the Atlantic side.

Over on the Pacific side they built a smaller dam and another lake at Miraflores, with two steps up to it at the locks there and another step up a mile away at Pedro Miguel. All they had to do then was connect the two lakes and let the traffic roll. Doesn't sound like much.

Standing in the way was the local stretch of the Continental Divide, the great spine of the Americas that stretches from the Rockies in Alaska and Canada to the Andes at the tip of Tierra del Fuego. The place they picked was only 330 feet above the

Pacific, but the terrain was the worst possible for digging. Time and again the earth shuddered and filled the Cut with slides, and it hasn't stopped yet. It costs millions every year to keep the dirt where it belongs. That's one reason why the average toll is more than ten thousand dollars per trip.

Uncle Sam pays to defend the canal. It's up to the Army and they've used some of the biggest guns ever cast, missiles and nowadays some fancier items.

One thing was pretty apparent, and I thought enough of the idea to speak up.

"Look, Captain, you say the canal is really the lake. The locks and all that are just to get ships up and down. Ships can cross the isthmus because we made the lake. To me that means that the best way to wreck the canal is to unmake the lake."

"Okay, let's see how you'd do that." He crossed to the scale model. "Probably the best place to try would be here at Gatun. It's simple enough, but big as it is, it would probably take the longest to repair.

"The heart of the dam is a kind of clay called hydraulic fill. It's impervious to water and compacts and sets as hard as cement. The facing is rock blasted out during the excavation of the Cut. Right here in the middle is the spillway and powerhouse. That's a regular concrete dam just like any other—reinforced concrete that you wouldn't want to tackle unless you had a year or more to work.

"Let's try for someplace easier to get at. After all, the dam is a mile and a half long and you should be able to find a nice spot. Of course, there are a few things you ought to know. It took over twenty-two million cubic yards of material to make the dam. At the base it's over half a mile thick and it tapers up to four hundred feet at the water line, and rises another twenty feet above there.

"I'm not a high-explosives expert, but we've got one of the best right here. What do you think, Sergeant Hutto? For the moment forget about the number of men you'd need and the time it would take. Just give us an idea of how much explosive it would take to make a nice hole for Captain Keefe."

Hutto, who hadn't said a word so far, got up and went to the model. He didn't slough it off with a glance and a fast answer. He really gave the thing a careful inspection before he was ready to commit himself.

"If you want an accurate estimate, sir, I'll need the slide rule and that calculator."

"Just give us a ball park figure. Something we can think about."

Hutto nodded. "Sir, there's not enough dynamite in the whole military inventory to make more than a dent in that thing. Just drilling and emplacing the charges would take months, with every man you could find the room for to work."

He turned and marched back to his seat, ready to be called on again when his expertise might be needed.

Murfree finally nailed the argument down hard. "There are other major dams, of course. There's Madden, up here, which impounds water during the rains and releases it as needed to maintain the level of Gatun Lake. That one's reinforced concrete, too, floodlit at night and under guard at all times. The smaller dams, Pedro Miguel and Miraflores, are right beside the locks, out in the open."

He was about to go back to his desk when Sidney Fox broke in.

"You said powerhouse a minute or so ago. Now, all the lock machinery is electric, isn't it? If you cut off the flow from the powerhouse to the locks and did a complete enough job, you'd force them to shut down until the repairs could be made."

"No, Doctor. It might take a few seconds but not much more. The power net would be reversed and the service resumed at once. If the supply was not sufficient, there are power barges available, old liberty ships fitted with power generators, which can be hooked into the net on connections ready for the purpose."

He had an answer for everything, but I knew that somewhere there had to be a weak spot and as far as I could see it must have something to do with water. After all, the whole thing worked only because man had put water where nature hadn't intended it to be. I know just enough physics to realize that in a setup like that water wants to go back where it belongs, and if you can give it a nudge at just the right place to help it along, you should, logically, get it moving. All the dams had been built with more than enough strength to hold it back, but there was a place where the water might drain away.

I held up my hand to get Murfree's attention and put it to him.

"You say that the lakes are the heart of the whole canal. As long as the water is held back the canal's okay. Still, there's one place where the water has to be free to move out. That's at the locks. If you can somehow or other get all those gates open, the water will just go roaring out to sea and the canal will shut down until you can get them closed. By that time a good deal of the water in the lake will be drained away and everything will stop until you can get the thing filled up again. For a guess, that would take months. That much time would meet the parameter that the general set."

Murfree waited for me to finish, standing there like a tennis player waiting to return a soft lob he knows he can't miss.

"You're getting better with your ideas, but that one was also planned for. Just on the outside chance that such a thing might happen, a case where all the gates in a lock or string of locks might be opened by accident or intent, each set is equipped with a movable dam, a big steel affair that can be set to hold back the lake. Each is electrically powered and takes only a few minutes to move into place. The engineers can get right at the trouble, repair it, and then the dam is moved out of the way and you're back in business."

"Okay, but that still means you've got to have electricity. If you could cut the power at the same time you'd be losing water until you could hook up again, right?"

"Wrong. The dam can be put in place by mechanical operation. It just takes a little longer."

He shot me down nicely, not as if he was getting any pleasure out of it, but cleanly, like a surgeon. Each time he did it I became more and more convinced that he was right. There was no way worth thinking about that even a well-organized group could put the whole canal out of service. I was just about to say so when Tiny came in.

Even before she opened her mouth I knew she had bad news.

"We've just had a call from the Zone governor. Early this morning the railroad bridge at Gamboa was attacked. It was another smoke device—a lot of noise but no real damage to the bridge. They'll need some time before we can get a complete report, but they did say that if high explosive had been used the bridge would have gone. No one was hurt or even shaken up, though it was a near thing. A train bound for Colón had crossed just a minute before. If it had been on the bridge when the device detonated, they would have been pretty well knocked about."

She looked around to see what effect her statement had made on the six of us. Sidney Fox was the first to speak.

"I don't know what advantage the FLP would get out of damaging the railroad, though. It doesn't have much to do with the canal."

Murfree got up from his seat and walked quickly across the room to the big survey map of the Canal Zone. He pointed his finger at a place right about the middle of the isthmus.

"That bridge is right there," he said. "That's the closest point that the railroad gets to the channel of the canal. It's only a matter of yards."

He walked slowly back to his place. Despite everything he'd told us about security, the FLP was still in there pitching. They must have been having all kinds of fun getting the Zone authorities half crazy trying to figure out where they'd get hit next.

So far nobody had been hurt and there didn't seem to be any property damage. The question was just how long it would be until they tried something a lot more serious.

• • •

4

When Tiny left there was a long silence, each of us deep in his own thoughts. Finally Sidney Fox hoisted himself up and went to the bookcases. He squatted down and began, methodically, to remove and inspect each book in turn, until he got to a heavy, large-format book in an ornate binding which he brought back to his desk. When he opened it and began turning the pages I saw that it was decorated on the front cover with a color picture of the big cut under construction, and from the style of the book, it had probably been published right around the time the canal was finished. Fox tilted his chin back to peer through the lower part of his bifocals and began to read. Apart from the periodic raising of his arm to turn a page, he barely moved, the book propped on his paunch taking all his attention.

Nagy was the next to get to work. He walked slowly down the length of the big survey, pausing every so often to move closer and retracing his steps to compare the overall chart with the inserts. Even with his fingers massaging and tugging at his cheeks, I could see his lips move as he carried on a silent dialogue with himself.

Captain Murfree was going over the working model of a typical lock mechanism, finally finding one point of special interest. He waved to Hutto and the sergeant went to join him. There was some quiet conversation between them and then Hutto returned to his place and came back with a pocket-size handbook. He flipped through the pages and he and Murfree compared something in the book with the model.

I looked around for Herbert Klingman, the only one left that I might go head-to-head with, but Herbert was back on his cot; as far as I could see, he was fast asleep. Whoever had picked him for the panel hadn't got much out of the choice. So far Herbert had barely said a word.

Whatever Murfree had come up with in his inspection of the working model must not have paid off. I saw him shake his head sadly when Hutto dealt out the card that busted what had probably looked like a real good four-card flush. He was still trying, though, and the two of them moved over to the scale model to explore some other idea. I took the chance to get a better look at the lock model for myself.

It must have been a labor of love for someone employed on the canal, who had put in years of work to make the model as perfect as such a thing can possibly be. There was a printed notice that identified each piece of the mechanism by number and what part it played in the sequence of operation. You pushed a button and somewhere deep inside things began to happen. The chain dropped, the gates closed and locked, the tiny motors and gears visible through glass-covered cutaways in the thick walls, each doing its particular thing.

I was still looking at the model when dinner was rolled in. The steward who brought it didn't say a word, even in response to something that Nagy said to him. He did smile and then went to the door and knocked to be let out. It must be true that thinking takes a lot of energy. I lined up with the rest, helping myself to a portion of everything on the cart to take back to my desk. Last man in line was Herbert. From where I sat I saw him help himself, avoiding the meat and not taking a hell of a lot of the rest.

The way our dining had been arranged, it didn't take long to eat. Without a table we could sit around, there wasn't much chance for talk to waste any of our thinking time. We were all finished by the time the steward was back for the cart. The others had picked up with what they'd been doing before the meal had come and I saw that Herbert had evidently finished his nap.

After he'd cleared the top of his desk, I saw him take off his shoes and use the surface to assume the lotus position, his eyes closed and his head tilted back. Awkward as he was in motion, Herbert had now composed his gawky frame into a graceful and harmonious composition, his deep, regular breathing the only visible sign of movement.

It would be a day or so before I discovered that this was his regular daily routine. He'd sleep for two hours each afternoon before dinner, eat his vegetarian meal, do his yoga bit and then settle down to read or write, working alone, the books his only source of information or inspiration, straight through to the following afternoon.

The meal we'd had was okay, having made the trip without any serious loss of heat, and while I would have liked a quick drink before we ate, or maybe a brandy to settle things, I felt pretty good.

It appeared that the only thing I could do was read, so I went over to look for something useful. Most of the books brought in were either engineering texts or scientific works. There were some pamphlets on the political situation, but I finally picked an old book published just before the canal had been opened, back in 1914, and took it back to my desk.

The author's name didn't ring any bell and when I saw his style of writing I wasn't surprised at that. The guy must have put in enough work on his book to dig a canal of his own. He had facts and data on every tiny facet of his subject and even his dull prose couldn't make the story uninteresting. It had been over sixty years since the canal opened and the work was still an engineering marvel. In a world where ships moved by sail or under coal-fired steam, where horses far outnumbered cars, homes were lit by gas or kerosene, stoves burned wood and Jules Verne was considered by most scientists to be a certifiable kook, the engineers had set to work.

It wasn't just the sheer size of the job but more the fact that they were meeting and solving problems that had never existed before. There had been plenty of canals built, but nothing like this one. The Suez, for example, was only a ditch dug through the desert, connecting the Mediterranean and the Red Sea with a couple of lakes that nature had been thoughtful enough to provide in the middle. There were no locks to worry about, no need to raise or lower ships. As long as the channel is kept free of silt and sunken ships, the job isn't much different from the the way canals were dug thousands of years ago by the pharaohs with nothing more than slave power.

The lock canals that had been built weren't much more. Single-lifts of a few feet to take small ships or barges over low rises in elevation or around an obstacle like Niagara Falls. Panama broke new ground in hundreds of different ways.

As if that wasn't impressive enough, the whole thing is still hard at work exactly as the designers set it up seventy years ago, without even minor changes. Somewhere I'd seen that the electric "mules" that haul ships in and out of the locks had been replaced after fifty years of service, not because they weren't doing fine but just because seagoing vessels were getting bigger.

I'd been reading for a couple of hours when the next flurry was set off. This time it was Nagy. He'd been standing at the chart for the whole time since dinner and I saw that the place he'd been looking at was where the Gaillard Cut slashed through the Continental Divide.

"Right here." His finger stabbed at the map. "This is the single most vulnerable spot in the whole canal, right? That's what took the most work. Hacking and blasting and cutting to get down to lake level and forty-odd feet still deeper to provide a deep enough channel for any ship they thought might ever be built."

Murfree had to agree. "It must have been a heartbreaker. Even after the French had taken off the top hundred sixty-one feet the Americans still had to haul out over a hundred million cubic yards. It took years, and every time they thought they were getting close to the end there would be a massive landslide and the ditch would have to be cleaned out and the wreckage of trains and tracks removed. Not only that, but they'd taken away so much, they altered the natural stresses in the earth and every so often the whole bottom of the ditch would heave up and have to be leveled again. They had a hell of a time, particularly during the rains. They didn't even think about giving up, like the French finally did. It must have been one whale of a day for those men when the water began to rise in the cut and when the first ships started through."

"So," Nagy announced, "if you want to block the canal at its most vulnerable point, what you have to do is get the earth moving again. Either side would probably do, and if you could start both sides, you'd be sure to narrow the channel enough to keep ships of any size at all from passing.

"Look," he went on. "You wait for the rainy season. Let the ground get really well saturated. You make a big bang, and between the extra weight of the water and the lubrication, you start things going. From then on it's back to Newton's laws. How about it, Sergeant?"

Hutto was at his side in a couple of steps. He took a good, long look at the place where Nagy's finger was pointed and then walked to the scale model and looked it over at the same spot. From there he went to the Gaillard Cut cross section, and as he began to jot down some notes, Murfree and Sidney Fox came to his side.

I stayed back a bit, letting the experts put their teeth into the idea. I knew they weren't going to get a fast answer from Hutto. Men who work with things that like to blow up if you get a little rough with them rarely make snap judgments. When he had the data he needed, he checked against his handbook and then went to work on the calculator. He got his total and checked it for a minute, his slim figure bent over the machine, before he straightened up and looked at the others.

"It could be done, sir. The more charge you lay, the more you'd move. Not a geometric increase, but a hundred-pound charge will do a lot more than ten times the effect of one of ten pounds. You'd want to do some tests, if you could, to find what effect the water content would have on the shock wave, but I'd say, offhand, that the wetter the soil, the better your results."

There was just one drawback to the idea, from my point of view. If I was going to take a team in on that kind of setup, I wouldn't want to do it with a lot of people looking and probably asking all kinds of embarrassing questions.

"Wait a minute, Sergeant. Suppose you had to do it at night or even under water? How would that affect it?"

He saw what I had in mind. "At night you'd probably be slowed down some. If you needed to be extra quiet it would take either more time or more people. Under water would depend on how good your team was. On the other hand, you could spread the work out over a period and not have to worry about your preparations being spotted. Now that you mention it, sir, I'd tend to think in terms of a smaller team, working under water and at night for a week or maybe more."

Murfree broke in. "Okay, Sergeant. How are you going to get that underwater team inserted and extracted every night for a week? You'd be working without a shore party. The whole deal would have to be totally covert unless you wanted some passer-by to get curious and call the Canal Zone police."

"Sir, that's not my department. From what Colonel Eriksen told us, I'd guess that kind of thing is more in Captain Keefe's line."

"Well, Keefe?"

I shrugged my shoulders. "I suppose so. You can do almost anything if you want it enough and can get the support you need. Look at it this way. If you'd asked the men who worked on the canal what the chances were that men would walk on the moon in fifty years, what kind of answer would you have gotten? We don't know how much these FLP people want to do the job and we have no idea of what resources they can draw on, but theoretically it could be done."

Sidney Fox had found something in his book.

"This is an analysis of the strata in the area. It's a geologic mess. There are all sorts of layers of volcanic rock mixed with fossil-bearing sediment and other kinds of material. The place has been heaved up and then submerged so many times that it's a mass of intersecting fault lines that barely hold together. Some have been identified by the canal engineers and steps are taken to prevent slides, especially during the rainy season, when the cleavage planes are full of water and are just waiting to let go.

"That's what kept happening while the digging was being done. When the cut got deep enough to affect the balance of the rock and soils, they just let go and came roaring down the sides and filled the excavation in again. When that was hauled away, the weight of the material on both sides pressed down and the whole bottom heaved up and had to be dug away. It says here that the slides totaled an extra twenty-five million cubic yards over what they'd estimated. By God, I think maybe we've got something at last."

We all turned to Murfree to get his reaction to that.

He thought for a minute, apparently weighing the whole idea.

"First of all, let me say that the idea has merit. The slides that happen in Gaillard Cut are still a major problem. Even without any outside help, nature keeps the canal people up nights. Somebody who really wanted to help along could make a hell of a lot of trouble."

He walked over to the map. "The critical area is here. That's the nine miles between Pedro Miguel and Gamboa. A whole fleet of dredges and drill boats and other equipment is always at work to keep it clear. The schedules are arranged so that any ship over eighty feet in beam never meets another there of any size. At night the banks are fully illuminated with rows of lights so that the turns are fully visible. Speed is regulated and the channel is marked to prevent collisions. Any ship with a hazardous cargo like gasoline or explosives or propane gas makes the trip through there alone, no matter how small.

"Now, let's say that the FLP is fully motivated to the job. They've got all the trained manpower they need and all the high-grade explosives they need. They are willing to come back night after night and plant charges in the banks below the water line, where they won't be seen by passing traffic. They take as long as they must, slipping in, doing their work and knocking off before daylight. Finally they have everything ready. They set a timing device and go home. An hour or so later they're all home and listening to the radio while they open the champagne. They may even hear the sound of the charges going off and hear the chatter on the canal frequencies. Total success."

He walked back and sat down, but he wasn't finished.

"While they're still shaking hands, things have begun to happen. The canal engineers are moving into the area by road, water and in the air. They're all busy photographing, locating, measuring and estimating the extent of the damage. Up at

Gamboa and elsewhere, the phones are busy calling the dredge crews in for the job and in a few minutes they're on the way to the site from either side. If there's anything these people know, it's how to pick up dirt from one place and get it out of the way. Some dredges are like gigantic vacuum cleaners. They suck up the dirt and rock and force it through huge pipes to where it's to be dumped. Others scoop it up in bucket chains and drop it into barges. Tugs are there to move out the full ones and push in the empties. All together they're moving tens of thousands of cubic yards on every shift and they'll have hundreds of men working around the clock."

He got up and went over to the scale model and pointed to the Cut.

"First they'll concentrate on opening enough channel to let one-way traffic begin to move. With the worst of the heat off, they can take it easier and let the bulldozers up on top move some overburden so that no more comes down. Other crews will be at work out of sight over the ridge line, making changes in the drainage to fit the new contour. Gradually the pace will ease up. Traffic both ways will be back to normal. A lot of money will have been spent and a lot of sweat expended, and the canal and the FLP will be right back where they were."

He took his seat again and then, almost as an afterthought, he went on.

"In the Canal Zone you get so that whatever happens, you begin to think of what it means to the political situation. It's not hard to figure out what a situation like that would mean in those terms. Frankly, it would be the best thing that could happen for those who want the American presence in the canal to continue. A slide is just the thing to demonstrate how well prepared the canal authorities are for dealing with the situation. There couldn't be a better testimonial to Yankee efficiency.

"I don't really think that's what the FLP has in mind."

It was a lot worse than shadowboxing. We had an opponent, but all he had, so far, was a name. They called themselves the FLP. It might as well be XYZ for all the information we could get from it. From the letter they'd sent to the governor they seemed like men of intelligence and balance. Most political nuts grabbed at every chance to spread themselves around and spout a lot of slogans, build up their egos when the person they were addressing couldn't talk back. Not this FLP bunch.

Everything was calm and almost matter-of-fact. They knew what they wanted and they looked as if they were perfectly willing to play every card they had if that was necessary. It made them a lot more frightening somehow.

I closed my eyes and tried to put some faces to them. There would be a leader—probably a little older and more articulate than the rank and file. There would have to be a wilder element, too. The ones with passion and a lot of hate who couldn't wait to begin the really rough stuff, with people getting hurt. Somewhere in the background would be the moneyman, another type with a grievance, who would use his money instead of his blood. The cost of terror can run pretty high. There are plane tickets to buy, weapons and ammunition to be bought at high prices on the black. Hideaways and safe houses have to be rented and stocked. Cars must be equipped with stolen license plates and phony registrations. ID cards and passports in different names made ready for the action men, who need to make quick changes of identity. Explosives and detonators have to be bought at the back door from bent dealers who know how much the traffic would bear. Everything the FLP would need would have to be bought, and for top dollar, at that.

They had to have a powder man—somebody who could make their charges without blowing everything up like those kids in Greenwich Village.

A good mechanic was a must. A man who could work miracles with only a screwdriver and a wrench.

People who do violent things get hurt. They must have somebody on hand with training and equipment to take care of the casualties without observing the niceties of calling the cops to report gunshot wounds and the like.

If we could only get a quick glimpse of one of them, he might lead us to the others. Right now that was all we had to hope for.

I was still thinking about it when the overhead lights were turned out. When I looked around I saw that Sidney Fox and Nagy were still reading, their desk lamps providing small pools of light in the darkened room. Murfree and Hutto were already asleep.

I stripped to my shorts and headed for the washroom, and that's where I found Herbert. He was seated in one of the cubicles, a heavy book on his lap. So far all our genius had contributed to Operation Paradox was his presence.

I showered, brushed my teeth and went to bed.

5

It was the overhead lights coming on again that woke me next morning. The witch-burner announced that breakfast would arrive in fifteen minutes if we wanted to wash up before we ate. I tagged along with some of the others to the washroom and used some cold water to chase the mild case of jet lag I'd picked up on the trip to Dulles.

While I ate I thought about Nagy's plan, which had looked so good until Murfree had torpedoed it with hard facts. It wasn't so much the plan itself that I was concerned with as the methods you'd have to use to bring it off. I've been on enough operations to know that the actual execution is the smallest part of the job. What takes time and work are the planning, the logistics and the training of the team. If you've done your thinking in advance, the rest of the job is just a matter of sticking to the plan. Maybe Nagy's idea had turned out to be a dud, but I'd learned something from it. When the food cart was taken away I put it to them.

"Look, so far we've been putting all our time into looking for any small gap in the canal defense that might be exploited by the FLP. What we've been doing is just what the canal authorities have done all these years. Each time we think we've found a place that might be penetrated, we learn they've already thought of it and taken steps to make sure it doesn't happen. In other words, we've been looking at this thing from the inside out. Our view is strictly from the point of view of the defense, if you want to put it that way. Now, what I'm saying is that we ought to look at it the other way round, from the point of view of the outsiders—the FLP in this case."

I had their full attention and I saw Dumbo switch on the recorder. Even Herbert looked up from his book.

"What it comes down to in practical terms is simply this. If we put ourselves in their shoes, if we can make a fair assessment of just what their maximum capability might be, we can rule out a lot of things that are possible only with resources beyond their reach. That is to say, we can stop wasting time thinking about operations that involve midget submarines or nuclear weapons or even huge amounts of high explosives and teams of experts to put them in place. Things like that are available only to large nations with unlimited funds and manpower to draw on. They'd be worth considering only if the deal was the other way around and the U.S. was trying to damage a canal that the Panamanians were trying to defend."

Nagy said, "I still don't see what you're driving at."

"Okay, let's put it like this. What kind of assessment can we make of the FLP's potential? With the manpower and equipment they can muster, just what can they take on?"

"Who knows? We don't know a damn thing about them except their name and the fact that they want the U.S. to clear out."

"No, that's not right. We know quite a bit about them and we ought to be able to make a fair guess about a lot more. Probably the best thing we have to work with is Colonel Eriksen's statement that the FLP has never been heard of before. That means they're undoubtedly a small group."

Murfree said, "How do you get that? There could be hundreds of them, for all we know."

I shook my head. "No, sir. With the coverage we've got in Panama, it's just about impossible. If they were that big, we'd have turned up some trace of them. A big group has to recruit, has to raise money, has to communicate with its members. They need publicity to attract support even if they try to limit it to the smallest possible number. The FLP hasn't done that and that fact is the first piece of evidence that makes me suspect there aren't very many of them."

Murfree nodded. "Okay, what else?"

"Take the two operations—or demonstrations, as they call them. Either one could have been done by one or two men. In fact, if I had the choice I'd do it that way myself. The very nature of the stunts they've pulled indicates that they're damn smart, ingenious and capable of using what they've got in the best possible way. They know the canal, maybe one or more of them even work on it every day, and they know how to use their heads and their assets. They chose targets that could be approached only by a small group and a device that anyone with a fair knowledge of explosives could put together out of easily obtained materials."

Fox leaned forward. "But the two things could have been staged by different teams from the same group. Why do you assume it was the same men in both cases?"

"Because a smart leader does things that way. The fewer people you use, the fewer things there are to go wrong. You cut down on communication and the need to explain things and train others just how to do them. A few men, used to working together, can get a hell of a lot more accomplished if—and here's the point in what I'm trying to say—if you tailor your plans to what you have to work with. Just for example, look at what we're doing here. There's only the six of us, right? But even though we haven't come to the point where we're productive, would we be any further along if there were fifty different heads at work? I don't think so."

Murfree still wasn't buying it. "Look at the claim they've made. They say they have a plan to block the canal for an indefinite period. That kind of thing requires a maximum effort, either a massive attack at a single point or a series of smaller ones at a number of places. That takes manpower and equipment either way. If what you say is correct, then their threat is an empty one. They'll never be able to bring it off. We might as well wrap up here and get back to what we're supposed to be doing at our regular jobs."

Nagy popped out of his chair. "Just a minute. Maybe Keefe has something here we can work with. What do we have to lose? At least it can be a starting point. Let's try Keefe's idea against that plan of mine about creating a landslide. How does it measure up against your yardstick?"

"Not very well," I answered. "The logistics of the thing is the weak spot. Hutto, you ran some figures. How much HE did you figure you'd need?"

"I didn't get it down to an exact figure, but I did find out one thing from the records. When they were working on the Cut they were using an average of twenty thousand pounds of dynamite a day. That brought down as much as they could haul off and dispose of with steam shovels and railroad cars."

"And you'd need a hell of a lot of highly trained men to even begin to emplace that much in broad daylight, let alone at night and under water. You see what I'm trying to say. Let's not waste our time on stunts that are within the realm of possibility but beyond the capacity of the FLP to stage. We're going to have to go on a basis of using a small, highly motivated and intelligent group of very talented men. We know they've got a good demolition man; we've got evidence of that already. Maybe he's the key figure in their big effort, maybe not, but there's always the potential provided we don't think in terms of tons of HE or any other massive application of force."

It took a while to really make my point, but finally, one by one, they conceded. Mostly, I guess, it was because no one had anything better to offer, so we all finally were agreed to accept the concept.

All except Herbert Klingman, of course. He was still keeping his own counsel, regarding his navel for all I could tell. So far his only contribution had been to mow down Nagy whenever our behaviorist felt the need of a chess game to relax him before going on with the job at hand. It was Nagy, in fact, who came up with the first idea that fitted the FLP's ability and imaginative powers.

"Eichhornia crassipes," he suddenly announced.

He looked around at our blank faces and explained.

"The common water hyacinth. You know the story. Someone imported a couple of plants for a lily pond in Florida. The damn things escaped and spread like wildfire. Now it costs millions every year to clear them out of the rivers and canals. They get tangled in a boat's propeller and the thing just stops.

"Now, let's just suppose the FLP had a source of plants, say their seeds. They wouldn't even have to get close to the canal. All they'd have to do is release them into the streams that feed in from the jungle and the water would carry them down to the lakes. If they grew fast enough they'd choke up the whole place."

Murfree didn't even bother to face him. "Sorry. The hyacinth is already there and it's no big problem."

"But in Florida it's a real menace. What's so special about Panama?"

"It's not my field, but from what I've been told, the plant has natural enemies in Panama as well as natural competitors for the same food and living space. Either way, it's never been a big problem. I've heard about what happened in Florida, about the way the plants spread, but even if they started right away they wouldn't have gotten very far in the ninety days before the international commission meets."

When the lights went out that night, only Herbert failed to turn in. Not that the rest of us had really got a lot done, but at least we were beginning to work as a team. Each new idea was broken down and we'd go to work on it in twos or threes and then put it together before dumping it for one reason or another, to wait for the next brain wave.

I don't remember who it was that got us away from our concentration on the canal hardware and thinking about the people who do the intricate jobs that keep the traffic moving. What we were looking for was the kind of thing that the aviation people call "human error," the kind of thing that even the best safety devices can't prevent.

The men in the control rooms were the first we tried. We got out the manuals and used the model lock to see if there was something we could do to evade the built-in protective devices. Apart from some minor confusion, which could be cleared up quickly, we couldn't find a thing that looked as if it might hold any promise.

We spent a lot of time on the canal pilots required on every ship that makes the transit. They're the real aristocracy of the Zone, highly paid, highly trained and sometimes inclined to be as temperamental as opera stars. Not only do they have to know every inch of the winding canal channel that threads through the islands in Gatun Lake and then the Cut, but they also control the electric mules that help the ships into the locks, one by one, and then out into the channel. With a big ship, that can be tricky as hell. It takes four pilots, port and starboard, forward and aft, guiding the vessel straight ahead in the locks, with enough speed to keep it moving, but slowly enough to halt it before it collides with the lock gates ahead.

We tried a whole bunch of scenarios, which included taking

their families hostage or doping their coffee to force them to mess up a transit and damage the locks. Some of the ideas we took time to pull apart were pretty stupid, looking back on it, but it did serve to keep things rolling. Even Murfree had to admit that the human element was worth concentrating on and we worked that vein until we finally had to concede that it was mined out. That was just before lights out and we went to sleep with a clean slate to start on in the morning.

That third day it had been easier to get started than you'd expect. First of all, we decided to do some role-changing. Murfree and Hutto agreed to start digging for the vulnerable spots and the others to point out the weaknesses in their schemes. Murfree went back to the first French attempt at building a canal. For all the waste and graft, they'd still got a hell of a lot done. When they finally packed up and went home, those who were still alive, they'd left a huge amount of excavation and all their expensive machinery. Some of each had been used by the Americans. Their overall plan was quite different, but some of the digging was in places where it could be incorporated into the new plan. Much of the machinery was pulled out, cleaned up and put to work. Murfree was searching for someplace where the French work could be used only to control through their channels extra water that accumulated during the annual rains. With the runoff impounded, the water could be held for later use during the dry season and anything over that could be diverted away from the canal.

A lot of that kind of thing was connected not with Gatun Lake but with the smaller lake at Miraflores, and finally Murfree found a place he thought might be the one. It would involve a certain amount of heavy work and charges laid at several places that would all have to be blown together, but it was within the FLP's capability. The question was just how far you could lower the lake level long enough to make it count. We got at it, working right through lunch to ready the figures for the computer.

There wasn't much I could do except errand-boy work for the ones who really knew what they were doing. Murfree and Hutto built up the data and Fox and Nagy programmed it. That took almost all afternoon. When everything had gone off to the computer, we stood around like a bunch of expectant fathers outside the maternity ward until the results came back a few minutes later. To every question we'd put to the machine there was an answer.

How much explosives would be needed? Too much for the FLP.

How far would the water level drop? Not enough to affect navigation to any noticeable degree.

How soon could the damage be repaired? Quickly enough to prevent any major loss of water.

A good try, but no cigar.

That one just about took the heart out of us. Dinner arrived but only Hutto and Herbert ate a thing. The steward came back for the cart and shook his head over the uneaten steaks sitting in a pool of congealing fat, and cast a long accusing look at us before he rolled the wasted meal out.

From then until lights out barely a sound was heard except the rustle of paper as Herbert raced through another thick volume. When the room went dark the rest of us were already in our cots, too discouraged to do much but look forward to the time when the brass would finally give up on Operation Paradox and let us get on with our lives.

We were still pretty subdued next morning when Dumbo came on duty and went through his regular morning routine and then Tiny arrived for her daily visit. That's when Nagy came up with his idea about the Jell-O. None of us had enough interest left to manage a smile at that one, but it didn't stop Tiny.

Instead she started down the line, asking us each for whatever contribution he might have. It all added up to the same thing. The exercise was pointless. We'd given Operation Paradox our best efforts and we still hadn't produced a thing. If they wanted to know what the FLP had in mind for the future, they'd do better to gather up a panel of mind readers. That, or words to that effect, was what she got from each man until she got to Herbert.

I didn't know why she bothered. Herbert had read, he'd written, he'd done his yoga and his breathing and slept his regular two hours a day. Apart from his silent chess games with Nagy, he hadn't added a thing, good or bad, to the effort.

Tiny put it to him anyway.

"Do you agree with the others, Mr. Klingman?"

I heard a snort from the direction of Sidney Fox and some low muttering and then, to my amazement, Herbert spoke.

"No; I think I've worked out what this FLP plans to do."

Fox swiveled around in his chair. "Do you mean to say, young man, that while the rest of us have been putting everything we've got into this problem you've worked it out all by yourself? Tell us, Mr. Klingman: where have we poor mortals gone astray?"

The sarcasm was thick enough to cut into slabs, but it didn't seem to have any effect on Herbert. When he answered he showed no sign of resentment at Fox's crack.

"Your problem, gentlemen, and with all due deference, is that you have approached the problem as any group of laymen might be expected to do."

Fox reacted as though he'd been jabbed with a hot poker.

"Laymen," he shouted. "Laymen indeed. Perhaps you weren't listening when the colonel introduced us. Each man in this room is a recognized expert in his field."

"Forgive me, but I was speaking as a philosopher, a person trained to think, to consider problems, abstract or concrete, and arrive at an answer. To experts in other fields the facts of any matter are an end in themselves. To a philosopher the facts are useful only to confirm and support his final conclusion. Each of you knows far more about high explosives, animal behavior, naval engineering, geodetics or covert operations than I care to take the time to learn. You are trained to use slide rules, computers, microscopes and other apparatus to help you in your researches. I have been trained to use my head.

"In philosophic terms, what we have here is an almost classic paradox; the person who chose that name recognized the fact and I assume it was the reason I was selected for this panel. The paradox can be stated simply. How do you block an unblockable canal? Clearly, the time you have put in on the problem has shown that there is no practical mechanical means to accomplish that end. You cannot block the Panama Canal. If your purpose is to achieve that result, you must go back to basics."

He had everyone's attention and when he paused for a moment Nagy spoke up. "Go on, Herbert. We're listening."

"It comes to this. If you can't block the canal, you can next ask yourself the obvious question: 'Why do I want to block it?' A child can answer that. 'I want to block it so that people don't go through.' Now, if you start from that point you get somewhere. If you cannot arrange matters so that people *can't* go through, is it possible to arrange them so that people *won't* go through, even when physically they can; so that even if the way is clear they will refuse to avail themselves of its advantages over some other course of action?"

I didn't know where he was going, but he hadn't been spending his time admiring his umbilicus.

"Let's go back to the French failure to build a canal across the isthmus. What caused it? Was it the graft and the incompetence and the waste? Not really. With the leadership of de Lesseps, even those things could have been overcome. Doubtless he could have found men as competent as the Americans did to solve the engineering problems. Still, the French failed and the Americans succeeded. Why?"

It was Murfree who answered him. "Because the Americans didn't turn a shovel until they'd cleaned up the environment first."

"Precisely. The French came and they died. The West Indians and the Chinese and the East Indians all died in the thousands just as the Spaniards had when they tried to colonize the area. Finally there were no more people that the French company could persuade to come to Panama no matter how much they were willing to pay them. There was no way to keep a work force on the canal project. Even if the French had not been plagued with wholesale greed among the promoters, if their company had been a model of recititude, they would still have been forced to concede failure. Nature wasn't ready to let them live in Panama long enough to get the job done."

When Fox spoke he wasn't sneering anymore. "Where does that lead us? How can that affect what happens now? The environment has been conquered long since."

Herbert answered him. "If I wanted to stop people from using the Panama Canal today I'd do the same thing nature did."

"And how would you do that?"

"To put it simply, I'd use disease. Possibly the one that finally stopped the French. I'd reinfect the canal with fever."

"Fever? What kind of fever?"

"I'd probably choose the yellow form. Yellow jack."

• • •

6

Apart from an audible intake of breath from Murfree there wasn't a sound to be heard. The whole idea was so far out that it was hard to know where to begin talking about it. Just the thought that anyone would wantonly bring back the plague that the Americans had fought so hard to wipe out was too horrible to comprehend. It hasn't been all that long since New Orleans and Baltimore and even New York played host to yellow jack. There was no way even to estimate how many had died in agony, vomiting out their lives. Now yellow jack lived mostly in medical history along with typhoid and diphtheria and the other killer diseases science has erased. I suppose the same thoughts were in all our minds, but it was Tiny who spoke first.

"Okay, Mr. Klingman, what else have you got to support the idea?"

"Essentially it's the only conclusion that fits the facts we have and those we can extrapolate. That answer is the only one that conforms to the laws of logic at every point. Just follow it step by step.

"First of all, it lies within the parameters we were given. It will show that the Americans cannot defend the canal against all comers. It will close the canal but still without doing damage of any kind to the waterway, its locks or any other installations. If it is the aim of the FLP to turn the operation of the canal over to others, they will be able to do so without difficulty or extended delay.

"The operation itself is well within the capability of a group such as Captain Keefe has described, a small unit of dedicated and intelligent men who have the courage of their moral convictions and are willing to risk lives to achieve their end."

Tiny nodded. "That all sounds convincing, but how about the time frame? How long would it take to get the epidemic started and how long before it could be brought back under control?"

"That fits the parameters almost perfectly. The time limit set by the FLP was ninety days. Is that correct?"

"Yes, timed to coincide with the opening of the commission meeting. You were told about that."

"And it also coincides with something else. The beginning of the rains in Panama, the time when there is more standing water available to the mosquitoes than during the rest of the year. Six months later the rains will end and the control measures will begin to eliminate further breeding. Once that is accomplished, the epidemic will end and the canal will reopen, probably under new management."

"Well, I'll be goddamned." Tiny leaned back and I saw her grope for a cigarette.

It was Fox who spoke up next. "Wait just a minute. Why yellow fever? There are lots of nice diseases that can be used. How about bubonic plague? That's a nice easy one to spread."

Herbert nodded. "Yes, and there's typhus as well. The reason for choosing yellow fever is based on a number of factors, not the least of which is that it's already endemic to the area. All the factors are still present, every link in the chain of the disease—the right species of mosquitoes, the virus and lots of susceptible host animals. Still, once it's detected, it's a lot easier to eradicate than typhus, with its rat-flea-man cycle, which tends to attack the bottom of the economic ladder."

Fox kept pressing him. "But if these men are the dedicated types you say they are, how can they consider killing thousands of their own countrymen? What kind of patriot do you call that?"

Herbert's answer was delivered calmly. "In point of fact, Doctor, the native population has a high degree of immunity to the disease. They contract it, but their survival rate is quite high, and of course, once you've had the disease you've got lifelong immunity. The death rate for foreigners is far higher. The Spaniards and French were almost wiped out and so were the Asians and other non-Caucasians who were brought in to work for them. We know from the epidemics that occurred in the States that our people survive at a very low rate. I would imagine that the FLP took that into account. To answer the question pragmatically, I think that those most likely to suffer would be those that the FLP already looks on as its enemies."

Of all the men in the room, only Murfree had actually lived in the Zone and I'm sure that his mind was racing as he tried to visualize what an epidemic might be like in terms of real people and places. Suddenly he stood up, his head shaking hard from side to side.

"It's preposterous. There hasn't been a case of yellow fever in the Zone in God knows how long. It's been eradicated, totally and permanently."

"I'm sorry, Captain, but that's not really true. There was a major outbreak in Central America in the forties and a small one in the seventies. The only reason it hasn't been seen in the Zone is that the spray program has eliminated the vector, the mosquito that passes it from man to man. As long as they can't breed, you've broken the chain. The disease is still out there in the jungle, but there are no mosquitoes to carry it to the places where people live in the Canal Zone."

"So there goes your argument." Murfree's voice had risen.

Obviously Herbert had given him a bad scare. "There are so few mosquitoes in the Zone, and in the city, for that matter, that people don't even bother to screen their houses any longer. Everywhere you go you see the sanitary squads spraying every drop of standing water, every stream, every ditch, every puddle on a regular schedule anywhere near an inhabited place. Grass is kept short, swamps are drained. I know damn little about mosquitoes, but I do know that they don't travel far, maybe less than a mile in their whole lifetime. If one does manage to stray close to a settlement, there's no place for them to breed. Anyway," he wound up, "they still have to bite someone with an active case of the disease before they can pass it on and there's just no chance of that at all."

He sat down, still shaking his head as if he'd been jolted by the mere thought that Herbert had even mentioned the idea. Nagy was the one who had the capper for him.

"The whole problem would be easy enough to deal with. When I went to West Africa I had my shot and that was that. They're good for ten years and you're safe as houses for at least that long. The Rockefeller Foundation developed the vaccine and the disease has been all but wiped out. A fast inoculation program and your plan would flop."

Murfree nodded in agreement. "Of course; no sweat at all. Everybody would line up and get his shot and that would be that."

It looked as if Herbert's brainstorm was dead and buried, but he still wouldn't give up.

"You're right if you are speaking of the classic yellow fever. It's now called the urban form because it's passed by the *Aedes* mosquito, the kind that like to live in houses and settlements. If one of the females bites a fever victim, it only has to fly next door to pass it on to the neighbors. It breeds where it lives and that's why it can be controlled, but—and this is the crux of the matter—it is not the only vector. It turned up first because it likes to live with man, but it's not the only mosquito that can pass the disease."

Murfree swung around to look at him. "What do you mean?"

Herbert took a deep breath and went on. "Urban yellow fever is only a form of the disease. There is another form, now known as the jungle type. It's a lot more potent and it affects many warm-blooded animals, man among them. It is normally passed by mosquitoes that live, not in houses, but at the top of the jungle canopy. They pass the fever from animal to animal, usually monkeys, the warm-blooded animal that lives there, but they can also pass it to man."

"I've never heard of it."

"That's understandable. There are few people living in the habitat and most of those who have been infected have been hunters or woodcutters, who go where the mosquitoes can get at them. From what I can gather, the laboratory animal usually chosen to infect for research is the rhesus monkey, which is very susceptible, but it can be given to white mice. Briefly, jungle yellow fever can be transmitted to a warm-blooded animal and can be passed by any mosquito that shares the same habitat. That may be a bit oversimplified, but as a working hypothesis, it will stand up."

He stopped for a second, gathering his thoughts. "Now, let's see if we can construct a viable scenario. There are three links in the chain. For a start, let's begin with a victim."

Sidney Fox delivered himself of one of his snorts. "Yes, where do you plan to get these heroes who will volunteer to be infected with a high-mortality disease like yellow fever?"

"From any supplier of laboratory animals, Doctor. The rhesus is used by the thousands, either shipped, wild-caught, from India, or raised for the purpose in many countries. They're cheap, plentiful and, as I said, highly susceptible."

"Fine. You've got a bunch of monkeys. Now, young man, how do you infect them? I don't imagine the virus is available at your handy corner drugstore."

"No, I'm sure it's not, but it is available at the commercial laboratories which manufacture the vaccine for sale all over the tropics, where the disease is endemic. Not for sale, of course, but a man who really wanted a virus culture and knew what he was doing should be able to get hold of a cultured egg from either a commercial lab or one doing research on the virus. The egg is light, compact and portable, easy enough to remove without difficulty. Kept at the proper temperature, it should last quite a while. With the live virus you infect one or more rhesuses and turn them loose."

"Okay. I'll concede that it's not all that hard to get hold of the virus if you know what you're doing. You infect your monkey and turn him loose. What does he do then?" Sidney Fox paused for a second. "I'll tell you what he does. He climbs the nearest tree and that's the end of it."

Herbert swiveled his head around. "Sorry. The rhesus is not an arboreal monkey. Though he may climb a tree to sleep, he lives and forages on the ground. He'll cover quite an area, but he likes best to live close to man, where he can raid a vegetable patch or a stand of fruit trees. That makes him a target for both the tree-living mosquitoes and those who live with man."

He raised his hand, fingers extended, and ticked off his points one by one.

"You obtain a vaccine culture. You admit, Captain, that wouldn't be too hard. You buy one or more rhesuses. There are hundreds of suppliers. You take your monkey to the target area, infect him with a hypodermic syringe and turn him loose. The mosquito closes the circle when the sick monkey is infectious."

Murfree was on his feet. "And that's where your whole scenario breaks down. To do any harm, that monkey has to be bitten by a mosquito. A hungry female mosquito of the right type. After more than seventy years of spraying, there are no mosquitoes living close to man in the Canal Zone."

Herbert shook his head. "No, that part is the easiest link in the chain to provide. The eggs and larvae live in water. Research labs raise them by the millions. A couple of pint bottles should hold more than enough to seed the whole area you're interested in. If you time their hatching to the point where the monkeys are most infectious, you should be able to make carriers out of hundreds of them. The wind will help spread them and each man they bite becomes a carrier himself."

"But as you yourself pointed out, there's a vaccine."

"There is. It's made from a specially developed strain, an attenuated, or weakened, virus that can still produce the antibodies in the person properly inoculated. The vaccine works perfectly well against urban yellow fever because what it does, in effect, is give a very mild form of the disease. You get almost the same degree of immunity as a person who has survived a full-fledged case of urban yellow fever."

Murfree broke in. "Okay. You said it. A weak form of the disease, isn't that right? How can you start an epidemic with that?"

"In the amounts given by injection you probably can't. If you want to produce a really virulent case of yellow fever, you have other options. Either an overinjection, or injection of a more virulent strain."

"And where do you get that?"

"From what I've just read, it is well within the competence of any trained researcher. Finally, he has one more option. If he can turn up an animal infected with the jungle form of the disease, he can always start his own culture."

Suddenly Sidney Fox's voice boomed out in the quiet room. "Let's get this straight. You get a virus, you infect a monkey, you let it loose where there's a mosquito to bite it and pass it on. Now tell me this. What guarantee do you have that you're not going to be the next one she bites? If you are, you're probably dead."

"No, not at all. It takes several days before the virus develops in the patient's liver and is released into the bloodstream. That's where the next mosquito gets it. The infectious period lasts only a few days because after that the patient is probably dead. Once in the mosquito, it takes another twelve to fourteen days for the virus to grow and get to the insect's salivary glands. With that timetable, the man doing the work has two weeks to finish up and get clear."

Maybe there was a flaw in his reasoning that an expert could find, but the way it sounded, Herbert had a watertight case. The only thing I couldn't figure out was where he'd got all his facts.

"They're all right here in the room," he said when I asked him. "That encyclopedia is a reasonably good one and it's all there. It was just a matter of reading the material and following up the cross-references."

He was nice enough not to point out that we could have done the same thing.

Suddenly Tiny stood up. "What do the rest of you think? Can this plan that Herbert's come up with really work?"

She looked at each of us in turn. Nagy and Fox each nodded and so did I, but when she looked at Murfree he didn't seem to have heard her question. She paused, waiting for him to finish his thought.

"Good God. Can you see what would happen? The moment word got out that yellow jack was back in the Canal Zone, every ship headed that way in the Atlantic or Pacific would put about and change course. If captains or owners insisted, the crews would simply refuse to obey orders. Even men who had been inoculated wouldn't want to take the risk. The people in the Zone would demand to be evacuated. The pilots and operators would leave their posts. At home the public would insist that the servicemen be withdrawn from the canal defenses."

His voice dropped until it was all but inaudible. The only other sound in the room was the whirring of the telephone dial as Tiny bent over the instrument.

I looked over toward Herbert's desk to see what reaction he had to the way his words had affected the others. If he cared at all, I couldn't tell. He was walking toward the washroom, his book raised to his face.

I heard Tiny's voice in conversation with someone she spoke to with a whole lot of respect. There was a delay and then she repeated her story to someone else.

When she rang off, a string of other calls followed before she got back to us.

"All right, gentlemen. The feeling is that there's enough in Herbert's idea for us to take it seriously. We'd like you to begin work at once to prepare a scenario of precisely how the plan might be reasonably expected to be put into actual operation. By morning, if it's ready, we'll have some people here to check the technical accuracy and give their opinions on what you've developed. At the same time perhaps we'll be able to supply the one thing that the whole concept still lacks."

Nagy looked at her. "I don't think there's a damn thing lacking. Herbert has me convinced. What more do you want?"

"Confirmation, Doctor. Any piece or pieces of evidence that we can get from any source at all that might show that what we've just heard is someone's actual intention. Once we have that, we can move ahead on Operation Paradox. We can gamble that we've discovered what the FLP is planning for the canal."

7

By the time we'd finished breakfast they'd arrived. Each new arrival had been given a copy of the scenario from the stack of duplicates that had been made of our original. Each had a red "Top Secret" cover sheet bound right to it. It was as complete as we'd been able to make it in the time we had. For once the lights had burned all night as we talked it through and then got down to putting it on paper.

Essentially it was the way Herbert had laid it out for us the night before, fleshed out with the necessary details the rest of us had been able to supply. Sidney Fox concentrated on what effect the rains and the prevailing winds during the period might have on the spread of the vectors—the introduced mosquitoes—and the best areas from which they might be launched toward the Zone towns.

Nagy had been allowed a call to the Columbian Institution and in a couple of hours a messenger arrived with a stack of books about the disease and the species of mosquito that were known or suspected to be carriers.

Murfree went to work to pinpoint the targets the FLP might be expected to select and concentrate on for their operation.

I got busy with Hutto, drawing a tactical plan and a timetable based on the factors we already knew. It must have already become light in the world outside when we finished and sat down to eat. When we got that done, the cart vanished and the general came in, followed by three men in Army uniform. Tiny brought up the rear; we hadn't seen her all night, but I could tell that she'd been up and hard at work ever since she'd left us the evening before, taking just enough time to change into uniform for the meeting.

There were no formalities. The general sat down and started right in without wasting a second.

"I've read your scenario, gentlemen, and I've got to admit I'm impressed. Considering what you've had to work with in the way of hard data, it's an extraordinary piece of work. I've been told that the original idea came from Mr. Klingman and I'm sure it must be a source of great pride to him to know he's used his gifts so well. Still, I'm sure that all of you have contributed to Operation Paradox in every way you could. I've asked these gentlemen to come into the operation for some expert opinion. Major Garcés has come up from the Canal Zone and I'd like to hear from him first."

Garcés was a neat-looking Latin type, who wore the caduceus and "S" of the sanitary corps. He spoke with the soft accent of an educated Puerto Rican and he sounded as if he knew his stuff.

"Sir, I've had time to read the document twice. I've looked for any flaw in the reasoning without finding a thing that is not completely feasible under the conditions in the Zone. Introduced mosquitoes would be almost impossible to eradicate until the dry season begins in December. Depending on how widely they were spread and in what amounts, it would take several months before they could be brought under control."

"There's no faster method than the one you use now?"

"There is only one and that would involve a massive toxic spraying of the whole Zone area, a procedure now prohibited by law and by international agreement."

The next person he called on was a tall, thin lieutenant colonel named Donlan, sent to The Rock from Edgewood Arsenal for the meeting. Donlan's thing was entomology, bugs of all types that carried disease, with a strong specialty in mosquitoes.

"The vector data is essentially correct. Jungle yellow fever can be transmitted by a number of species, but since it's never been a real hazard in populated areas, there's not too much known about the full range of insects or much about their habits. Urban yellow fever is transmitted by what you might call an urban mosquito and all the methods used by the sanitary teams fielded by Major Garcés are based on the habits of the *Aedes.* That species breeds at ground level and there's where it's controlled.

"That's not the case with the others. There are dozens of species, all potential vectors, that are found only at the top of the jungle canopy. They're adapted to breed in the tiny amount of water held in the plants that grow high off the ground in trees and they don't usually travel out of the jungle, probably because the leaves shelter them from the winds that move lower-living insects. Whether they'd breed elsewhere if they were transplanted is debatable. One thing is certain, though. Wherever they are they'll bite, and if they're infected, they'll transmit whatever disease they carry. We know they carry the jungle form of the disease. We suspect they may be able to carry the urban form as well."

"So if you had the problem of controlling these species, what would you do?"

Donlan shook his head. "I don't know. Methods could be worked out, but the only thing that comes to mind would involve cutting down every tree in the exposed areas, including parts of Panama that adjoin the Canal Zone."

The last visitor was a short, gray-haired, dapper little colonel, a medical officer named Simpson, given to tugging at the short mustache that was penciled across his upper lip. He was wearing a clutch of ribbons, one of which I recognized as a Thai order usually given to the senior tropical disease specialists who had worked at SEATO Laboratory in Bangkok.

"The report is not written in medical terms, of course, but it is essentially accurate. The disease is about as described—short, intense and usually terminal for those from areas where it is not endemic, particularly those of European stock. Prophylaxis is generally achieved by standard methods and techniques, which are common knowledge, essentially by inoculation with a weak form of the virus in a carefully controlled dosage. Long-range control is not a medical matter but is based on the need for the vector. Eliminate the mosquito and you break the chain."

He probably could have gone on for quite a while, but the general wasn't about to give him the chance.

"The plan, Doctor, the plan. Is it workable, from your point of view?"

"Oh, yes. Quite. Any person with knowledge of the basics and some degree of technical training should have no difficulty in assessing the known control methods and working out a method to circumvent them. Given virus, host animal and vector, you have everything you need to start as big an epidemic of yellow jack as has ever been seen in Panama or anywhere else."

It looked as if he had something further but wasn't quite sure about speaking of it. A prod from the general got it out of him.

"There is one possibility that almost frightens me to think of."

"Go ahead. Let's have it all, no matter how bad."

"It's just this. Like any life form, a virus can mutate, produce a new form never before seen, with characteristics different from those of the parent stock. They turn up every so often and a skilled worker learns to look for them to appear quite often in simple organisms like viruses. That's how things like attenuated strains often appear. Their ability to attack is far less than that of the parent stock. You get sick if they attack you but nowhere nearly as seriously, and you still get the immunity. It's the other kind of mutant I'm speaking of. A new virus so much more potent than other strains that it can override the immunity they give."

"And what does that mean in terms a layman can understand?"

"First, that existing inoculations will not work. The mutant will be too potent for the protection to be effective. Second, the mutant will have to be isolated and identified before we can begin to develop a new vaccine. Until then the area will be lethal."

"Just a moment. This new strain, the mutant, will still need to be spread by a mosquito. When the control measures begin to work, the disease will end."

"No, sir. We haven't even wiped out the present form. We've kept it at bay, dormant, at a safe distance from the Zone. It's still out there, though, and if we drop our guard anywhere around the areas occupied by man, it's ready to move in."

"Okay, so we move everyone out of the area and there's no one to pass the disease on. Wait a minute—monkeys get it, too? Then we move them out as well."

The doc shook his head. "Sorry, sir. Men and monkeys are highly susceptible; a single mosquito bite will serve to infect them. Other animals need more, that's all. Give a cow or an elephant or a cat a big enough shot and they'll get yellow jack. The only immune animal we know of is the tree sloth, and we don't know why. We do know that any sick animal, no matter what species, can infect a mosquito."

He had more data, all of it discouraging. When he finished the general left, accompanied by Tiny. The rest of us killed time until the door opened again and Tiny strode in. She was carrying a fistful of teletypes and she shuffled through them for a moment before she began.

"We've got a couple of hundred men in the field and these

are the first reports to come in. First off, we've made a check of every place that might be a source of the virus. As you'd guess, there aren't too many. Maybe we've got something. There's a small outfit in New Jersey, just outside Philadelphia, that makes several vaccines, including yellow fever, for the export trade. There's just the owner and about a dozen employees, mostly members of one family, who used to have a place in Havana. When our man got the owner out of bed he asked if any shortage had been found in their stock of virus cultures.

"The man wasn't sure. Normally they make a count at regular intervals, but they'd had a rush of work, a big order to fill, and they'd been just too busy to get to it. It's not the kind of thing anyone would be likely to steal, so it's more of a safety precaution than anything else. The field man got the owner to go down and open the place during the night and he took a quick inventory. The eggs that hold the virus are kept in a special receptacle and they could see that everything looked to be okay until it was found that one of the eggs in the case had not been opened for inoculation and then resealed with clear tape. In other words, it was just a plain egg.

"I won't go into the whole thing, but it seemed like a good idea to find out just who works there. The owner could vouch for almost all of his lab people. Some of them he'd known in Havana and the rest are relatives. There was just one man he was evasive about, a man named Benitez, Alejandro Benitez. It turned out that Benitez had turned up a couple of months before, looking for work. He really knew his stuff; in fact, he was way over qualified for the kind of job he seemed willing to take, yet he agreed to take a lot lower salary than he was entitled to with his training.

"There are quite a few people in the States now, mostly Latin Americans, in the country without working permits and willing to do anything to get a job. The lab owner took him on, glad to get him at the price. The only thing about Benitez was that he wanted permission to use the lab after working hours for some research of his own. He was willing to work out the cost of anything he used, and on that basis, he stayed there until about two weeks ago.

"What still gripes the owner is that right in the middle of their rush Benitez called in sick. He promised to be back as soon as he felt well enough to work. Busy as they were filling their big order, it was more than a week before somebody remembered Benitez and called his rooming house to see if he was okay. He'd departed the day he'd called in sick, and left no address. We sent a man over to the place and went to work on the lab owner as well for a description of Benitez. Here's what we got from the few people who worked and lived with him."

She picked up a message form.

"Height, from five seven to five ten. Weight, one thirty-five to one sixty-five. Complexion, olive; hair, dark; age, twentyish. Facial hair, bushy mustache, long sideburns. No visible marks or scars." She looked at the next item carefully before she went on. "One thing all the witnesses agreed on. Benitez has blue eyes."

"Blue eyes?" Garcés and I said it together.

"That's right. Otherwise he looks like any other young Latin."

Garcés shook his head, but I had another question.

"What kind of accent did he have?"

"It's something the field men tried to find out, too. Most of the people said he'd spoken only Spanish and the only thing they agree on is that he wasn't a Cuban, although he said a few things that led them to believe he'd been there." She looked at Garcés. "That mean anything to you, Major?"

"The blue eyes are not very common and people tend to notice them. About the accent—there's one thing, I think. They have excellent research facilities in Cuba. Thanks to the Russians, they are replacing the losses of trained professionals who left when Castro came to power. They even offer training to young men from other Latin American countries."

It wasn't the kind of evidence you'd want to be hung on, but it did make Herbert's proposition seem to be on the right track. Better still, we might have a line on the first man in the FLP we could hang a name on. To carry out Herbert's scenario they had to have a man who knew the medical side and it looked as if he was Alejandro Benitez, the blue-eyed Latin.

There wasn't much opportunity to gloat over that. We had too much work. We didn't have time for any fancy variations on Operation Paradox. It was set up like any counter intelligence deal, one group playing the opposition, the other the defense. Stanley Nagy and Sidney Fox played the FLP, with Major Garcés as technical adviser. The others, with Simpson and Donlan, set up to catch them at it. I took over as coordinator, moving back and forth between the teams and generally keeping the ball rolling.

Herbert did nothing. He finished his yoga and then moved his chair back out of the line of fire and began to read. This time there were no cracks made about his method of attacking a problem. It worked too well.

Tiny had gone out to keep an eye on developments from the field. Dumbo was still manning his desk, ready to run errands or be helpful, but there wasn't a lot for him to do. Probably he was the one who ordered sandwiches for a lunch that could be eaten without breaking the pace of the work. Tiny must have skipped some meals as well as her night's sleep. When she came back she was looking tired, though it didn't appear to slow her down a bit. She grabbed a sandwich for herself and started to munch it while she gave us the latest.

"We've been checking out the laboratory animal suppliers. The day after Benitez called in sick, a man named Charles Davis was in Boston. He bought three rhesus monkeys from a dealer there, paid cash and left with the animals in a shipping cage and enough dry food to hold them for several weeks. The field office was going on the assumption that Davis would ship the animals by air, but a check of the airports didn't turn up a thing. Finally somebody used his head and they started checking the shiplines. Then they hit something in Providence. The same day the three rhesus monkeys were bought, a man named Ernesto Fernandez arranged to ship them to the port of Colón, consigned to someone named German Henriques. I've got a call in to our detachment in Panama for arrival data on the ship, the S.S. *Felicidad.*"

We had three more names to work with. "Did they get any kind of descriptions of the two men?"

Tiny shook her head. "Not much. Young, dark, slim. The man who sold the monkeys to Davis said he spoke with a New York accent, whatever that is, but it may be that he got that idea from the New York license plates on the station wagon Davis drove."

"How about the one who did the shipping, Fernandez?"

"Same general description. Davis may have had a small mustache and Fernandez may not. The agent remembers him best because he had to use an interpreter to make sure Fernandez was clear on the terms. He paid in cash and they called a cab for him."

"Either one have blue eyes?"

"If Davis did, they don't remember. Fernandez wore sunglasses."

She stuffed the last of her sandwich into her mouth and I got her a container of coffee. She had time for just one gulp before the phone rang. I shoved her a pad and pencil and she stabbed away at the paper, scrawling diagonally across it. When she hung up she was smiling.

"That was New York. Ten days ago, almost a week after the first three rhesuses left Providence, a man named Irwin Jones bought twelve monkeys, four from one dealer and eight from another down the street. He insisted that he only wanted young males and that's why the first dealer couldn't fill the whole order and passed him on to a competitor. Jones paid cash, loaded the animals in two shipping cages along with a supply of food.

"Now, both dealers remember Jones. They didn't care much about selling to him. Said he looked too much like a hippie, with long blond hair and ragged denims. He was driving a beat-up old van all painted with flowers and birds. They didn't remember the license number, but one said he thought the car was from New England. When Jones left he asked for directions to the Jersey Turnpike, though."

"How about the eye color?"

She looked down at her notes. "Nothing. No mention."

Something funny about the report was bugging me, but it took a minute for me to pin it down.

"Wait a minute. You said he bought nothing but young males. How about the other guy, Davis? Did he buy males, too?"

It took a minute on the phone to check and confirm that those three were males as well. I didn't know why, but it seemed to me that it was important. Tiny had something else on her mind.

"Why do you suppose they would first buy three monkeys and ship them off and then wait a week, buy a dozen, and send them separately?"

I had an answer for that. "It looks to me like they're setting up for a dry run. They'll turn the first three loose to get an idea of what the rest will act like when they really go for the roses. Maybe they don't want to take a chance on what the rhesuses might do when they get a taste of freedom."

Tiny shrugged and we got back to work. We'd done over an hour's worth when the next report came in.

"The morning after Jones bought the monkeys, a man named Luis Martínez shipped twelve rhesus monkeys in two cages out of Baltimore on the M.S. *Mercedes Pineda,* a banana boat bound for Port Everglades, Belize, Puerto Cortés and Colón. Martínez was told that if he cared to wait a few days, he could ship on another vessel leaving two days later for Colón but arriving a couple of days earlier than the *Pineda.* In spite of that, he said he preferred the first ship, and his monkeys were delivered to shipside by a commercial trucker.

"Martínez is described as a conservatively dressed stout man, about forty. He spoke good English but with a marked accent. The thing that impressed the shipping agent was the way Martínez tried to keep from touching anything around him. He paid cash in advance for his shipment and consigned them to the same man in Colón that Fernandez had named, German Henriques."

It was beginning to build now. The fact that two shipments of rhesuses had been made to Colón and to the same man, Henriques, had to tie them together. If our luck held, we could begin filling the dossiers on each of the FLP as fast as we could gather up information. The next break came a few minutes later.

"That was Major Art Ross in Panama," Tiny announced. "The first three rhesuses arrived in Colón two days ago. German Henriques, the consignee, picked them up at dockside. He had their health certificates and there were no problems at all. He raised a fuss because they hadn't been cared for to his taste, but finally he left with them."

"Did Ross get a description?"

"Nothing that's worth anything. Average, average, average."

"Maybe they'll get a better one when he comes to meet the *Pineda.*"

"That won't be for another week, at least."

I was still bothered by the same thing. Finally I decided to put it to the others.

"Why do you suppose these people are using nothing but young male rhesus monkeys? They all get the disease, don't they? Why be so fussy about whether they're male or female?"

Nagy had an answer for that. "Even an Army officer should be aware of the joys of sex, Captain. Don't you know the usual outcome?"

"Sure. In this case it would be a lot of little monkeys."

"I thought we'd already agreed that the FLP are not a gang of desperadoes. They appear to me to be men of both education and dedication. Has it occurred to you that they may have heard what the result was when some idiot introduced the rabbit into Australia? The little bunnies that the English love to hunt had no natural enemies in Australia and the hunters couldn't keep up with the rabbit's natural urge to propagate. Before anyone knew what the hell was going on, they were up to their pelvises in rabbits. They've been working like hell ever since and spending millions and still they can't do better than to barely stay level.

"If the FLP is going to introduce a new species of monkey into their country, they want to be sure the same thing doesn't happen to them. They'll set out boy rhesuses, but they don't want any of the other gender around to start a flood of little monkeys they may not be able to control when they get loose."

That had to be the answer.

Tiny was smiling for the first time since we'd left Honolulu, and of course it had to be at my expense.

"Is there anything bothering anyone else?" she asked.

"Yes, Colonel."

It was Herbert. He hadn't said anything since the night before, but now it looked as if he might be having another of his flashes.

"The man Jones. Does he spell his first name with an *E* or an *I*?"

Stupid as the question was, it was even worse coming from our resident genius. Tiny went along with it, though.

"It's spelled here with an *I*. Why do you ask?"

There was no answer. Herbert was back in his shell.

8

For the next couple of hours it was pretty hard to get much work done in the room. When we'd moved in there had been plenty of space, but it began to fill up fast when the teams of technicians started swarming around us, setting up equipment, stringing cables, adding desks for the operators who would man the gear as fast as it could be put into service. I'm supposed to be a Signal Corps officer, if you go by what I wear on my collar, but I didn't recognize half of the stuff being installed.

When it was finally all in place, we had our own switchboard, which tied us to both commercial service and the worldwide military AUTOVON and AUTODIN networks, with a special tie line direct to Southern Command in Panama and another that wasn't identified except by the bright red color of the handset. There was a scrambler for classified conversations, a high-speed encoder/decoder machine, and lots more.

Our desks and cots were pushed down to the end of the room to make room for new desks for Tiny and the three experts and for a row of easels and plotting boards. The door was hooked open and the rule that we couldn't leave the room was forgotten. We were too damn busy to leave even if we'd wanted to go.

Better places probably existed in The Rock for a command center for Operation Paradox, but there just wasn't time to make the move. All the data we needed—maps, charts, books, tech and logistic material—were there, sent over from the Map Service, the Smithsonian and Columbian and the Library of Congress for use in the think tank. Now that we'd gone operational, they were more important than ever.

The same thing applied to the command group. They could have been replaced by a team of trained professionals, but there just wouldn't have been time to stop, fill them in on the whole situation and then turn over the reins. We saw that right away. We were used to working together and had the three medical specialists aboard for expert advice, so we wouldn't have to waste a minute to break in replacements.

That was when we began to draw a timetable for the FLP. We had a pretty good idea of the date when they planned to hit—the time when the international commission would convene, which was the start of the rainy season. Working backward from that point, using all the known data, like the incubation periods for the fever in man and mosquito, and allowing for a time cushion at each phase, we could see that our schedule matched up almost exactly with what we now knew of the FLP's movements. The first shipment of rhesuses on the *Felicidad* had been delivered in time for the FLP in Panama to make their field test. The second, the dozen animals on the *Pineda,* would be coming in with just enough time to inoculate them, turn them loose ready for the hatching of the transplanted mosquitoes, which would be fully virulent for the winds to carry them to their objective on schedule.

That's when we had our first big disagreement. One side insisted that the *Pineda* be boarded on arrival and the rhesus monkeys confiscated. They insisted that even having them in the country was too big a risk to take. Murfree was the spokesman for that point of view.

At first I was inclined to agree. Confiscation of their host animals would be a big setback to the FLP. Then I heard the other side. Nagy put it this way.

"Let's say you do seize the rhesuses. What's the result? First, you let the FLP know right off the bat that they're being watched by the authorities here in the States and in Panama and that the nature of the operation has been discovered. You put them on guard, but do you stop them from going forward with the plan?

"It's my belief that you won't. Everyone in this room agrees that the FLP are smart. They know the country down there and they have a full understanding of what's involved in their scheme. Very likely they already have a contingency plan, ready to use if the rhesus is either not suitable or not available. That's the reason they sent the first three animals down. To establish the feasibility of that animal for what they are trying to accomplish. If you deny them the use of the monkeys they'll switch to their alternate plan and go right ahead, fully alert to the fact that we are on guard."

Murfree was unconvinced. "You mean you're willing to risk letting the FLP take delivery of the monkeys and just go right ahead with their plan?"

That was when Tiny broke in. "Just a minute, Captain. I see your point and I can assure you that when this man Henriques turns up to claim his shipment he won't be unobserved. From the moment the ship docks we'll flood the area with our people. He'll be under observation every second, and with any luck at all, he'll lead us to others in the FLP. This might just be the break we need. If we time our move, we may even be able to hit them hard enough to force them to call off the whole operation. That's what we're trying to do, isn't it?"

Murfree still had his heels dug in. "Then I must request that you refer the matter to higher authority."

Tiny shook her head, but she got on the phone and it was only a matter of minutes until the general came in. He heard both sides of the argument and asked just one question. He put it to Colonel Simpson.

"If these monkeys are confiscated, will it force the FLP to call off their plan?"

"Medically speaking, the answer is, Probably not. They have other host animals available, plus the option of getting more rhesuses from another source. The best we could gain out of the action would be a short delay."

That did it for the general. "Carry on, Colonel Eriksen. Let me know when you're ready for Phase Two."

I didn't know what Phase Two was and, frankly, I didn't give a damn. We had one more thing to wipe up and then Paradox would be ready to go operational. If that was Phase Two, I had nothing to offer the poor suckers who'd get stuck with it but my heartfelt sympathy.

Our last job was to make our best assessment of where the FLP would choose to launch their operation. There's more than five hundred square miles in the Canal Zone and they had their choice, you'd think, but as a matter of fact, the choices weren't all that many.

Much of the Zone is just water or small islands that are surrounded by it. A hell of a lot more is inaccessible except for a few trails, which are easy enough to guard. All the routes across the isthmus, highways and railroad, are on the east side of the canal and so are most of the towns and settlements. The west bank, the side that you take to go to the north, has no crossing of any kind and the few roads it does have all end at the west arm of Gatun Lake.

We started out on the assumption that it was the east side of the Zone the FLP would pick. That cut the target-area choice in half right away. Tiny came up with the thought that made it possible to narrow it down even further.

"Look at what they've done so far. They've deliberately

drawn our attention to the installations of the canal. The smoke bomb in the lock and the other at the Gamboa bridge. They promise us more of their 'demonstrations' and I'll bet a month's pay that the next is directed against a similar target, at either terminal or something connected with the canal. There are just so many men we can use to guard the area and it stands to reason that we'll concentrate on protecting what we think is most vulnerable. It's my opinion that if they keep up the pressure in certain areas, that will be the strongest indication that their real effort will be launched somewhere else."

That still left a lot of territory, the whole stretch from Gatun Dam and the locks on the north and Pedro Miguel on the south, or so it seemed at first glance.

Unless the FLP had learned either to fly or to walk on water, they were going to have to be able to get in and out of their target area. That meant we could forget about the narrow stretch of lake from Gamboa north to Darien and the place where the channel swung away from the shore and out to the middle. There's nothing but one road along there, which finally comes to a dead end at an arm of the lake that juts over into the Republic.

There was a tiny possibility that the FLP planned to stage in by water, in which case they could have set up shop anywhere along the shore, but no one could really make a case for the idea. With all the work they'd have to do, it seemed inevitable that they'd choose a place they could get at easily from either Colón or Panama City by car or truck. What clinched it was that from the dissemination angle, there was a place that met every test we could think of: easy to reach, close to the canal traffic, well sited for the release of the mosquitoes and with a Zone town just a few miles downwind.

That was the stretch of about ten miles along the narrow strip between Gaillard Cut and the Gaillard Highway. The Panama Railroad runs through the area between canal and highway and there's a net of secondary roads as well. We gave it to the computer and the results were conclusive. Given what the FLP was expected to do, you couldn't find a better place. If the people in the Canal Zone wanted to throw a spoke in the FLP's wheel, that's where they were advised to concentrate. It might be smart to take a look elsewhere every now and then, but it was my own conviction that the first sign of FLP activity would be seen in that part of the Zone.

As usual, we broke the problem down into parts and got to work on a report that would list our estimates on the FLP site selection possibilities, together with our conclusions. As far as I could see, that would finish up our job. There was still a chance for Tiny and me to salvage our leaves if we could get out of there and back to the Islands.

With all the people in the room, it took longer than it should have to get the site report done; not until late evening did we have it finished and ready for the general. It didn't take long for him to read it. There were no questions and he got up for what looked like a farewell speech.

It was. Short, congratulatory and still direct.

"You've all done an extraordinary job. Considering what you had to work with in the beginning, I must admit that each of your theoretical conclusions has been supported by the evidence. I think we can declare Phase One, the preliminary stage, complete and initiate Phase Two, the counter effort in the field.

"Captain Murfree, you are to remain here at The Rock to coordinate the support for the group in the field on the military side. Dr. Fox, we'd appreciate it if you would agree to remain with the operation here and handle the scientific side. Colonel Simpson and Colonel Donlan will remain on call at their own stations to be contacted as needed.

"That brings us to the group we will field in Panama. Major Garcés will return to the Zone but will be detailed to Paradox until relieved. Sergeant Hutto will also go on a temporary duty basis, attached to the Southern Command EOD team but under control of Paradox.

"Dr. Nagy, we would like to ask you to accompany the field team. For the record you will be visiting the Columbian Institution facility in the Zone, but your duties will be with the team."

Nagy nodded. "I am honored that you ask me and, of course, I am most proud to accept." Tired as he was, Nagy was obviously moved by the request. He bowed slightly to the general and, in his slightly accented English, asserted, "I am much in debt to my adopted country, far more than this small service can ever repay."

"That brings us to Mr. Klingman." At the sound of his name Herbert looked up. "I don't think I can really express how we feel about your contribution, but I know that everyone connected with Paradox is aware of how important it has been. Now that we're moving into the field I think we cannot, in conscience, keep you from your own work any longer. Transportation to New York has been arranged and you may depart, with our thanks, at your own convenience."

Before he could go on, Herbert's voice broke in.

"Would it be possible for me to go with the others to Panama?"

Even the general was surprised at that one.

"I'm not sure of what I can do to justify it, but there is a chance that I may be of some use."

The general looked up at Tiny and I saw her shrug and nod her head.

"All right, Mr. Klingman. You will join the others—Captain Keefe and the rest."

My jaw dropped, but before I could get it closed he was on his way out of the room. I saw Tiny regarding me and I gave her our signal that means, "Look, lady, I want to talk to you right now."

She walked out into the corridor and I was right behind her.

"What the hell does all this mean? I didn't volunteer for this and I want out right now. If you want to come with me and try to still make something out of our leave, okay. If not, I go alone."

"No good, Mike. You're going to Panama. I'm staying here as part of the command group on Paradox. That's an order."

"All right, Colonel Eriksen, if you want to play it like that, then I know my rights under the regulations. I want that order from the next higher in our chain of command."

"Wait a minute, Mike. That's the general."

"I don't give a damn if it's the Archbishop of Canterbury. 'Leave will not be withheld.' That's what the book says. Now, do I see the general?"

"Okay, if you want to try that route I can't refuse. In fact, I'll go in with you."

She turned and I followed her down the corridor. There was an aide in the outer office and in a couple of minutes he had managed to slide us into the general's schedule. I hadn't said a word to Tiny as we waited and by the time we were in the office I was building a good head of steam. I didn't take the chair he offered, but stood in front of the desk and spoke my piece. I ended it up with this:

"Sir, I did not volunteer for this assignment. I'm afraid that just as in the past, someone has volunteered for me. My approved request for leave was suspended so that I might take part in this exercise. Now that my job is done, I ask that the leave be reinstated. I have the time and if I don't use it soon I'll lose it."

He had every right to blow me right out of the room. Captains don't usually bother four-star generals with their minor personnel problems. Instead he got up and spoke very quietly.

"You seem to be a trifle confused, Captain. No one volunteered you for Paradox. It is an assignment, recommended by your commander in the States and approved by me personally. It was based solely on your record in unconventional operations. For your further information, the officer who did volunteer for Paradox was Colonel Eriksen. I gather she also gave up a long-awaited leave to join the group."

He sat himself down. "Request for leave not approved. Carry on."

I saluted and then messed up the about-face and marched out of the room, my face flaming.

As if I didn't feel bad enough about misjudging Tiny that way, when I got back to my desk I found she'd kept right on looking out for me even when I was acting like a brat. My orders were cut and waiting, detailing me for temporary duty for up to ninety days, at which time my leave would begin, or sooner, if possible. Right under my name were two others, Chief Petty Officer Sam Wynn and Staff Sergeant John Potter. Tiny was still worried about the safety of my skinny butt.

That part was fine, but it also meant something else and when I could get a minute with her I asked.

"Does this mean you want me to stage another one of our phony photo missions?"

"That was the general idea."

"What for? We're operating on our own real estate. At least, it's our own if the FLP doesn't scare Uncle Sam into giving it away. There's no reason for us to hide."

"Didn't you read your own report? Your answer is right there."

"Of course I read it. I wrote it! I still don't see the need of a covert operation."

"Mike, your report says that the FLP is making a show of their 'demonstration' close to the canal facilities to draw our attention away from the Gamboa area, where they really plan to work. Okay, we're doing the same thing. The command down there will react the way they're supposed to, by making a show of strength in all the wrong places. That leaves you to cover the target zone."

"How am I supposed to do that? With a handful of men how can I keep an eye on a stretch nine or ten miles long?"

"You can't, and you couldn't with fifty, not without tipping the FLP to the fact that we're on the lookout for them. On the other hand, you and your few men, if they're supposed to be doing something explainable but harmless, like making a film, can wander around anywhere without being suspected of doing anything threatening. Once they get used to your being in the neighborhood, if you get in their way they'll just back off until you leave and then get on with what they're doing."

"What good will that be? They'll be doing just what we're trying to prevent."

"Because you'll be keeping your eyes open for any trace they leave. They can't be in the area without making some kind of trail. Good a tracker as Potter is, he'll be on the lookout and able to tip you to whatever he finds."

"And what is this horsed-up film supposed to be all about?"

"Whatever you like, but I'd suggest something about animal life and ecology. That kind of thing."

"About which I know precisely nothing."

"Of course you don't, but Nagy does and so does Garcés. Don't downgrade the major, Mike. He's got two Ph.D.s, one in his own field and the other in entomology, and he's as smart as they come."

"And he outranks me. For that matter, so does Art Ross, the agency man at Command Headquarters."

"Garcés won't be any trouble on that score. You're the boss, as far as Paradox is concerned. That goes for Art Ross as well. You know him, don't you?"

"Yes, from Saigon. He worked for Colonel Humphries."

"Well, you won't have any problem with Ross. If I know Art, he's sweating freely as it is and he's going to be happy as the little Dutch boy when you come along with some spare fingers for the dike. He'll back you every way he can."

"All right. Now, what's the drill?"

"It works out pretty well. Just outside Gamboa the Columbian Institution has a field station. That will be your base. You'll have to brief the director, Calder, but it's okay. He's cleared all the way. The rest of the staff will buy the cover story as long as you make it look good. Calder has quarters for you and you can get your meals there and call on him for anything you think you need."

"When do we leave?"

"Just after daylight from Andrews. I'll have you all called at about three so you can get some breakfast before the cars come to take you over there. Potter and Wynn have been alerted. They'll have the film equipment and meet you at the plane."

"What am I supposed to do with Herbert?"

"If I were in your shoes, I wouldn't try to do anything with him. Just let him alone to do things his own way. I don't know how he does it, but I sure know that for him it works."

"What time is it?"

"About twelve-thirty."

"Okay. If you get out of here maybe I can get a shower and a couple of hours of sleep. By the way, what did you do about all those cash deposits we laid out?"

"I told them to hold on to the money because we were still coming, but we'd be a little late. Now go get some sleep."

9

Whoever had to wake me at three in the morning must have had a hell of a time. At best I don't come awake easily, and beat as I was, it must have been a problem. He kept at it and finally I lurched out of my rack and went in to shake my head under the cold-water tap and then do something about the red stubble on my face. Down at the end of the row of sinks, Herbert was brushing his teeth to a measured cadence, after which he did his gum massage. He was the source of all my troubles.

What did we really have to go on anyway? His word plus the shaky confirmation that had been interpreted from what might have been the perfectly innocent actions of some totally harmless people.

Benitez was a lab technician who had quit his job without notice. Maybe he'd taken a virus culture and maybe he hadn't.

Somebody named Davis had bought three monkeys. Maybe he was just plain lonesome.

Another guy, named Fernandez, had shipped three monkeys to Panama to his friend Henriques, who had picked them up, perhaps for some perfectly legitimate use.

A man named Jones, Irwin Jones with an *I,* as Herbert had confirmed, was a hippie who bought a dozen monkeys, possibly to turn over to a fussy man named Martínez, who had arranged to send them to Panama and the above-mentioned Henriques, the man with the legitimate use for them.

There was no shred of evidence to tie them all together, really, or to deduce some dastardly intent on the part of the FLP, who were most likely a palpable bunch of kooks trying to play heroes.

By the time I'd finished, I had pretty well convinced myself that Herbert was the kook and that we were all nuts for believing him. If we found out that Henriques was perfectly entitled to import all the rhesus monkeys he liked for a valid purpose of his own, the whole basis of Operation Paradox would fall apart like a paper house in a typhoon.

By the time I'd dressed and was having my coffee I was convinced that the whole exercise was charging off in the wrong direction. I was on the second cup when Tiny came in.

She went straight to her desk. She didn't sit but bent over and looked at what had come in while she had got a little sleep. It had been too damn long since I had seen her without a large audience around to keep us on a formal basis. I couldn't help but think of other times when I'd seen her bending over like that. In the morning when she was trying to tease me awake. In the shower washing her long auburn hair. Brushing it out as I sat on the lanai of her house on the side of the mountain above Kaneohe. I was giving up a month of days like that because Herbert had a vivid imagination.

I finished the coffee, tossed the carton into the trash and headed across the room. She looked up and saw me coming. Before I could say a word she straightened up, a message form in her hand, the perforations of the decoding machine on both sides of the paper.

"This came in a little while ago. At 0023 this morning a Canal Zone policeman was cruising the Gaillard Highway between Summit and Gamboa when a monkey ran out into the road. The headlights of the car must have blinded the animal and it was hit and thrown quite a distance.

"The patrolman looked around until he found the animal. It was dead and it didn't look like any monkey he'd ever seen before so he put it into the cruiser and took it up to the Summit Gardens, thinking it might have escaped from the zoo there. He got one of the staff up to look at the dead animal. It was established right away that it hadn't escaped from the zoo and that it was a rhesus.

"The cop used his head. He called for some help and went back to the place where he'd hit the thing. They took a good look around and established that someone had stopped by the road, probably just a minute or so before the cruiser came by, and had released the monkey. The poor thing still wasn't oriented and bolted when the police car came by."

"What happened then?"

"Well, he reported what had happened and the desk man called Art Ross. He had orders to do that if anything peculiar happened in that neighborhood. Ross got this message off and went out to check up."

"Was the monkey sick or anything?"

She shook her head. "It's too soon to know. I signaled Art to get a vet to look at the rhesus right away, but it's going to take a while."

Everything I'd decided while I was shaving sounded pretty stupid. I'd just have to get used to the idea that Herbert was a lot smarter than I was and quit resenting the fact.

"Better get ready, Mike. The cars leave in fifteen minutes."

The sky was just beginning to lighten when our little parade of sedans drove out on the ramp at Andrews and up to the twin-engine jet. There was a small knot of people standing at the foot of the steps taking turns looking at wrist watches and shaking heads. Tiny was the first out of our car and she went directly to an Air Force type with enough scrambled eggs on his visor to feed the whole bunch. She saluted and handed over our orders while the rest of us helped the drivers unload our gear and pass it to the flight crew for stowage.

All but one item, that is. It was a well-padded bundle about the size of a golf bag which Potter insisted on hand-carrying aboard. This time he wasn't going to take chances on being able to find his favorite item of hardware on the scene. He was bringing it himself in violation of six or seven Army Regulations.

Gently, but very firmly, we were urged up the steps and into the aircraft, the old cost-conscious Air Force all too aware of the exact cost per minute that was being expended on special transportation for Operation Paradox. At the top of the boarding ramp, I took a second to look back at Tiny, standing beside the sedan that had brought us. It wasn't the first time she'd stayed home, keeping a light in the window while the rest of us went off to where the fun was happening, and it probably wouldn't be the last.

Not that there is ever any doubt about who the boss is. Tiny runs a tight ship and if you work for her you keep that fact in mind at all times on the job. Off duty we have a different relationship that's nobody's business but our own. It's still based on mutual respect, even when I sometimes get the urge to throttle her.

She's the one who got me into DPOE in the first place. The Defense Photo Operations Executive is supposed to be the hottest thing in military photography. It's listed on all the organizational charts and its mission is to supply the Joint Chiefs, the Secretary and the White House with film and photo reports on anything they want special data on. DPOE is staffed with officers and men drawn from all the armed services, people with established reputations, and once in, a man rarely leaves except to retire.

We cover wars, small and large, maneuvers, tests of new and

secret hardware, international shindigs, and when we're not doing that, some of us work for Tiny, her boss and their outfit.

Don't bother looking them up. They don't appear on any of the charts and they're not listed in the big Department of Defense phone book, but don't think they don't swing a big stick. They can, and do, communicate with the very top without bothering to go through the steps in between. Which means that when they want something to happen, it's as good as done. They're backed and backed fully and they draw a lot more water than their ranks indicate. I'll never forget seeing Tiny chew the tail off a full colonel, a line officer ten years older and a grade higher. He didn't like it, but he took it.

The WAF flight attendant steered me to a vacant seat and I got the belt on just as the plane started taxiing out for takeoff. I was looking forward to my first glimpse of the sun since we'd gone into The Rock, though not until we broke out of the cloud cover that had dumped rain all night did I get confirmation that the world was still running right. I unstrapped when the seat-belt light went out and headed up the aisle to Potter and Wynn.

When we'd boarded I almost hadn't recognized Sam Wynn, probably because it was the first time I'd ever seen him in his regular Navy winter uniform. As a rule Sam is so quiet you forget that he's a senior chief petty officer, the same grade as master sergeant, with over twenty years service and the ribbons and hash marks to prove it—about ten yards of gold braid and three rows of top-drawer ribbons under a clutch of special qualification badges. He's a lot older than I am and in a hell of a lot better shape, no more than five pounds over his weight when he enlisted during the Korean fuss. As a cameraman he's as good as you'd want, production or news, hand-held or tripod, plus underwater and aerial. I've never seen him get the slightest bit excited.

Staff Sergeant John Potter is a quiet man, too. He's been with me most of the time I've been in uniform, going way back to when I was a reserve lieutenant doing active duty in Vietnam. Officially John is a still man, a good one, cross-trained to work with a chief cameraman like Sam, but that's not his biggest asset—and he's got a lot of them. For one thing, he's a powerful man, though not the musclebound type that lifts weights. The way he uses his strength with grace and efficiency is a real pleasure to watch. Farm raised, he has an instinctive feeling for terrain and the ability to read the ground like a printed page. The only thing I've ever seen him afraid of was the possibility that he might run out of his supply of toothpicks, one of which is always in the corner of his mouth. His only vice is a weakness for vanilla ice cream; his greatest love, the Army; his greatest talent, his ability with every individual weapon in the inventory. In the last category his favorite is the ten-gauge shotgun, and I was sure he had one in the bundle he was keeping between his knees.

We don't talk about it, but there have been times when, but for John's courage and quick thinking, they would have closed out my personnel file and started looking for my beneficiary.

Naturally, he and Sam didn't know anything, as yet, about Paradox. I gave them the copies of our reports and while they read I went to the pair of seats that Herbert and Nagy were sharing. A magnetic chessboard was on the fold-down table in front of Nagy, who was staring at it fixedly, muttering and tugging at his cheeks. I waited until he made a move and nudged his opponent. Herbert put down the notebook he'd been writing in, gave the board a quick glance, made his move and announced, "Mate, in four moves."

Nagy looked down in disbelief, then slammed the board shut, folded up the table and shot out of his seat. I saw him go back to the little galley, shifting around until the WAF handed him a cup of coffee.

I slid into the vacant seat and tapped Herbert on the arm to get his attention. He made a last notation and then shifted in his seat to face me.

"You're wondering why I asked to come to Panama with you."

It wasn't a question and he was right.

"It's not that we don't want you, Herbert, but I was curious about your interest in taking on something that's not really in your line of work. If it's just for the sightseeing, I'm afraid there's not going to be time for much of that."

"No. If that was my intention, all I needed to do was buy a ticket. I'm quite well off, you know."

I suppose I must have shown surprise, because he went on to explain.

"No, I haven't devised a system to win at roulette or anything like that. The stock market takes only a minute or two a day and an occasional telephone call."

"Is that what you're doing now?"

"As a matter of fact, it's related in a way. I've taken what we know of the FLP and on that basis I'm trying to make an informed guess about their future movements."

"We don't have much beyond a few names and some partial descriptions. You can't get much out of that, can you?"

"Actually we've got quite a lot to go on if you arrange the data properly. Take the first man, Benitez. He's a highly trained medical laboratory man. We've got expert testimony on that. He's young, Latin and has blue eyes. To achieve that level of training he must hold, at the least, a master's degree in science and possibly a doctorate. That amount of formal training is also a form of conditioning. Benitez will act and react in a highly predictable manner. His training will be, to a degree, modified by his Latin background, which in turn will be affected by the fact that he may not be only of Latin stock, as witness the blue eyes. Given his training and the modifiers, it becomes possible to form a statistically viable picture of his personality."

Maybe what he was doing might be useful, but I didn't feel equipped to judge it one way or the other.

"Based on that, we can make a fair prediction on how this type of person will react to given situations. This may not be of value right at the moment, but I believe that as the situation in Panama develops it may help."

He went down the list of the names we had, picking out the few facts we had from the witnesses and expanding them. It added up to a great deal. Taken as a group, the FLP had revealed a lot to Herbert.

The outstanding characteristic was their ability to plan. Every step of the way you could see that. No member of the group had made more than a single appearance, even in the business of buying the rhesuses and arranging for their shipment. They'd even changed vehicles to eliminate the possibility that they might be connected with each other.

Despite the ultimate aim of generating an epidemic, they appeared unwilling to do unnecessary harm. Even the welfare of the animals they planned to use concerned them. The two Americans, Davis and Jones, had taken pains to provide proper food for the monkeys rather than trust a steward to bring them what the ship's cook might take from his own stores. Henriques, the man who'd picked up the first shipment at Colón, had raised a fuss about the way the monkeys had been treated when he might have taken them quietly and not attracted the notice of the witnesses Ross had found.

The fact that all the monkeys were males showed a concern for the long-range effects of what they planned to do, something that less sophisticated men might not even consider.

He had a lot more and I probably should have listened, but I had an idea of my own to offer.

"It looks to me as though there are two main parts of the FLP in action right now. There's the bunch in the States, Benitez and the others, and a separate team taking care of the demonstrations down in Panama. Benitez is a medical specialist and the leader of the others is a skilled man with explosives. While one outfit prepares the big effort, the other keeps the pressure on and the defense all worked up and off balance."

"Still, they both have to be controlled by a central authority. That's the man I want to meet and that's the reason I wanted to come with you."

"You think it's a matter of one-man control? Not some sort of council?"

"Oh, yes. In fact, it may be even more than that."

"What do you mean?"

He paused a moment before he answered. "Let's say that as of right now I'm not far enough along to be sure, even though my instinct leads me to a certain conclusion."

"Okay. Now, what do you think about this leader, the mastermind?"

"More than any of the individuals we have reports about. For one thing, the overall plan he conceived is a remarkable achievement even for someone of his evident intellect. He's under thirty, because after that age any mind begins to lose the resiliency needed for such meticulous planning and execution, let alone the ability to create such an original concept. Even allowing for his years of training, he can't be any older. Next, he must have a phenomenal I.Q., probably in the same range as my own."

He said it without the slightest trace of pride or false modesty. To Herbert his intellect was just a fact of life, as I'd speak about my red hair. I suspected it would take something pretty earth-shaking for Herbert to take pride in it.

"This man has the ability to see through all the distracting details right into the heart of a problem, the essential crux, and devise a truly innovative way to achieve his objective. Take the way he arranged to introduce the explosive device into the canal mechanism. With even less detail to distract, it took me quite a while to find out how he'd done it."

"Wait a minute. You know how the smoke bomb got past the guards and was put in place and exploded? How did you figure that out?"

"By applying the same rules and tests our friend of the FLP did."

"Then maybe you'll explain it to me."

"Of course, but let me do it my way. Let's take another situation and apply the same method. We'll use the philosophic approach, the application of pure reason. Now, Captain, during the days we spent in confinement, how many people were actually in that room?"

I took my time answering. "Well, the six of us were there. There were the three watchdogs, one at a time, usually. There was the general and Ti—Colonel Eriksen."

"That's everyone? No other officers or anyone else?"

I checked back in my mind. "No. That's the lot."

"And if necessary you'd testify to that?"

I nodded, still not able to see where he was going.

"And how did we get our meals?"

"That steward brought the cart and then came back later for it. You can't count him. He belonged there, didn't he?"

"Of course. Now, one more question. Was it always the same man?"

"I don't know. I didn't bother to look every time he came in."

"In other words, because the man belonged there, just like the cart and the tables and chairs and walls, he didn't really register, did he?"

"No. He just belonged and there was nothing unusual about him."

"Still, a minute ago you'd forgotten all about him to the point where you would have sworn that only the people you named had been in the room during that period."

"All right. I concede that. What does that have to do with the other case?"

"First, every man in that canal lock area swore up and down that he had seen no unauthorized person in the place in which he worked every day. Not one could say that he'd seen anything like the bomb, or whatever you call it, being brought in. It and the man who brought it were, to all intents and purposes, invisible. Why? Because when he got in he did it by looking as if he belonged."

"I still don't get it. But they all know each other. They'd have spotted an outsider right away."

"All right. Now remember the man with the food cart. There are no food carts around the canal locks, but there's something very like it, so common that every visitor to the Canal Zone notices even if the residents don't even look up."

"What's that?"

"The mosquito-control men. The squads that are seen everywhere spraying oil on any bit of standing water. From what I've read, they are as much a part of the scene in the Zone as the lampposts or the palm trees or the fire hydrants. They belong and because of that they're as invisible as Japanese prop men in a Noh drama. When those workers stated that they hadn't seen anyone around who didn't belong, they were speaking the literal truth. They hadn't."

"Okay, I'll buy that much. A man who looked like he belonged could get in unobserved. That still doesn't explain how he got a good-sized explosive device past them."

"Oh, I'm sorry. I thought you'd get that for yourself. He had it in his spray can slung over his shoulder, of course. Probably didn't take more than a few seconds to slide it out, set the timer and move on."

"Well, I'll be a son of a bitch. Herbert, how the hell did you work that out?"

"Partly by applying pure reason, even though I confess that

part of it, for want of a better term, is intuition. When you begin to question evidence that is purely sensory, you sometimes get a funny feeling when things just don't add up properly. In this case it was made a lot easier because I was able to put myself inside the mind of the man who actually worked it out first. The solution fits precisely with what I already knew of his personality."

"What does that mean?"

"With his intellect, he's perfectly able to make an assessment of his own importance. Up to a point, intelligence and ego rise proportionately. Above that point one is able to really assess its true meaning and to accept what you've been given as something more than the right to look down on others. What that means in this case is that our friend could slide right into the role of sanitary sprayer and not look like a debutante carrying out the garbage. From the pictures, the sprayers have a highly characteristic posture and gait, due, probably, to the heavy weight of the tank and the need to look down constantly for anything that needs spraying. To make his masquerade work, our man had to look exactly right or he would have been spotted at once as an intruder. He's far superior to me in that respect," he added matter-of-factly.

He was a seven-day wonder, our Herbert.

"What else have you got? For instance, how many do you think are in this thing?"

He shook his head. "I'm still not sure, but the number keeps getting smaller, the deeper I look."

"Well, we've got six names already."

"Yes, we've got names, but not a man for each name. For one thing, I'm sure that the two men who shipped the rhesuses were actually one."

"That's Fernandez and Martínez. Yes, I'd say that was likely."

"Then the man on the receiving end, German Henriques. I think that was just another alias for the same person."

"How could he be in the States and down in Colón at the same time?"

"He didn't have to be. Remember how one report said that there was a faster ship leaving after the *Pineda,* but the shipper turned it down for a slower boat? There's only one reason for a man who was concerned with the welfare of the animals to keep them confined longer and that was so he'd have time to be on hand for their arrival. They went by the slow boat; in fact, they're still on their way. He had the choice of arriving first on a faster boat or by air."

That was something to think about and there was an added possibility.

"There's even a chance that Benitez is the same man, as well."

If Herbert heard me, he didn't bother to acknowledge what I'd said. He was back at his notebook. I got out of the seat and let him do things his own way, as Tiny had recommended. You don't tell Henry Aaron how to hold his bat.

I got back to my seat and looked down. We were out over the open sea and I realized how high we were flying when we passed a clutch of islands and I saw a tiny airfield. We had to be high enough to avoid any nervous Cuban gunner, and with that thought to comfort me I fell fast asleep.

• • •

10

The jet made its long, gliding descent through a scattering of clouds until Colón, the Atlantic terminus of the canal, came in sight off to the right and then we made the turn south to cross the isthmus. Those with window seats made room for the others and we all looked down on the locks at Gatun and the expanse of the lake. There were some ships in the canal channel, their wakes leaving a widening V across the barely ruffled water. Between the green masses of the clumps of jungle the open areas were brown and dusty-looking, waiting for the rains to come and start their cycle again. After all the time we'd spent looking at the scale model and the maps back at The Rock, it was easy enough to identify what we were seeing—the bulk of Madden Dam and the reservoir behind it, the deep slash of the Cut—and by the time we were over Pedro Miguel and ready to enter the military airfield pattern, we were low enough to see the men at work on the locks.

The plane kept dropping as we shot out over the Bay of Panama, giving a clear view of the city beyond the mass of Ancon Hill, the tangle of crooked streets and ramshackle buildings close to the Zone in the older section and the long boulevards stretching away to curve around the bay, lined with skyscraper hotels and office buildings. Then the right wing went down as we turned one eighty and in a few seconds we were on the ground, hearing the old familiar *crumph* of the landing gear as it took the shock and the brakes squealing in protest.

After the five-hour flight my uniform was, as usual, a mess, but somehow the others in the military, Hutto in particular, looked as though they'd stood all the way. We left the plane to face the heat, and I had to squint against the glare after the dim coolness of the plane. Among a group of men at the foot of the steps I finally spotted Art Ross, the major commanding our local detachment. He had a couple of civilian sedans waiting for us—regular cars, not OD, with Canal Zone plates—and a GI pickup for the baggage and gear. There was the usual milling around until we could all get sorted out. Garcés would go to his quarters and then drive up to meet us. Hutto would be quartered with the local EOD team, on call if we needed him.

I'd assumed that I would travel with the others, but Ross had other plans. When the rest drove off I got into his car and he headed for Balboa. Traffic was heavy and I let him keep his mind on his driving.

He looked about as he had when I'd seen him last. Ross was anything but your conventional idea of a spook. As far as I knew, he'd never done a thing in covert operations, and a good thing, too. When Ross was worried it stood out all over his face. Right now he was trying to break his own record for the course.

Not that Ross wasn't a top man. He'd have to be to get a sensitive station like Panama. He spoke Vietnamese pretty well and it was a cinch he knew Spanish for the slot he was in. I knew from Tiny that he ran a few nets, including one high-visibility operation to draw attention from the ones that really did the work. He had a pretty good staff of junior officers and some top NCOs, and I was sure I'd get the best possible backup from him.

That's not as usual as you'd think. Without a good man strong on detail to back it, a covert operation can come unstrung, usually at the worst possible moment, because somebody you're relying on has to take his wife's cat to the vet. I didn't have to worry about Ross.

He was heading up toward the mass of Ancon Hill and shifted into a lower gear for the climb to Quarry Heights. I assumed he was taking me to command headquarters, but instead he turned right to a sprawling oversized bungalow, heavily planted with lush shrubbery and with a white-helmeted MP trying to find a patch of shade. A houseboy in a crisp white jacket let us in and we followed him through a formal living room to a large lanai furnished with white wicker and hung with orchid plants.

Two men were waiting for us, one a heavy-set type with three stars on his collar, the other in a white suit. Ross and I saluted and I took the tall glass of iced tea that the houseboy handed me before he left, closing the glass doors behind him. I found a seat and waited for the conversation to begin.

It was Ross who led off. "If you gentlemen will allow, I'll fill Captain Keefe in on our structure here." The man in uniform nodded and Ross started in while the two of them got a good chance to look me over.

"Under the law the canal is operated by the Panama Canal Company, a wholly owned instrument of the United States, with a president and a board like any commercial firm. It runs the business, collects the tolls and pays its bills, at no cost to the U.S. taxpayer. The whole Zone is administered by the Canal Zone government. They act like any government, with schools, police, fire and water departments, hospitals and courts and a prison. The president of the Canal Company and the governor are the same individual, a general officer of the U.S. Army Corps of Engineers."

The man in the white suit raised his hand. "That's me."

Ross went on. "The defense of the canal is the responsibility of the U.S. Armed Forces, with a general or flag officer commanding the Southern Command, which has operational control over elements of all services stationed in the Zone."

The three-star nodded. "That's me."

"You have to understand this," Ross said. "By law, in case of danger to the canal or the Zone, the military commander takes over. That's a decision made in Washington by the President. We've had a signal from the Pentagon that such a situation now exists, although no announcement has been or will be made for the time being."

The governor interrupted. "That's fine with me. I just don't have the resources to deal with anything like this. I have my police and they're at your disposal, along with anything else in my power to give, but the main effort we're going to have to leave up to you people."

The general nodded. "That's our job, Ed. The trouble is that in a situation like this Operation Paradox, we're not up against a conventional threat. It means that we've got to bring in the people who are specially trained for that kind of thing, like Ross and Keefe. To a large degree we're going to have to be guided by what they recommend. That's the purpose of this meeting." He turned to me. "Now, what can we do to support you?"

I didn't want to give him a fast answer, the "don't worry, we've got everything under control" kind of response we usually come up with for senior officers who don't have to be told details. I wanted to make sure he'd act the way we wanted him to, like a man scared and committing everything he had.

"Sir, our assessment is that the FLP is conducting a two-pronged operation. One consists of the type of attack that was made in the lock and on the Gamboa bridge. That's the kind of thing that your own staff is far more competent to handle than someone from out of town. We are going to ask that you make a maximum effort at every sensitive spot. A full-bore, everything-committed alert condition. We think this should be done openly. All leaves canceled, quick-reaction forces in place, manned checkpoints—the whole gamut. That's not only for the obvious reasons—to protect the installations—but to convince the FLP that we're thinking only in terms of an attack of that nature."

"All right. It's going to play hell with the troops, but if that's what you recommend, you've got it, effective as fast as we can move."

"Remember, sir, it's to be an effort with no attempt to cover it up. Nobody inside an installation without an ID, packages searched, patrols increased, the whole bundle."

The governor spoke up. "The ambassador is going to raise blue hell over that. If we start shoving our Panamanian employees around, he's bound to get a blast from their ministry. Next thing, he'll be over here demanding an explanation. What do we tell him?"

"That's up to you, sir. The effect we're trying to establish for the benefit of the FLP is that we're going all out to protect the locks and the other vital installations."

"What's the purpose of that?"

I took a long breath. "Because we have every reason to believe that the other prong of their attack, the main thrust, if you will, is going to be directed elsewhere. That's the part we're taking on."

"Can you handle it with the manpower you've got? Don't you want some help from us?"

"No, sir. I've already been told that if we think the situation gets out of hand in the sector we're going to cover, we can have anything up to a full airborne division. So far I've made no such recommendation, although I'm not giving up the option."

"But what are you going to do with your handful of people?"

"First of all, I'm going to make a film."

"You're what? A film?"

"Exactly, sir."

"You mean that with this FLP ready to hit, you're going to fiddle around making a movie?"

Ross spoke right up. "That's our cover story to explain Keefe's presence in the area where we expect the FLP's main effort. It's a cover we've used in Vietnam and other places."

I picked it up. "You see, sir, our estimate is that the FLP is a small, highly organized group, hard to detect and able to evade a conventional defense. If they see too much pressure where they want to operate, they'll just pull out and try somewhere else. We want them to make their move just as they've been planning. The presence of a small photo team won't look like any problem to them. They'll go right ahead, not dreaming that we're aware of their plan and in place to make sure it doesn't pay off."

"Then what am I doing acting like an old biddy with twenty chicks and the hawk overhead? If the attack is going to come elsewhere, why am I reacting as if the Apaches were just over the ridge?"

"They are, General. You're going to get your share of action. At the same time, you're going to be doing what any sensible tactician would do. By denying the enemy certain areas, you're going to be forcing him to make his move where you can best deal with it."

"And if they get past you while you're trying to look like you're just a harmless photo team?"

"Then you'd better get ready to evacuate all dependents and nonessential personnel and line the rest up for booster shots. Unless, that is, a decision is made to give up the Canal Zone altogether."

He strode across the room and then swung around to face us.

"God damn it, I've got troops, planes, ships, missiles and everything needed to fight a young war all my own, and what good do they do me? How do you defend against this kind of thing?" He stopped right in front of us. "I know. You leave it to the experts. Well, gentlemen, I sure as hell hope you know your business, because if you don't . . ."

He didn't need to finish it.

We got out of there and Ross drove down the hill and through Balboa. We went along a series of winding streets lined with well-kept homes, tree-shaded and everything immaculate. There's no such thing as private property in the Zone and with the company both landlord and sole employer, everything is kept up to standard. Our way led under the soaring rise of the Thatcher Ferry Bridge and into Fort Amador. Most of the land around us had been made by dumping the spoil from the cut into an old tidal swamp, improving the real estate and at the same time eliminating another mosquito breeding ground.

The buildings were chiefly tropical-type barracks built between the two big wars, with broad galleries at each level, high ceilings and big windows. Ross parked in his reserved spot and I followed him into his office. I already knew some of his staff and he introduced the rest before we got down to business.

"Another monkey turned up this morning. A Chinese truck gardener spotted him trying to get through the fence to a stand of banana trees and called the cops. By the time they got a car up there, the animal was gone. According to the witness, the monkey looked okay—just hungry and frightened, not sick or injured."

"How far is that from where the first one was hit?"

"A couple of miles north. Just before the bridge to Gamboa."

"What have you got on the *Pineda?*"

"She's still on the way. If she stays on schedule we've got a few days."

"Do you have enough bodies to cover the site? If you want more, Tiny said she'd get us some help from Miami."

"No, I think we're okay. It takes less than two hours to drive over to Colón, even with traffic."

"Don't think I'm trying to run your shop, Art, but these guys are smart. If your people get in too close they're going to be spotted. If this guy Henriques gets the wind up, we've lost the only lead we've got. We better not blow this shot; we may never get another."

"Don't worry, Mike. I'll have at least twenty-four hours warning, plenty of time to set it up. This isn't Saigon, you know. There are just so many roads he can take to leave the docks. Just one question. Which do you want most, the man or the monkeys?"

I thought about it and there was only one answer. "The man. If we go for the animals the FLP will just switch to another plan. The thing we need most of all is information. Just let him lead us and let him alone unless it's a matter of his getting away clean. Only in that event is he to be picked up."

"And suppose that happens outside the Zone, over in the Republic? It could lead to a real mess if we picked up one of their citizens in his own country."

"Then I'd say use your judgment. If I had to make the choice, I'd weigh the risk against what it could mean if the FLP goes through with their plan."

Neither of us had eaten lunch. I wasn't all that hungry, so we walked over to the yacht club and had a sandwich and a beer. When we'd finished, Ross told me something about the place I'd be working out of.

"The Columbian Institution has had their field station at Gamboa for years. They're real big in anything dealing with the tropics, and while a lot of their research is done in Washington, they still need a place in the field. They've got a complete layout here—labs, equipment, animal houses and plenty of space for visitors.

"They've done a few jobs for us, and Williams Calder, the headman, has full security clearance. You're authorized to brief him on Paradox. All he knows now is that we're staging into his area and that it's a priority operation. Doc Calder will give you support for both the main effort and your cover activity. He's set aside a guesthouse for you, three or four bedrooms and a living room and kitchen. You'll be able to get your meals at their dining room and if you plan to be gone all day they'll even fix you up with box lunches."

"How do I contact you?"

"You've got your own line in the guesthouse, but it's not secure. Just in case you need it, I've sent up a radio that's netted with mine and the one the MPs use. Be careful how you use it, though."

"Why?"

He nodded his head in the direction of the city. "Our friends over there monitor it." He saw my expression change. "Don't let that bother you. We monitor them, too. It's one of the facts of life you have to get used to if you operate down here. Now, my people have orders to stay strictly away from you and your team. I'll be your only contact. Officially the word is that we're old friends and I'm just being sociable. You keep the two sedans and the pickup. If you're ready now, I'll have one of my people drive you up."

He obviously had plenty of work, so I thanked him and got into the staff car, sitting in front with the driver for a better chance to see the sights. The man was a chatty young Spec 4 and he gave me the full treatment. After all the time we'd spent with the maps, I thought I'd have no trouble recognizing the high points, but as usual, things look a lot different from ground level.

We went straight through Balboa, past the shopping center and over the tracks into the dock area before the road straightened out and headed for the high ground up ahead. The kid driving had an interesting theory he was dying to spring on me.

"This whole place is just like communism. Everybody works for the government and the government owns the whole place. They rent you the house you live in, they run the grocery stores, the bakeries and most of the other services you need. They rent space to doctors and dentists and the banks and any other things they don't run themselves, but they've all got to follow the rules or out they go.

"It's a pretty good life. The streets are clean, the schools are good, the outdoor life, like hunting and fishing, is great. Prices for food and gas and tires and anything else that has to be brought in are set at the same levels you'd be charged in the States."

He must have made quite a study and was more than happy to trot out all the facts for a newcomer.

"This is a big churchgoing community—something like fifty-five registered congregations just here on the Pacific side. Big for lodges and service groups, too. Most of them run a restaurant and bar, and that's where most of the night life is. A lot of Panamanians come over from the city. I guess the prices are a lot less and you hear more Spanish than English in most places."

While he talked I took in the scenery. For the first couple of miles we went past a bunch of built-up areas—the Albrook air base and the army post at Fort Clayton with the Miraflores Locks a few hundred yards over to the left. The ground had been rising steadily, climbing up toward the hills ahead. At Pedro Miguel we waited for a train to clear the crossing and for a short way the road ran right beside the locks and the narrow channel cut through the ridges by the French and then the Americans.

We flashed past a sign that marked the Continental Divide and past the clipped fairways of a golf course, the grass brown and dusty in the dry season, with only a patch of bright green showing around each hole. There was a railroad underpass ahead and just beyond it the road forked, one arm leading to the Atlantic side and the other, the one we took, going on to Gamboa. There were cars in the parking lot at Summit Gardens, tourists probably, and off to the left a scatter of towering antennas, draped with aerials, that marked the Navy communications station. There's a riding club there, but beyond that not much but jungle. The other highway, my driver told me, crossed over into Panama and was policed by the Guardia Nacional all the way to Cristobal, where the Canal Zone jurisdiction took over.

The road we were on ran almost straight north, holding its elevation above the Cut, a few hundred yards away across the railroad tracks. A couple of times I heard a ship or a tug hooting, but all I could see was the jungle, held back a few feet from the pavement by the road gangs, but ready to reach out and close the way if given half a chance. No wonder the Army had picked the Zone as the place to train troops for Vietnam. A couple of whiffs of nuoc mam and I'd have felt right at home.

I had a map and a look told me that up ahead was the Canal Zone prison, the bridge where the FLP had made its "demonstration," and then Gamboa, but we didn't get that far. Instead we took a right onto a graveled road, the dust boiling up behind us, and a short way farther on my driver swung to his left and went between a pair of whitewashed gateposts that marked the grounds of the field station.

The entrance road wound through an open tree-shaded area of lawns and plantings to a group of wide-spaced one-story buildings. There was a line of concrete-block lab buildings, a cluster of family quarters, a big dining hall, which doubled as a social center, and a wooden administration building.

If we were going to accomplish anything useful with Operation Paradox, then this was where we would get it done.

• • •

11

"So you see, Captain, the field station has quite a number of monitoring duties in addition to supporting research into new areas."

Williams Calder leaned back in his desk chair, his extended fingertips forming a basket, tapping together to punctuate what he had to say. Doc Calder was sprung from the bluest of Back Bay blood, prepared at St. Paul's, polished at Harvard and brought to a high gloss at a variety of institutions, each of which had tacked a few more letters to the string that followed his name in learned publications. Even Nagy, who'd come with me, was impressed with him.

He really talked that way, as if he were addressing a seminar that never adjourned, or a congressional hearing at which every word he spoke was being taped and might be played back later. I always thought of what his answer might be to the challenge "Your money or your life." Chances are Calder would have taken longer to reply than Jack Benny. Not that he couldn't afford to make the cash contribution. The nineteenth-century Calders had made enough so that no member of the family had worked for wages or salary since the McKinley administration, preferring to devote their lives and efforts to Good Works and Science.

There wasn't anything unfriendly or stand-offish about Calder, though. I gave him our reports to read and used the time to look him over. Despite his casual clothing, he still managed to project an air of formality, like the photos I'd seen of Calvin Coolidge in overalls pitching hay and making no attempt to cover his highly polished shoes. Calder was a lot happier with a tie and jacket no matter what the thermometer read.

He read the reports carefully, leafing back every now and then to check on something. Through the octagonal lenses of his rimless glasses I could see his eyes narrow and when he finally turned the last page and handed the file back, it was clear enough that he knew a bad scene when he saw one.

"What can we do to help you, Captain?"

"I'm afraid I can't give you a complete answer to that until we know a lot more about how this situation is going to develop. As far as our real mission is concerned, we're stuck until the FLP makes a move. Meanwhile we would like your help in our cover operation."

"That would be the film you spoke of, correct?"

"Yes, sir. Dr. Nagy is supposed to be the technical man, but he's never been in Panama and he's going to require some expert help in selecting material and in locating it in the area we want to keep under surveillance. Maybe he'd better explain what he needs."

I managed to understand the first three or four words of Nagy's explanation and then he lost me in a spate of technical and scientific mishmash, which appeared to be clear enough to Calder. It wasn't until later, when I got Nagy to explain it in words of less than five syllables, that I understood what they'd worked out.

Way back when the Panama area was mostly under water and

the Caribbean and the Pacific were connected naturally, the plants and animals evolved what Nagy called an "ecosystem." That was the way in which every living thing was interconnected with all the rest—the ones they ate, the ones that ate them, those that were nourished by the dead remains of others, and so on.

Everything worked out fine until one day the earth heaved and shook and the mountains rose out of the sea and split the whole isthmus in two parts, one side draining its waters into the Pacific, the other into the Caribbean. The animal and the plant families, just as with humans when they are separated, changed their life styles over the years, developing subspecies and new species, which elbowed around until they found their own place in the ecosystem. What it amounted to was that on each side of the Continental Divide there were life forms that still had a general resemblance to their common ancestors but were just different enough to survive under new conditions.

They'd had a lot of time to do it and things were just dandy in each ecosystem until along came some busybodies who just had to dig a canal that would put the two sides of the Isthmus of Panama in touch again. That's what the film would be all about: how the mixing of the two life styles was affecting each of them and what could be learned as a result.

Best of all, from our point of view, was that the ideal spot to do this research was along the sides of the Gaillard Cut, where man had made the greatest alteration in the scenery.

"What we're going to need first, Dr. Calder, is a person who is knowledgeable about the area, both physically and biologically," Nagy said. "I don't imagine that there is anyone of your staff so generalized as to know the whole field, but might there be someone who could pass us on to the experts in the various specialities?"

Calder thought a moment. "Yes, I think the ideal person for such a project would be my deputy director, Dr. Wagner."

"When do you think it would be convenient to meet with him?"

"Her," Calder said. "Dr. Felisa Wagner. A most remarkable young woman." He ran off a string of academic credits that didn't mean a thing to me but did to Nagy. "Dr. Wagner is, by specialty, a taxonomist, with strengths in each of the phyla. Much of her work here is in coordinating the efforts of the various specialists and she is much more familiar with their backgrounds than I."

I had one important question. "Is she an American?"

Calder said gently, "Captain, if you're going to spend much time here, you're going to have to remember that all the people from Alaska to Tierra del Fuego consider themselves Americans. They refer to us as North Americans."

"Okay, I'll try to remember. I asked for a reason, though. Is your Dr. Wagner cleared for classified data?"

He went to a file cabinet and selected a folder.

"Dr. Wagner is the daughter of a Panamanian mother and a North American father. As such she was entitled to select either citizenship at her eighteenth birthday. She chose the Panamanian. As a rule I do not like gossip, but it may be pertinent that her childhood was rather difficult. Her father abandoned his family, leaving the mother to raise the children by herself. She did rather well, since she saw them through school and the university before they were able to begin to support her.

"There is no mention here of a security clearance being requested, granted or denied, but were the decision mine, I'd have not a moment's hesitation in vouching for her complete integrity."

"You know her background that well?"

"If you mean names, places, dates, all that sort of thing, I must say I don't, but I do know this. Dr. Wagner is not what might be called a political person. In all the time of our association I have yet to hear her express views on any subject other than her work here. In any case, you'll meet her and make your own evaluation at dinner tonight."

"All right, Doctor, but I think that for the present at least, we don't talk about Operation Paradox with Dr. Wagner. In a way, that may be a good thing."

"I'm afraid I don't understand."

"Well, let's put it this way. If she stops around to tell you that she thinks there's something not quite kosher about us, we'll know our cover isn't all we think it is." I stood up and held out my hand. "There's just one more thing we might ask of you."

"Of course."

"If you're a churchgoing man, you might say a word for us. We're going to need all the help we can get."

He gave me a thin smile and Nagy and I walked back to the guesthouse.

They'd got a lot accomplished while I was with Ross. Garcés had probably done little more at his quarters than kiss his wife hello and goodbye before he'd checked into his own office and then driven up to join the others. He'd brought a full set of maps and he was mounting them on the walls while Sam and John were unpacking the camera and giving it a trial setup and check.

Nagy had already been to the field station library and withdrawn a stack of books he thought we'd need. Herbert was working away on some project of his own in the room they were sharing. Sam and John were sharing another room, leaving one for Garcés and another for me.

Mine was a nice big room, twin beds and two closets, each with a bulb mounted just above the floor that would be kept lit during the rainy season to keep the damp and mildew out of the contents. One wall, the outside one, was open and screened, with a door leading out to the porch that surrounded the house on all four sides, keeping out the glare of the sun and sited to make the most of the breeze coming from the lake.

Off in the distance I could see the bridge, and just beyond, the channel and the ships leaving and entering the Cut as they slid past. I unpacked my bag and set out my things in the bathroom. If we'd had nothing to do but make the film, it would have been just about perfect.

I didn't know what Dr. Wagner would be like. Probably about five foot and a hundred and forty-five, built like a duck pin, with thick glasses and a bad skin, the sworn enemy of the whole male sex. What with Paradox, though, it didn't make a lot of difference. I was going to be too busy to worry about Dr. Wagner even if she looked like Helen of Troy.

When I came back to the living room, Garcés and Nagy were huddling at the map and I saw that a number of points along the highway had been marked in red crayon.

"Those are the mosquito traps we've already got in place," Garcés said. "That's our early warning system, for want of a better name."

"I hate to sound stupid, but what's a mosquito trap?"

"Nothing very complicated. It's a portable kind of screened-in horse stall. They're put out in the jungle with feed and water and a horse inside. That's what draws the mosquitoes."

"Isn't it kind of tough on the horse just to stand there and get bitten?"

"Not really. As a matter of fact, the mosquitoes never get that close to him. They fly into the trap, but the screening keeps them from getting to the bait. The trap is inspected on a regular schedule and a count is made of the mosquitoes inside. Any rise in the *Aedes* population is noted right away and the controls are increased in the area around the trap. What we're working on now is whether we should add some more traps and step up the frequency of the count."

"Wouldn't it look funny if you suddenly started adding more for no apparent reason?"

"Not really. They're always being shifted around as a check on the control program. It's a perfectly normal thing."

"Then I'd say go ahead."

While Garcés phoned to his foreman, I sat down to reread our reports. The part I really wanted to review was the timetable we'd projected for the FLP. When Garcés had finished his call, I got together with him on it.

"The way it looks, the easiest part of their operation is the deployment of the rhesus monkeys. They just have to drive along the road and drop them off to get the best coverage they can. The hard work is going to be getting the mosquito eggs and larvae spread around so they'll be all ready to hatch when the monkeys arrive from Colón. Logically, they're going to do the longest job first. Get the mosquitoes in place and ready to bite when the time is right."

Garcés agreed. "There's not much standing water now, and that means that the eggs or larvae may have to be in some kind of container. It shouldn't be too hard to spot a jar or a tin can in the area."

It was starting to get dark and my stomach was sending up signals to the effect that it wanted something besides a sandwich or a paper cartonful of coffee. I told Sam and John to knock off and eat whenever they were ready. Herbert would go when and if he wanted, so Nagy and Garcés and I walked over to the dining hall together.

The others had been there before and knew the drill. Instead of going directly to the dining room, they led the way to a small bar off the main lounge. Calder was there, standing with a member of his staff and a slim girl with her back to me. She was almost as tall as Calder, who saw us come in and waved to us to join him.

"A local custom, gentlemen. The director buys the first drink. After that you're on your own."

We told him what we wanted and when he turned away to pass it on to the barman, the girl turned to face us. That was how I met Felisa Wagner and it's not something I'll ever forget.

Don't get me wrong. Felisa was not the type you'd expect to see walking down that ramp in Atlantic City, weeping under her rhinestone crown while the MC sings his soppy ballad. If Felisa wasn't an all-American girl, she sure as hell was an all-girl girl. She was female, but she was neither proud nor defensive about it, accepting her gender just as she did the fact that she had two eyes and one nose. To her, being a woman was neither an asset nor a liability, but a simple fact of life.

The way she dressed showed that. She was wearing an unbleached cotton dress, some kind of native fabric embellished with enough colorful embroidery to bring out her own coloring. The dress was belted at the waist with a strip of bright woven material that showed her slim figure and made no attempt to conceal the fact that, by the usual standards, Felisa was just a trifle flat-chested.

What you saw first were her eyes. Even without all the goop that other girls use, hers were outstanding, large, wide-set and bright, but the thing that caught you most of all was their expressiveness. When she looked at you you felt about ten feet tall because she seemed really interested in what you had to say. Later I found that you could have a whole conversation with her and neither one had to utter a word. Those wonderful eyes made you forget that her nose was just the slightest bit crooked, her lips were a shade thin and her teeth weren't like pearls.

Don't ask me what we found to talk about. There's not a whole lot I had in common with a lady Ph.D., but I kept babbling on, and on the whole, she seemed to find what I had to say interesting. I do remember telling her about the time we flew a chopper over a herd of wild elephants in the jungle along the Cambodian border south of Pleiku and the sense of wonder I had at seeing those huge animals completely free in their own environment.

Doc Calder didn't have a chance to do much more than make the introductions before I all but pushed him out of the conversation. It didn't seem to bother him, though, because when I finally woke up to how bad my manners were and turned to him, he was smiling with just as much curve to his lips as Harvard had taught him was correct under the circumstances. I finished my drink and he got me started toward the dining room. He took his place at the large table in the center of the room and offered me the seat at his right. Felisa wound up a few places down and on the other side. I was disappointed and I suppose I showed it, but it did force me to pay some attention to our host and the food that was served. Still, it seemed like hours before we left the table and went into the lounge.

Looking back, I can see that she stayed just long enough to be polite and not give the impression that she was offering me a fast brush. She was friendly enough, but there was no doubting the fact that she wasn't the kind who goes rushing into anything without devoting careful thought to it. When she said good night and left, Calder moved over to sit beside me.

"A very dedicated type, Dr. Wagner," he said. "She has worked so hard that I'm afraid she has had to miss some of the things that other girls her age enjoy so much."

He didn't say any more, but his meaning was clear enough. Mind your manners and don't mess with the natives.

12

When we left the dining hall, the starlight was so bright we could see the way back to the guesthouse without a bit of trouble. Off to the southeast the sky glowed with the reflected lights of the city. Even though we were only about a hundred feet above the level of the ocean, we were high enough to catch a soft breeze coming off the lake. Early as it was, I had a lot of sleep coming and all I wanted was a shower before I got better acquainted with my bed. Nagy and Garcés had been yawning openly and I knew they felt about the way I did.

In the guesthouse living room, Sam was watching an old movie on the Armed Forces TV station and Potter had just finished checking out his Speed Graphic and its supply of film and flash bulbs. There was no sign of the long bundle he'd carried aboard the plane, but I was sure that what it contained had been cleaned and stacked, ready for use.

I'd seen the film that Sam was watching and I was sure he had, too. His way of watching was something special. He paid no attention to the acting or the story, but if you were to ask him after it ended, he could give you a complete rundown on every move the camera had made, the lens and focus and a pretty good estimate of the exposure. I watched with him for a minute and then went to the window and looked out toward the south, enjoying the thought that in a few minutes I'd be starting a full night of uninterrupted sleep. Off to my left I could see a jetliner rising from the civilian airport at Tocumen. I was turning away when there was a sudden flash of light from a point just about due south.

It was so brief that for a moment I thought it might be from a revolving beam like that of a lighthouse. Then there was a second flash and immediately after, a third. I waited to see if there would be more and tried to recall if anything located in that direction might explain what had caused the three brief bursts of light. I didn't remember any lighthouse on the map and I was just about to check what we had in the way of detailed surveys when I heard a dull, muffled boom followed by two more that blended together as if they'd been amplified when the vibrations were funneled through the Cut.

To take that long to arrive, the sound had to be from a place a hell of a long way off, and to come that far and still be audible meant that it had been a lot more than a firecracker. I swung around just in time to see Sam switch on the radio and tune it to the MP network. Potter was beside him, bent over to catch whatever transmission could be heard that might explain what had happened.

There was a burst of static and then a youthful, very excited voice.

"This is Mike Papa Seven. Ten—one. I repeat, ten—one."

"What the hell is that, Sam?" I asked.

"That's Clear the net. That kid's got a real emergency."

"I have a ten—two on Venado Beach Road just west of the Howard strip. Repeating, ten—two, ten—five."

"That's Send assistance and Send ambulance."

"Mike Papa Seven, what is the nature of your ten—one? Over."

"It's the ammo dump for Howard, Sarge. I can't see much for

the smoke, but there's been a real big blast."

Whoever the young MP—or Mike Papa—was, he must have been badly rattled to forget his regular communications procedure. The calm voice of the dispatcher showed that someone was keeping his head and trying to steady his trooper.

"Mike Papa Seven, do you require additional ten—fives? Over."

"I don't know yet, Sarge. There's two men lying by the side of the road and I know there's supposed to be two more inside with the guard dog, but I can't see them around."

"Mike Papa Seven, stand by."

A whole string of other calls began, but I didn't need to hear them.

"Do you have a set of car keys, John?"

"Yes, sir."

"Then grab your camera. We're going to a fire."

It was almost daylight before we were done. That was at Ross's office at Amador, his whole team on hand while I did what I could to help. Then, leaving Art to deal with his own problems, I contacted The Rock and reported to Tiny.

"Do you think it was overt, a sabotage deal?"

"Right now I don't see how. They've doubled the guard at every point and every man has orders to be on the alert. As soon as I get anything I'll call you back."

She wasn't happy, but you couldn't blame her. Our team hadn't been in place for twenty-four hours when the stuff had hit the fan.

Potter and I had gone directly to the site. It wasn't hard to find it. All we had to do was follow along behind the string of emergency vehicles and try to stay out of the way of the ones coming back. Our way led over the big bridge across the Pacific entrance and into the post, which somehow manages to be an Army fort and an Air Force base at the same time.

At the south end of the airstrip we hit the first MP roadblock and wasted a couple of minutes until they could radio in to Ross and get us cleared to proceed. We started across a heavy timber bridge but had to pull to one side to let an ambulance, lights flashing and siren howling, go past us on its way to Gorgas Hospital before we could make the last couple of hundred yards to the site. There was a heavy cloud of smoke and the burning chemicals made my eyes sting.

Enough vehicles were clustered around to make the area bright as day with their headlights and their revolving red roof beacons, all blazing and flashing. There was a big group clustered around a double gate in the chain-link fence that surrounded the area and I saw Ross huddling with Hutto and a bunch that I took to be the EOD detachment. With Potter blocking for me, I managed to make a long, off-tackle slant and finally got through the mob around the locked gates.

For once Hutto was doing all the talking and the others, Ross included, were listening respectfully. When it came to high explosives, you'd be a damn fool to do anything but listen to the top man. I nudged Potter to get his still camera ready to start shooting before the rest of the mob got loose inside the magazine area and began leaving tracks all over the scene. I wasn't going to let him go in until Hutto had checked out the possibility of more blasts, but I wanted him to be first in when the place was declared secure.

"There's a whole bunch of these beehives running back into that little draw," Hutto explained. "They're sited by the book so that if any one of them goes it can't detonate any of the others."

"So there were three separate incidents timed to go off just about together? Is that what you mean?" I asked.

"It had to be, and it's got to be intentional. One magazine in a million blows accidentally. For all three to decide to go within a few seconds isn't possible. As far as we can see, it was the second, third and fourth that went, but we'll know for sure when the fires burn out and we can get inside for a better look."

Hutto left us and jogged over to a truck loaded with the special gear he'd need when the smoke cleared away enough for him to get in closer. Still another police vehicle arrived, with a tall Air Force captain who identified himself as the base munitions officer.

He'd brought his keys with him and the first thing he did was to unlock the big brass padlock that secured the gates and swing them open for Hutto and his team. He had the stricken look of a man who was looking forward to a mountain of reports and investigations and boards of inquiry looming up in the months to come. If he was a reservist, expecting to get out of service soon, he was going to have to take care of this mess before he could even hope to return to his life.

The poor guy stood in front of the gates looking bereft until Ross called him over to give us the details of his security setup.

"This is the first night under the new alert condition, but it's just as we had it before, with the guard doubled. There's supposed to be two men out here at the gate. They don't even have a key. If somebody has to get in he has to show a written order and the key to the individual beehive he's cleared to enter. Once the men outside are convinced everything is okay, they go ahead and call to the roving patrol inside, two other men with the dog. They pass the gate key out and when it's open the men escort the guy to the beehive and check to make sure he takes only what's authorized. He's never left alone for a second."

That was right by the book. Two teams of guards and two sets of locks and keys. Everything had to match up like the combination of a safe. Yet there were three magazines in there still sending out clouds of smoke through their open doors.

"Did I do something wrong, Major?"

"Not as far as I can see, but when the MPs came by they found the gate unmanned and two of your men lying on the ground across the road in the ditch."

"Dead?"

"No, and this is the goddamnedest thing. There wasn't a mark on either one of them. The medics thought maybe they were either asleep or dead drunk. They tried to shake the men awake, but neither one would budge. They were both out cold, just like they'd been drugged or something."

"How could anybody do that without raising enough fuss for the men inside to come for a look?"

It didn't make sense to me, either. "Have you any idea about what happened to them, the inside pair?"

Ross said, "I've got a couple of MPs circling the outside right now to see if they can spot anything through the fence."

Hutto and a couple of his men were ready to go in for a close look. They pulled protective masks over their faces and shouldered air tanks, then walked carefully through the gates. They passed the first beehive and then went out of sight in the smoke and darkness. We waited there until a pair of MPs came trotting along the fence on their way back from checking the sides and rear from the outside.

"There's a good-sized hole cut in the wire back there, sir."

"Any sign of the inside men?"

"Yes, sir. They're just laying on the ground a couple of yards from the hole with the dog between them. They're not moving, but it looks like they're breathing."

That was too much. Maybe somebody could drug the pair at the gate, but how could the two inside, not to mention the dog, be laid out?

"Do you think you can get them out through the hole in the fence?"

"I think so, sir, with some help."

"Okay. Get hold of a couple of medics and take them out that way."

In a minute the MP was leading a half-dozen men and three stretchers around the fence. They returned with the two men and the dog, each on a stretcher, and as the ambulance went screaming off I saw Hutto coming back to the gate.

He'd pulled off his protective mask and perspiration, mixed with streaks of soot, was streaming down his face. One of his back-up men handed him a canteen, and after he'd had a drink, helped him take off the air tank on his back.

"They got three of them—the second, third and fourth. Probably skipped number one because it can be seen from the road. The fifth one was opened but not blown. The three they did hit were totaled, of course. What's burning is just the packing cases and the wooden racks."

Ross broke in. "How the hell did they get the doors open? They're heavy-gauge steel with a tempered padlock. I guess you could cut one of those things with a hacksaw if you had about a week and didn't care how much noise you made." He stopped for a moment. "They didn't lay the charges outside, did they?"

Hutto shook his head. "No, sir. That wouldn't work. The doors are too heavy for anything you could lay in a hurry. Anyway, the doors are all on their hinges and standing wide open. I'll want to take another look later, but I think I know how they got past the locks."

"Go on."

"It's an old safe-crackers' trick. They used to pour straight nitro into the lock and then blow it from the inside." He shook his head in admiration. "I sure would like to meet the man who did it. He must have measured the charge with an apothecary scale. There was just enough to blow the mechanism and still not damage the hasp or the door."

He reached into the pocket of his coveralls and brought out a padlock. There wasn't any sign of damage on the outside, but the thick staple was swinging loose and when Hutto shook the lock I could hear disconnected parts rattling around.

"They didn't need any charges inside, of course. Probably they just taped a detonator to whatever was handy and wired it out to where they could close the circuit safely. All they had to do then was pack up their gear and go home." He shook the mangled padlock. "I really would like to meet the guy that could pull off something like this."

"How many men would you say it took for the whole stunt?" I asked.

"Hard to say. You wouldn't need, or even want, more than a few. I don't know about the entry, but for the explosives work maybe as few as a couple. One to carry and the other to work. I'll know better when I find the wiring."

"How come?"

"By the splices. No two men splice wire exactly the same way. It's like a fingerprint or a signature. You know, Captain, good as this guy must be, he could even have done it alone. Boy, would I like to meet him."

After I'd made my call to Tiny we went up the hill to Gorgas Hospital. The four men and the dog had all been taken to the emergency room, and while the doctors tried to figure out what had happened to the guards, a vet was working on the big German shepherd. When we walked in they still hadn't come to, almost two hours after they'd been found.

The vet was a sandy-haired captain named Putney, a Yankee with a flat New England accent, and while he didn't have much to say, it was obvious that he was just as worried about his patient as the regular medics were about theirs. He really knew his stuff, working smoothly, step by step. He took a blood sample and some of the dog's saliva and went off to the lab to run his own analysis.

The first of the men to stir was a big chubby kid. He started to move a little on the examination table, his fingers beginning to twitch and his lips working as though he were trying to speak but just couldn't open his mouth.

Ross bent over him. "What happened, son?"

Slowly the man opened his eyes and looked into Ross's face. I had to fight down the giggle I'd be sure to come out with if the kid said, "Where am I?"

Whatever it was he was trying to say, it emerged in a confused mumble as if he were having trouble getting his tongue wrapped around the words.

"Try again."

This time the words were clearer, even with the Georgia accent thick as sorghum molasses.

"Goddamn hornet stang me."

The effort must have been too much for him and he closed his eyes for some more shut-eye to build his strength for another try. If we wanted further information from him we were going to have to wait.

As it turned out, we didn't need him. Putney was back from the lab, and after he'd looked again at the shepherd, he had some word.

"I don't know anything about the men, but the dog was tranquilized. The saliva test was positive and the blood backed it up."

Ross said, "You mean somebody gave him a pill?"

"No; I'd say it was injected. His coat is pretty heavy, but I expect we could find the point of injection if we looked hard enough."

"Look, Doc, there's no way in the world anyone but the dog's handler could get close enough to do that."

Putney gave Ross a cold look. "I didn't say that, Major. If you want my professional opinion, I'd say the dog was injected with a dart gun, one of those air rifles they use for tagging game animals or those too dangerous to get close to in a zoo."

"Have you used this stuff?"

"A couple of times. Unless you can do it in a regular animal hospital, most vets try to stay away from the tranquilizers. Too much risk if you can't be accurate about your patient's real body weight and physical condition. Getting the exact dosage to put the animal under long enough to do your work, and still not kill him, takes an expert. Too little and he wakes up before you're ready, too much and he's your ex-patient. Still, if you really know your stuff, it's a damn good anesthetic."

"Well, maybe that's what happened to the dog, but you can't explain the men's condition that way. If anybody shot one of them with an air gun, he'd start yelling and warn the others. That's right, isn't it?"

Putney shook his head. "Nope. If you hit a major vein he'd likely go out like a light. If you got the dart in where the blood supply was good he'd start getting groggy in seconds and before he had a chance to yell he wouldn't care anymore."

I'd heard enough. With one of the doctors to help, we lifted the fat kid from Georgia and got off his fatigue jacket. It was when we rolled him on his side that we saw it, a bright spot of dried blood on his undershirt, high on the back of his shoulder.

From across the room I heard Putney's dry voice. "That would be a good place."

There was no delay when I asked for Tiny. She must have been sitting right beside the phone waiting for my second call of the night. She scrambled and set the recorder and I gave her as much as we'd been able to piece together.

"And they did the whole thing without really hurting anyone, not even the dog?"

"That's the report. The men will be groggy for a day or so and the shepherd is off his feed, but nothing permanent. There's one more item for the computer. The medics say that the man who figured the dosage hit it just about on the button and put it at just the right place anatomically to do the most good. I looked over the ground and the distance to the nearest cover means that the one who fired the air gun is a marksman in the Expert class."

"Okay. We'll feed that into the computer. One FLP man is a highly skilled explosives expert, one a medical type and one a crack shot."

"Tiny, what good is that damn computer? We've given it names, dates, places, special characteristics to match against everybody in the Western Hemisphere, and what have we got?"

"You just keep sending in data. Now give me the rundown on last night's party as far as you people have reconstructed it."

"It couldn't have been simpler. There's a gravel road that runs past the magazine area or ammo dump and then along the beach to the Zone border and a village just over the line called Vera Cruz. That's where it dead-ends. There's very little traffic on the road after dark and that's when they hit. They probably shot the two men at the gate first while the other pair were cruising. They pulled the gate guards into the ditch where a passing car wouldn't see them and then worked their way around to where they could get the inside pair before the dog winded them. When all the men and the dog were down, they cut their way in with bolt cutters and went to work. They blew four locks and set charges in three of the magazines."

"Why not the fourth if they'd gone to the trouble of breaking in?"

"We don't know yet. That beehive is used mostly for flares and pyrotechnics. There's some other stuff and I'll have an inventory made in the morning to see if anything is missing. Anyway, they blew the first three, one at a time, packed up and went home."

"Did they leave any physical evidence?"

"Some wire. Hutto's checking that. Otherwise they took it all. The bolt cutters, the firing device, the air gun. They even took time to retrieve the darts they'd expended."

"Mike, is there any way to keep this under wraps?"

"No way in the world. The Info Officer has announced that the whole thing was an accident. If I heard the blast over ten miles away, you know the population a lot closer had to hear it, too."

"And nobody hurt; just property damage."

"Let's hope they stick to that policy."

As I hung up, Hutto came in. He hadn't waited for daylight to search the area and he had already found the wiring. Potter had photographed it just for the record, but the important thing was Hutto's analysis.

"All the wiring was the work of one man. I found the cut ends and traced it all out, and the splicing is identical. Just to make sure he didn't get a hang-fire, he touched them off one at a time."

"There's just one thing I don't get. The nitro. Why nitroglycerin?"

"I'd say that if it's power you want without a lot of fancy gear and the extra weight, you couldn't make a better choice, always assuming you're crazy enough to work with it. He didn't even need a detonator for it. Plug the holes with clay and stand back and toss a rock at it and it blows." He thought for a moment. "It's easy to get, too."

"You don't mean you can buy it at the corner drugstore?"

"No, but it's easy to extract. The old-time safe-crackers used to take regular blasting dynamite and cook it down. The Vietcong even had a way to extract it from the HE in our artillery duds way out in the jungle over a charcoal fire. If you know the chemistry it's no big deal."

"Okay, Sergeant. You've had a busy night, but I've got one more thing for you. As soon as that munitions officer finishes his tally, I want to know if it's all there, and if not, an exact list of what's missing. Turning a bunch like the FLP loose in a magazine is like giving a kid the key to a candy store. There are just too many things in a place like that to attract somebody who's looking for ways to make trouble."

"Are you going to stay here, Captain?"

"No. I'm going back to Gamboa, where I'll try to look like a man who's just dying to make a film about ecosystems. Come on, Potter. Will you drive? I've got to try to get some sleep in the back seat."

"Wait a minute, Mike." That was Ross. "The Old Man has been screaming for us. Potter can take the car and I'll get you back after the meeting."

He must have read my mind. "I'm sorry, but he's the man I work for. It won't take too long."

I picked out the one comfortable chair in the office and dropped into it. Ross said something else, but I didn't hear it. I was asleep.

13

"What in the name of pluperfect hell is going on, Keefe?"

We'd gone a long way past the stage of polite conversation. The general wasn't just scared now. He was scared and mad and all too aware that the security of any military installation, when the chips are down, is the responsibility of its commander. When questions came tumbling out of the Pentagon, he was the one who was going to have to field them.

This meeting wasn't quite as informal as the first. In his office, with his Chief of Staff and the G-2 beside him, he was a hell of a lot more impressive. Somehow it didn't seem like the right moment to point out that I was just a guy from out of town who'd been sent in to help and not his own hired gun.

"Did you know this was going to happen, and if so, why in hell didn't you give us some warning? Isn't that your job?"

Now, I'd been up for two nights running. I'd had a couple of cat naps and I'd missed most of the more important meals. It wasn't my kind of assignment and I've got red hair. The only thing that kept me from doing my famous impersonation of Vesuvius in a bad mood was the fact that it's damn hard for a cashiered officer to get a job.

"Sir, we've all had plenty of warning that the FLP intends

going on with their 'demonstrations.' My orders are to do my utmost to stop their main effort, the one we call Paradox. That's the extent of my mission. It goes without saying that I do everything I can to work with Major Ross and the rest of your own staff. It does not mean that my people are any smarter than your own just because we work for a higher level of command."

That last was just to freshen up his memory. It's any commander's prerogative to climb all over his own troops, but that doesn't go for people who work for somebody else. If he didn't like the way I did my work, he had the right to make his beef to my boss.

"I'm free to admit that I was as surprised as anyone at what happened last night. That doesn't mean I'm surprised that the FLP hit us again, but only at the way they did it. Not after all the warnings they've given us." I saw his eyes narrow, but kept right on. "I'm not trying to pass the buck, sir, but I don't think this is a matter that has my name on it."

I don't know how long it had been since a three-star general had a captain speak to him this way, but it did serve to slow this one down.

"Now, what does that mean?"

"General, your people have done everything right. Take that magazine area. The base commander doubled the guard. They tightened up the entry procedure. The men were properly deployed. They added an extra dimension with the guard dog. There's not a thing you can fault those people on."

"Then what happened?"

"To put it bluntly, we're up against a group that so far has been a lot smarter. The FLP team went right through that defense without a slip, did what they planned and got away clean. Not only that; they did it without hurting a single man or even the dog, just as they did in the first two incidents."

He thought about that for a moment and when he spoke again he'd dropped a few points on the Richter scale.

"You're right, of course. We've lost some government property, but the men are okay so let's be grateful for that. There's just one question. Do you think they'll try again?"

"Why not? They're batting a thousand right now, doing exactly what they said they would. Why would they quit when they're ahead?"

"Any ideas on what they might try next?"

"No, sir, and I'd be a liar if I said I even had a guess."

"How about you, Ross?"

Ross just shook his head and the general swung around to face his G-2, a young-looking full colonel with a shaved head.

"You have anything to contribute, Stan?"

"Nothing on the positive side. We've deployed every man we've got ever since this thing began—military personnel, civilians and our local nationals. We've had full cooperation from the other intelligence outfits and none of us has even had the hint of a lead. As far as we can tell, no one has ever heard of this FLP. They don't do any of the things we usually expect from any far-out group. They don't recruit and they don't raise money. They don't put out handbills or pamphlets or run a clandestine radio. They've never staged a public demonstration of any kind. We have no line on their ultimate aims beyond the one they announced to us—to get the U.S. out of the Canal Zone.

"So far one thing is the most peculiar. When they pull off one of their raids they don't want any credit for it. Most terrorists run for the phone and call the papers or radio stations. This FLP has sent us just the one warning letter and that's all. They know we're aware of who's behind these acts, but they don't bother to call up afterward and rub our noses in it."

"But it still doesn't make sense. All these small attacks serve to keep us stirred up and madder than hell, but they're not going to make us pull out. What do they get out of it?"

G-2 shrugged his shoulders. "Maybe the Operation Paradox

team has some ideas on that, sir. They don't stand as close to the problem as our people do."

"Well, Keefe?"

"I think the answer to that is in the character of the men in the FLP. Everything we have on them shows them to be highly trained, highly motivated, highly intelligent people. They are not a ragtag gang of terrorists who destroy things for the sheer feeling of power it gives to little men. As the colonel said, they don't give a damn if their attacks get them any publicity. It's my estimate that they make them for a far different reason."

"Okay. What's that?"

"If we're right about the final phase of Paradox—the initiation of a full-scale epidemic of high-mortality disease—that's a step the FLP will take only when they are satisfied that to get what they want a lot of people are probably going to have to die. It's a step they won't take unless they're sure that it is the only way they've got to go. They know what any civilized person would say about what they threaten to do and they know how history will report their action.

"To sum it up, what they want is moral justification for their actions. They want to be able to tell themselves that we are the guilty ones, guilty because we failed to heed their repeated warnings. Right now they are trying to convince us that they are able to do anything they elect and that we're powerless to stop them. When they think that we've failed long enough to heed their warnings, they'll feel justified in going on to play out the final stage of Paradox."

"Then they don't really believe that what they're doing is going to make the United States just pull up stakes and leave?"

"No, sir, they don't, as far as I can see, and they never did. That's why they need justification for an act they think will force world opinion to do it for them."

"And they'll feel they have done the right thing even though a hell of a lot of innocent people are going to die, and die horribly?"

"Sir, if you ask the IRA or the urban guerrillas or the Puerto Rican nationalists how it is they can toss a bomb into a school bus or a theater or a crowded department store or bar, they'll tell you they're patriots. You've got the Palestinian Arabs, just for an example, who prefer to attack people before property. At least so far, the FLP hasn't hurt anyone."

"You don't mean you agree with them?"

"No, sir, but I sure as hell admire them. They know what they want, right or wrong, and they seem to be able to think rings around us. So far they haven't made a single error that we can exploit."

"Sooner or later they've got to make a mistake, don't they?"

"Sir, I sure as hell hope so. If they don't, we haven't got a prayer."

When he dismissed us he was a lot paler and a lot quieter than he'd been when we came in.

When I got back to the guesthouse the only ones there were Potter, who was asleep after his night out, and Herbert, who was doing his yoga. He came out of it long enough to say that the others had decided to get familiar with the area and look around for any sign that the FLP had begun their preparations. Felisa had gone along to work with Nagy. Sam was supposed to be getting the feel of the terrain and the photo problems he'd be up against when we actually started filming. Garcés would be looking for sites where he might want more traps set up. Even if I'd gone along there wasn't much I could do. I pulled off my clothes and went to bed.

When I sleep during daylight I always have nightmares, and I must have been having a real Oscar-winner when Potter shook me awake. The others were back and it was almost time to go over for dinner. When they'd got cleaned up, we gathered around the map.

Considering that it was their first day in the field and that they really didn't know what they were supposed to be looking for, they still had accomplished a lot. While Nagy had kept Felisa busy, Garcés and Sam had been using their eyes.

They'd started at the place where the police car had clipped the first rhesus. It was just north of Summit Gardens, about a mile from the overpass and the point where the Gaillard and Madden highways split. There was a secondary road there that went off to the left, across the tracks, and then turned north to run between the railroad and the Cut. About two miles up it turned again and rejoined the main road. The map called that stretch La Pita Road and, on paper at least, it looked tailor-made for the FLP. Not much traffic at any time and only yards from the canal. Rough country interesting to no one except an occasional iguana-hunter.

They'd spent the morning in that area and after lunch moved to the place where the second rhesus had been seen. From what Garcés told me, it was just like any of the other roadside markets all over the Zone, located in or near the towns of any size—an open-front shed with tables of vegetables and fruit, mostly grown on the acre or so of garden right behind. They're operated by the descendants of the Chinese laborers, imported by the French, on leases granted by the Zone government. You can get all kinds of native stuff at them, chiefly food, but an occasional parrot or monkey is for sale.

The team had parked near the place and scouted around for some sign of the rhesus, but apart from some droppings, they didn't see any trace of the animal. In spite of that, both Garcés and Nagy agreed that given a choice and the problems the FLP had, the place was just about ideal for their purpose.

It was easy to get at by road and with a minimum chance of detection. There were a number of side turnings, mostly little cul-de-sacs, where a car or light truck would be invisible to anyone passing by. The terrain was a mixture of standing jungle and open fields of high, dry grass that would serve to hide the monkeys they planned to release.

Best of all, strictly from their point of view, an infected female mosquito needed only to fly a few yards down to Gaillard Cut, where the ships pass at slow speed, giving her a good chance to come aboard and get a free meal from any sailor out on deck to admire the view. The ship would take the nonpaying passenger right to Balboa or Colón; then the lady could fly ashore to spread the infection while the crewmen sailed away, to get sick a few days later at sea.

Of course, any mosquitoes who didn't care to travel by boat had the chance to ride the wind down to Paraíso, a few miles south, and then on to Pedro Miguel and the heavily populated areas below, spreading the virus as they explored new fields.

"There's just one thing about that stretch," Garcés pointed out. "Anyone coming by car from either side of the isthmus has to go past this point right here." His finger indicated the place where La Pita Road branched off. "If they have to get in and out, it has to be past there."

"Wait a minute," I said. "They may not look at it that way. Remember that as far as they know, we're unaware of the last phase of Paradox. There's nothing in the area that needs any special protection. If our cover's any good we won't worry them. As soon as it gets dark every day, they'll figure they've got the place to themselves."

We were still at it when the door opened and in walked Ross. He looked like hell, but he was plugging away. They'd had a report on the *Pineda* and he was on his way to Colón to set up his operation to cover Henriques when he came to pick up the monkeys.

Ross had some news, none of it good.

They'd searched the magazine area as soon as it was light enough to see, both inside and outside the fence, but the only thing they'd found were some tire tracks that led down to the beach and they turned out to belong to some women who had been collecting shells on the night low tide. The ladies hadn't seen a thing, but the explosions had shaken them up pretty badly.

The beehive magazine that had been opened but not blown had been inventoried. Missing were some parachute flares, the kind that come in a metal tube about the size of a rolled-up magazine, a belt of NATO machine gun ammunition, and three thermite grenades.

Ross said, "It's hard to figure out what they want with this kind of stuff. You can't do any damage with the flares and the ammo is only useful if you've got a NATO weapon. The thermite grenades are used against tanks or armored vehicles and fixed fortifications. I guess they just grabbed, because if they'd gone back in the magazine they'd have found frag grenades, high explosive in blocks, some detonators and even a couple of cases of tear gas. That's the kind of stuff terrorist outfits love to get their hands on."

I tried to think of what they might be able to do with the stuff. The flares just go up in the air, ignite and then parachute down. The ammo is only good, as Ross said, in NATO weapons. The grenades were another matter.

Each is about the size of a can of soup, with a handle and pull-ring like any other kind of grenade. You pick out your target, get within throwing range, pull the pin and run like hell for cover after you toss it at your candidate. When it blows it burns with an unquenchable flame hot enough to melt steel. If your target is big and full of other things that like to blow up, you'd better pick a good deep hole to hide in unless you don't mind turning into shish kebab. As a rule, it's not recommended that you use them on things like fuel tanks, which are apt to go up in a mushroom-shaped cloud before you can get clear. The tank blows up, but then, so do you. Unless.

Unless you're as smart as the FLP.

I pointed that out to Ross and he didn't need a lot of convincing. He was on the phone asking for increased protection for every fuel storage tank in the Zone. Whoever he talked to didn't care much for the request. There was just so much manpower available and it was beginning to spread a little thin. If there were any more demands, it was going to be pretty hard to fill them. Most of the guards would be troops who had already done a day's work, and the added strain of night duty wasn't going to provide men with the alertness they'd need to stay on their toes night after night.

When Ross finished his call he slumped back in his chair.

"Mike, are you real sure about all this yellow fever stuff?"

"I have to be, Art. We haven't got anything else to go on. Why?"

"I checked with the sanitary people. They haven't seen anything like an increase in the yellow fever mosquitoes, the *Aedes.*"

"Art, I'd like to tell you that I was sure about anything connected with the FLP, but they don't operate that way. All we can go on are the tiny pieces we've put together. They just aren't the kind of people who leave big, muddy footprints on the kitchen floor that lead right to the cookie jar. If you're asking me for enough evidence to convict, I simply don't have it. If you ask me if I'm sure, all I can do is ask if you've got anything that looks better. We're agreed the FLP is ready to stage something big. If this isn't it, what is?"

He shook his head sadly and pulled himself together enough to get out of the chair. Ross was too good a man to give the job less than his best. The trouble was that we were all human and there's just so much punishment you can hand out before a man begins to crack.

I walked out to the car with him and watched as he turned around and headed for Colón. At least I had one thing to look forward to.

With any luck at all, I'd see Felisa at dinner.

14

"Actually taxonomy is giving things names."

Felisa was doing her best to explain what it was she did, without making me look like an uneducated jerk.

"Anyone can see that a zebra isn't a horse. The taxonomist's job is to discover all the differences between them, and then go on to find out how one kind of zebra is different from another. He has to draw on a lot of other disciplines—genetics, embryology, anatomy—to determine that things that look and act a lot alike are actually two different species. That makes us very different from the other specialists. A man who knows everything in the world about flatworms doesn't need to know the difference between a horse and a donkey. We do."

She had been alone at the bar when I'd come in for dinner. The rest of our team had gone directly into the dining room, but when I'd seen Felisa was not in her usual place I went looking for her. I may have been kidding myself, but it seemed as though her face lit up when I came in and asked if I could join her. The barman brought my order and a fresh one for her and asked if he could shut down.

When we were alone she began to open up. At first she kept the conversation to things she had a direct interest in. When I mentioned I'd spent time in Southeast Asia she had a lot of questions, only a few of which I could answer. About the only experience I'd had with the local wild life had been to try to keep it out of my quarters. Before I got a chance to ask about her, someone came in from the dining room with word that if we wanted to eat we'd better come right away.

Just about everyone had finished and left and we took a small table beside a window that looked out toward the lake. The room had been partially darkened when the others had left, and after our food was served, we had the place to ourselves.

I don't know what we ate and I don't remember much of what we talked about except that something was beginning to build between us. In the quiet room her voice took on a new warmth, projecting only across the width of the table as though what she was saying was meant only for my ears. We finished quickly and then went outside.

"This is the time I take for caring for my babies," she said.

I didn't have any idea what she meant, but tagged along past the laboratory buildings. The last in the row was set off by itself and surrounded by a high chain-link fence topped with barbed wire. Running beside the long dimensions of the building were good-sized cages that could be reached from the inside.

Felisa unlocked the gate in the fence and after I'd followed her inside, she carefully closed and latched it. There was another key for the door at the end of the building and she opened that and went in.

When she switched on the lights I heard a mixed chorus of squeaks and the rustling of scampering clawed feet. The whole inside of the place was filled with banks of shelves loaded with cages of all sizes. As we walked to the far end I looked into some of them and saw the usual assortment of experimental animals—mice, rats, hamsters and guinea pigs—as well as some local small animals and birds, none of which I'd ever seen before.

At the far end of the room was a food preparation setup for

the animals on special diets and a couple of straw-filled pens. While Felisa was busy there I inspected the rest of her zoo. I was still looking them over when Felisa called to me.

"These are a little special. Come and see."

She was holding a pan of freshly mixed mash and a large baby bottle and I watched as she opened the door of one pen and edged in carefully. She laid the pan on the floor and there was a sudden burst of high-pitched squealing as the pile of straw in one corner erupted and out burst a tiny piglet, its little hoofs skidding on the cement floor. It buried its snout in the mash, snuffling loudly as it wolfed down its food.

"He's a wild one," she said. "A farmer brought him in. Sometimes they get too close to a garden and when the older ones are driven away the little ones get left behind."

"I'm surprised they didn't keep this one for dinner."

"Oh, I pay a small reward and then keep them until I can be sure they will be big enough to get along on their own. There are several bands of the wild ones over in the Forest Preserve and I'll take him there and release him soon."

She backed out of the pen and hooked the gate before she turned to the next enclosure. Opening it, she stepped back to let me go in. The tenant was a small fawn, still in its spotted coat, lying on a bed of straw. It tried to get to its feet, but one of its forelegs was encased in plaster and it couldn't quite make it. Felisa knelt down beside it and holding the bottle firmly, slipped the big nipple into its mouth. The fawn nursed hungrily, its eyes half closed. I squatted beside her and watched as she smiled down at the little deer, her cheeks glowing and her eyes bright as the level of the milk dropped quickly.

When most of it was gone, the fawn's pace slackened. Its eyes closed and a thin dribble of milk escaped from its mouth as the last bit was consumed. Felisa eased the nipple from between the fawn's lips, but before she could rise I reached out and put my hand on her shoulder. Still kneeling, she turned and looked into my face, lifting her chin slightly as I kissed her.

With our lips still together, we rose slowly to our feet. As I put my arms around her I heard the bottle drop to the floor, then her arms slid under mine and around my back. Beneath the thin material of her dress I could feel her muscles respond as she tried to draw herself even closer until I raised my mouth from hers.

Now, there are lots of more romantic places than an animal house lit with long strips of fluorescent lights and perfumed with the social lapses of various rodents and birds, but that's where it happened. I took time to look down at her, wondering at the beauty that shone from her like a beacon, and then I kissed her again.

The first kiss had been a message, loud and clear. "I think you're wonderful and I love you very much."

The second message, her answer, was: "I think so, too, so let's get out of here and do something about this marvelous thing we've found."

That sounded sensible and when I released her she cleaned up quickly, took a last look at the two animals and then took me by the hand. She locked the door and the gate and then we walked up the slope to the row of living quarters, my arm around her firm shoulders while hers around my waist drew me close.

Her bungalow was next to Doc Calder's and as we passed I could see him moving around inside. I knew he was a bachelor and I assumed he was alone in the place. How he would react to my paying a visit to Felisa was a problem. He'd been clear enough when he'd warned me off the night before.

If any such thought had occurred to Felisa, there was no sign of it. When we got to her place, a smaller one than Calder's, with a carport for her little sports car, she steered me to the front door. She swung it open and then turned to look up at me when I hesitated.

"Will you come in?"

I didn't know what to do. Part of me was screaming that I was being a first-class damn fool and to get moving and let nature take its own sweet course. Felisa was old enough to make her own decision, but I was acting like a schoolgirl in a back seat.

"That's Calder's place, isn't it?"

A tiny frown was beginning to show. "Yes; why do you ask?"

"Would he approve if he knew I was visiting?"

"That doesn't concern me. I don't tell him how to live his life."

"But he might think a little the less of you."

She looked up at me, clearly puzzled, but she wasn't any more puzzled than I was. I knew I couldn't put it into words for her, but I wanted desperately for her to understand. What I had in my mind was something more important than a casual roll in the hay for myself. I knew it would mean more to her, that it would be a commitment she was making, sure that it meant the same thing to me.

Maybe it was all the frustration I was having with Paradox. Whatever was happening to me, it was the first time. I started to make the attempt to tell her what it was and I managed to get the first few words out before I suddenly stopped.

At a lit window in the house next door the shade was being pulled down by an unseen hand. We both saw it and then Felisa turned away and went into her house, closing the door firmly behind her. I stood for a moment and then walked away, hating myself for the clumsy idiot I was.

A few yards away, I turned and looked back. Her house was dark and when I got to the guesthouse and looked again the lights had still not come on.

There was no sign of her when we all came in for breakfast. We ate quickly, anxious to get out to the location and begin work. The night before, Garcés had broken the whole stretch into search zones. He would take one side of the road and Potter the other, heading south, while the rest of us started to film. We drove out to the starting point, and while Sam assembled the camera I got a look around.

The terrain was pretty much like what I'd known in Vietnam and in Thailand, a mixture of open savanna and stretches of jungle where there was enough topsoil to sustain really big trees. Most of what was around us was single-canopy jungle, the huge trees rising straight without limbs to seventy-five feet or so, where the boughs sprang from the trunks to interlace with their neighbors, the whole affair bound together with heavy vines and creepers. The ground was soft and springy to the foot, the loosely compacted fallen leaves and rotten twigs disintegrating quickly into fresh soil. Walking was easy in the dimness, where the sun barely penetrated the solid mass of greenery high above. Only when one of the giant trees fell victim to age or the hand of a woodcutter would the sun reach the ground to permit the low bushes and shrubs to flourish, creating a tangle of lush growth that was passable only after a lot of work with an ax or machete.

Out in the open the going was easy enough through the tall, dry grass, but as the sun rose higher we found ourselves seeking the shade more and more. Luckily our subjects were doing the same thing.

Nagy was starting us off with insects and we didn't have to go far to find the right actors. The first scene featured a sedan-size beetle that made its living shaping balls of dung and then playing a game of one-man soccer with them. Why this was important to it Nagy didn't explain.

Next he turned up a larger type, the tractor-trailer size, with a pair of horns like one of John Wayne's steers in *Red River.* It took a lot of coaxing to get this lens louse to follow the script while poor Sam lay stretched out in the dirt trying to stay with the critter on the longest lens he had.

There wasn't any point in telling him that the film would most likely never see a screen and that he might just as well be shooting with an empty camera. He would have replied by pointing to his name on the camera slate and gone on doing his best to keep up with whatever he was given to film, whether it was eight inches or eight miles away.

We tried to stay close to the road and show a high profile to anyone passing by. Some people slowed down to see what we were doing and a couple even got out for a closer look. For a few minutes we played host to a father and son, Panamanians out for iguana with a pack of mixed-breed dogs that showed the extreme variations possible within the species *Canis familiaris.* The father stood off a way, but the kid came right up close to watch the crazy gringos at play. I hoped that when they got home he'd tell his buddies what he'd seen and pass the word that way to the populace.

Even though it was just a few miles to the field station, I'd asked for box lunches, and when Garcés and Potter got back we took a break and sat under a tree to eat. Neither one had seen a rhesus or any further trace that the two not yet accounted for were in the area. They hadn't noticed any cans or jars with standing water in them or signs of anything that didn't belong.

When we finished eating I sent Garcés and Potter north. We'd be moving, so I gave them the word that we'd be at the railroad crossing at about four to collect them. We drove over to the main road to set up and that's where Ross found us. He'd finished his preparations in Colón and was going back to Balboa until the *Pineda* was due to arrive.

"There's nothing fancy about it," he said. "The shipment of monkeys will be off-loaded and put into a warehouse we can keep right under our eyes. When Henriques shows up we'll be prepared for him. I've got foot patrols ready and four teams in cars to shuttle behind him. Luckily there are only two routes he can take, one that leads into the Zone and the other that goes to the Republic."

"You'll have radio control, I guess."

"I don't dare."

"You mean you think the FLP will be likely to intercept?"

"No; they're not the ones that worry me. It's the Panamanians."

"How do they figure in it?"

"Look, this Henriques is almost certain to make tracks to get out of the Zone. Whether he takes Randolph Road or the Bolívar Highway, it still takes him to Panama. If I try to control the surveillance by radio, it's not going to be long before the Guardia Nacional wakes up to the fact that I'm running a covert operation on their real estate. They're going to start asking questions, and if I don't have a lot of answers handy, we're all in for trouble."

He had a point. We'd been playing Paradox so close to the vest we'd forgotten all about our opposite numbers across the Zone line. If things kept breaking wrong for us and right for the FLP, we were going to have to let the Panamanians in on the story. Their health authorities had to be given a chance to tool up for what was going to happen or we'd be as guilty as the FLP for the deaths that followed.

"One more thing," Ross said. "There was another demonstration last night."

"Jesus, what did they pull this time?"

"A helicopter on the pad at Albrook blew up."

"How did they get close enough to do that?"

"They fired a round into the fuel tank. Totaled the chopper."

"Wait a minute. That wouldn't be enough to make it blow."

"That's what I thought. Hutto finally figured it out. Remember that missing belt of machine gun ammo? Every fifth round is a tracer. That's what the sharpshooter used. It only took one to do the work."

"Anybody get hurt?"

"No. There was a walking guard on the chopper and he'd gone off a way—for the usual reason, I guess—and when his back was turned the thing went up."

So while we were worrying about thermite grenades and fuel tanks, the FLP was using a ten-cent round to blow up a quarter-million-dollar helicopter. Whatever we were doing, it wasn't right.

"Art, maybe we'd better pick up this guy Henriques and his monkeys. We've got to do something."

"What can I charge him with, Mike? As far as I know, there's no law against owning all the rhesus monkeys you want. We can't even tie him to the 'demonstrations.' If we try an old-fashioned snatch-and-grab, there are going to be questions asked when he's missed. Right now, with the talks scheduled to begin, it could be a four-star mess. Hell, we can't even charge him with mopery."

"What's mopery?"

"That's an old law school gag. Mopery is defined as 'the felonious defloration of young owls.' "

If Ross could come up with that kind of gag, he was still in good enough shape to handle his end. I got out of his air-conditioned car and watched him drive off, then got back to work.

When we finished I drove up to the railroad crossing. Garcés was sitting at the roadside with nothing to report. His side of the road, between La Pita and the tracks, hadn't shown a thing. At some point he'd got too close to a black palm and the damn thing had reached right out and stabbed him with its thorns, leaving a bunch where he couldn't get at them. Sam went to work with a pair of tweezers from his tool kit and while he was busy extracting thorns, Potter turned up.

He was holding something in his hands. It was a half coconut shell and when he took one hand away, I saw that it held about a half cupful of water.

"What is it, John?"

"I'm not sure, Captain. It was so well hid I almost missed it."

"Why did you bother to bring it back here?"

"Well, sir, for one thing it just didn't look like it belonged. There's no coconut trees anywhere around here, far as I can see. I just figured he must have put it there."

"Who, John?"

"The man I was tailing. I found where he'd pulled off the road and parked. It was right near one of those horse stalls and the truck that came in to check the trap this morning had gone right over most of his tracks. That's where I picked him up. The way it looks, he'd walk along a certain number of paces and then stop and look around for a place to put one of these. It wasn't until I got to the last one that I found out he'd been planting them."

Garcés said, "Let me see that thing, Sergeant."

Potter handed it to him, careful not to spill out the liquid.

"I'm sorry I didn't find the others, sir. I guess they just sort of blended in. I would have missed this one if my foot hadn't kicked the big leaf it was under. Then when I saw the water I got to wondering. Anybody can see it hasn't rained around here in a hell of a long time."

Garcés took a good look at the contents of the shell and then, without a word, passed it to Nagy. I didn't know what they found so interesting until Nagy looked up.

"Let's get back to the station," he said, his voice peculiarly strained.

• • •

15

If someone had walked in on us he'd probably have thought we were all nuts. Nagy had carried the shell half as if it held a dose of the FLP's nitroglycerin, and when we got back to the guest-house he held it while Garcés got the lid of a coffee container and Potter pulled up a lamp. Nagy poured the liquid into the shallow lid, and for the first time I saw that the water was teeming with tiny darting and diving creatures. Garcés pulled out a small magnifier and the two of them took turns staring at the little swimmers.

From what I could see with the naked eye, they didn't look like much. If this was the creature that spread yellow fever, it didn't appear very frightening.

Garcés was shaking his head and finally he put down the hand glass.

"Well, it's not the *Aedes.* Doesn't even look like the same kind of larvae."

"This isn't the mosquito that spreads yellow jack?"

He was positive. "It is not the *Aedes.* I'm as sure of that as I am that it's not a swan."

Nagy wasn't willing to let it go at that. "Okay, if it's not the mosquito we've been looking for, then what is it?"

Garcés said, "You're asking the wrong man. There are over seventeen hundred species already described that can be called mosquitoes and there are probably just as many more that science hasn't gotten around to yet. For all we know, this may be one of them."

"Wait a minute," I said. "Mosquitoes carry all kinds of diseases, don't they? Maybe we've been wrong in thinking just about yellow fever. One thing is certain, though. Those little things didn't just happen to be where Potter found them. Somebody had to put them there and he did it for a purpose."

Garcés nodded. "Okay, let's settle it."

He got up from the table and went to his room for a moment, returning with a heavy volume, one that he'd borrowed from the station library. He opened it on the table and spoke to Nagy.

"You describe and I'll check."

Nagy took the hand glass and bent over the mass of wrigglers. Then for the next few minutes he delivered a stream of technical terms that didn't mean a thing to me, while Garcés leafed quickly through the book. As far as I could see, they were narrowing down the field, concentrating on the species that matched the specimens we had, and eliminating the others.

When Nagy stopped describing, Garcés looked up from the book.

"Well, we've eliminated the Anophelinae and the whole Aedes family. That means we can rule out not just yellow fever, but malaria and dengue as well."

Nagy wasn't ready to quit. "Keep going. I'll find out what these things are even if I have to microdissect the little sons of bitches."

He looked up, frowning. "Anybody have something sharp?"

Potter reached into his pocket and came up with one of his pointed toothpicks. Nagy poured a little of the water on a sheet of white paper and used the toothpick to shove one of the wrigglers to one side. He swiveled the second lens of the hand glass into position and looked at the specimen he'd isolated.

"Okay. Now I need a needle or a pin."

Sam had a needle in his camera cleaning outfit and Nagy started to describe again. It was slower going now, but it ended when Garcés suddenly looked up from the book and said, "Oh, my God. No."

Nagy straightened up. "Have you got it?"

Garcés nodded, unable to say more for a moment.

"For a moment I hoped I was wrong, but there's no doubt."

Nagy said, "It's *Haemagogus,* isn't it?"

"Haema—what?" I must have sounded like an idiot, but I couldn't see what all the fuss was about.

Garcés looked up at me. "These little things are the larvae of a mosquito belonging to the group known as *Haemagogus,* God help us, the vector of general mammalian yellow fever. When it feeds, it can take the virus from any infected animal and pass it to any other susceptible to the disease."

"Including man?"

He nodded slowly. "Man most of all. One bite will deliver a lethal dose. It will also make any higher ape damn sick and do almost as much for other species, such as the rhesus. The greater the susceptibility, the better the chance that the next mosquito to bite the victim will pass it on to another host. If the *Aedes* mosquito is Jack the Ripper, then this little beauty is Attila the Hun."

If we'd had any doubts about the final step in the FLP's plan, they were gone now. The circle had closed. They had the virus, stolen by Benitez. They had the rhesus, shipped to Henriques. Now they were planting the vector, the *Haemagogus.*

Garcés briefed us. "The characteristic of the whole group is that they like to breed in the tiny amounts of water held in plants high at the top of the jungle canopy. Many plants, like the epiphytes, collect water during the rains and hold it for use during the dry season. These mosquitoes use that tiny bit to breed in, a perfect adaptation to their chosen environment. They will not descend to ground level unless they are forced to do so. If you want to have the *Haemagogus* live below the canopy you've got to put him there. That's just what somebody has been doing."

"Wait a minute. How did he get them in the first place? He hasn't been climbing trees and gathering them like a farmer's wife?"

"He'd only need a few for a start. They're not hard to breed if you know the technique. Give them the right conditions and you can breed all you want. We do it all the time with *Aedes* for research use. There's even a technique for artificially inseminating the females."

I looked up and saw Herbert standing in the doorway, listening to the conversation. As yet he hadn't contributed a thing on this leg of the job and bringing him along had so far been a total loss. Not that he got in the way or anything like that. He was following the same routine I'd seen back at The Rock, doing his yoga and his breathing, sleeping a couple of hours every afternoon and then spending the rest of his time reading or looking at his notebook.

What we needed was some information on how the FLP had got the mosquitoes into place, and the best source was Potter.

"Okay, John, just exactly what did you see?"

Potter shifted a little from one foot to the other, embarrassed at having every eye in the room on him.

"Sir, could I get a drink? It's pretty dry out there."

He looked dry, his uniform streaked with dust and sweat.

"I've got a better idea. Let's all take a few minutes to clean up and maybe we'll be able to do a lot more."

There was no argument to that and the whole bunch felt a lot fresher after a drink and a shower.

"Okay, John, let's take it from the top."

He took a last pull at his bottle of beer and set it on the floor at his feet. There was a fresh toothpick in his mouth and he seemed a lot cooler in the slacks and flowered shirt he'd brought with him from Hawaii.

"Well, I almost missed him. He'd pulled into one of those little lanes leading to a mosquito trap with a horse. Like I said before, when they checked the trap this morning they went over most of his tire marks. Then I saw where he'd parked on the grass."

"Okay, what did he do then?"

"He took off on foot, heading north, cutting right along, cross-country, not staying on any kind of trail. It looks to me like he was counting steps or something, because every so often he'd stop and walk around a little. I guess that's when he planted one of those shells and then went on, counting steps until he figured it was time to drop another. Now that I think about it, he must have stopped and used a flashlight to find a good spot and then gone on again. My bad luck I didn't know what he was doing until I just kind of stumbled over that last one."

That was as much as I'd ever heard Potter say at one time.

Nagy said, "He must have had a larger container and a supply of smaller ones to fill when he'd found a place. How many times do you think he stopped?"

Potter thought for a minute. "Maybe a dozen or so in the two miles he covered last night."

Garcés looked at me. "First thing tomorrow, Mike, we've got to get those things, every last one. Do you think you can find them all, Sergeant?"

"I think so, sir, now that I know what he was doing."

Nagy asked, "How soon before these things hatch and fly away?"

Garcés shook his head. "I don't know this species, but it can't be long. Once that happens we can forget about trying to do anything about them." He thought a moment. "That doesn't mean that the same people won't be out there again tonight and every night planting more."

"Wait a minute," I said. "Something you said earlier, remember, about there only being one way to get into the area? Anybody driving in has to get past that one point, right?"

"That's right. What do you have in mind?"

"Well, if we had people right there where the area begins, they'd be able to spot a car coming in and grab them."

Garcés shook his head. "No. My guess is that if they saw people around they'd just pick up speed and get out of there."

"That's right. A real roadblock would spook them and at the same time it would tip them off to the fact that we're onto their plan. If we had just a couple of men, well hidden, they'd be likely to roll right past and get to work."

"Probably. They'd be anxious to get to work, finish up and get out."

"Okay. Now, John, how many sets of tracks did you see?"

"Just one, Captain. I guess one man stayed with the car. If there were any more, I didn't see their tracks."

"Now, how long would you say it took your guy to cover his route?"

Potter thought for a minute. "Maybe three hours or so."

That meant the planters could wait until after midnight, when the traffic on the road would be at its minimum, have enough time to work and still be away by daylight.

Garcés agreed. "That's the only way that makes sense. By the way," he added, "who gets to cover the detail? It'll take a couple of men, at least."

There was only one answer to that. It would be our ace jungle tracker, John Potter, and guess who else?

Dinner wasn't much fun. Our whole bunch went over to the dining room together, and as I came in the door, I saw Felisa at a table for just two with an older woman I hadn't met. She didn't even raise her head, but I could feel the temperature drop as I followed the others to the table they usually ate at.

I took a seat where I could look across at her—where, if she'd wanted to, she had only to raise her eyes to tell me what I wanted to know. She was eating at her normal pace, making no visible attempt to finish quickly and get away, but the message was clear. If a move was to be made, it would have to be mine.

It couldn't have come at a worse moment. I had absolutely no intention of bowing out of her life, but this just wasn't the time.

I ate as quickly as I decently could and left the table for some rest before I had to leave and get into position. If Felisa was aware of my going, she gave no indication that it concerned her one way or another. The only one who seemed to have the faintest idea that something had happened was Doc Calder. He gave me his usual small smile when I came in and another when I left. If he had seen us together the night before, he kept it to himself.

If you think the jungle is deathly quiet at night, filled with slinking creatures that creep up on you and then pounce, you're wrong. At least, you are about the one we were in. There must have been hundreds of creatures within earshot of where we were parked, all contributing to the racket. Like our friend Herbert, they'd had a good rest during the heat of the day and now they were all out for choir practice. There was a steady din of squeaks, twitters, chitters and grunts, punctuated, every now and then, by the roars and yowls of the bigger beasts confined just down the road in the small zoo at Summit Gardens.

I'd backed the sedan off the highway where it would be screened from headlights coming from either direction and killed the engine. The noises ebbed and flowed around us, reaching a peak a few minutes after we got there, when there was a deafening crash from somewhere beyond the horse stall a few yards back. That set off a general shrieking and cursing from a colony of parrots spending the night in a low tree, for all the world resembling a bunch of frenetic teen-agers at a rock concert.

Potter was out of the car like a shot, his riot gun in one hand and a flashlight in the other, both aimed in the general direction of the ruckus. When he switched the light off and turned to me, I saw his teeth gleam in the darkness.

"One of those sloths. Picked a branch that didn't hold his weight."

I took my flashlight and walked back toward the place for a closer look. A sloth is an ugly-looking beast by any standard, and this one was typical. It appeared to be not a bit hurt by the fall and was trying to right itself. Maybe I should say wrong itself, since their normal position is, by our standards, upside down. When it got turned I could see a little one hanging on for dear life and the mother began to crawl, like a swimmer in slow motion, back to the tree. I started to get a little closer and I must have crossed the sloth's warning line because she swiveled her head around and hissed at me.

I switched off the light and let my eyes get accustomed to the semi-darkness. In the stall trap a few yards away, the captive horse snuffled and stamped and nickered a little when he caught my scent. I had no trouble getting his, a sharp mixture of manure and urine that brought back a vivid memory of my old man's barn. Maybe it was Chanel No. 5 for mosquitoes, but all it did was make my tail ache. It was out in the barn that I used to get whacked. I went back to the car and tried to settle down.

For the first half hour or so there was a small amount of traffic, probably people who'd spent the evening in Balboa or the city coming home to Gamboa. A Canal Zone police car went by, heading south for the change of shift, and then we had the place to ourselves. The local population of fauna settled down and the noise level dropped. Every so often there would be a brief outburst when some predator, snake or cat, murdered a bird or a monkey for a late snack, but after a while even that stopped.

Potter sat beside me, his riot gun propped against the car door, ready to hit high gear if he had to react in a hurry. He didn't make a sound, but I was sure he was fully alert. Every once in a while a small cramp would make a muscle in my thigh begin to twitch and I'd get out and walk around the car to get the blood moving.

I looked at my watch so often that finally I took it off and slipped it into my pocket. Potter would let me know when it was time to go.

The high point of the night was when the moon rose, casting long shadows across the road, and it was by its light that we saw the first sign of something on the road.

It was a tribe of about ten or fifteen coatimondi, a big one leading and the rest tailing along in its tracks, with a little guy, less than half size, playing caboose. The leader knew we were there; it didn't bother him, though. He gave us one glance, his big rubbery nose twitching, but he didn't pause or miss a step.

If the mosquito-planter was coming at all, he should have got to work already in order to finish before daylight. I was just about to say something about it to Potter, when he spoke first.

"It's four o'clock, Captain. Do you want to wait any longer?"

I started the car and drove back to the field station. Just our luck that the night we pick to keep an eye out for the FLP they had something else on the schedule. I told myself that it was worth the effort just to be sure that they hadn't planted any more larvae for us to gather up, but that wasn't much help.

There was only one light at the guesthouse. Herbert was coiled up in the wicker chair he'd preempted as his regular place. From somewhere he'd promoted a sheet of illustration board and I went to his side to take a look at what he was doing. It didn't tell me much.

He'd covered the whole board with circles, squares and triangles, all interconnected with solid or dotted lines and labeled with notes in what looked like shorthand. Before I could ask him what it meant, he looked up.

"Major Ross called earlier. He asked me to tell you that the ship was in and would be unloaded in the morning. Then he said that you'd had a call from someone named Tiny, who wanted you to call back."

I wanted to talk to Tiny about as much as I wanted a root canal job, but there was no way to get out of it. I'd have to get to a secure line and that meant a trip to Balboa, though it turned out Ross had thought of that, too.

"The major said if you wanted you could place your call from the office in Colón. He gave me the directions in case you preferred to go there."

He handed me a carefully written note and I made a quick decision. If I went to Colón I could get a look at Art's arrangements to keep track of Henriques. I could even treat myself to a couple of hours' sleep before I took off, and I was on my way to my room when Herbert called me back.

"I was wondering if you'd like to go over this with me."

He held up his chart. Leave it to Herbert to feel chatty at four in the morning.

"If it isn't something red hot, I'd rather look at it when I've had some sleep."

He didn't show any disappointment, just nodded and went back to looking at his work. If he didn't think it was all that important, there was no use losing any of the little sleep I'd still be able to get.

16

"I hate to bother you when you're so busy, Captain." Tiny only called me captain when she was pissed about something. "Perhaps you can take a minute from your duties to let me know what the hell is going on down there?"

There wasn't any point in telling her that we were still running a couple of laps behind the FLP and not much chance of catching up. She switched on her recorder and I gave her the story as I knew it. I had to stop and explain about the jungle mosquitoes and then tell her about my night out with Potter.

"You're sure nobody showed?"

"There's only the one way in and nobody went past us by car or on foot."

"I don't know, Mike. If the monkeys are there, they should be loading the area with bugs ready to bite. Maybe somebody in the FLP goofed."

"They haven't slipped so far."

"Let's just keep hoping. What's happening right now?"

"The team is out trying to locate the larvae. Just in case the FLP sends somebody up to check, they've got orders to dump them and refill the shells with water. That way it may look as if they've hatched and flown off."

"What about the monkeys?"

"They're still on board the *Pineda* or just being taken off. Ross gave orders to put them into a warehouse he can keep under surveillance. When Henriques takes them out he'll be followed. Depending on what he does, we'll decide what to do next."

"You mean you haven't developed a plan?"

I was beginning to get a little hot.

"That's exactly right. You get that computer you're all so in love with to tell me what the FLP has in mind and then maybe I'll be able to know what I'm going to do. Right now I'm flying by the seat of my pants and getting damn little help at it."

"Okay, take it easy. Call me back when you get something."

I hung up and had one of the men show me where Ross had set up a command post for the stakeout. It was a second-floor room with a clear view of the big loading doors to the warehouse. There was a good bit of traffic as the *Pineda*'s cargo was off-loaded and brought in for storage.

Ross was sitting by the window. "The monkeys are right inside the door. They're in two shipping cages. I got somebody to clean out the mess and give them fresh food and water, but the poor things are still a little rocky from the trip."

"Anybody taking a special interest in them?"

"Not so far. I saw one kind soul go in with a hand of bananas and I suppose he fed them to the rhesuses, but nobody's come to claim them."

"The FLP man is going to have to show pretty soon. The mosquitoes they set out are ready to hatch and it's going to take a couple of days before the monkeys are infectious."

Ross was worried. "Mike, there's just so long we can keep this many people tied up. I'm using every man stationed here on the Atlantic side and all I could spare from the other posts. If anything big is to break, I just won't have the bodies to cover it."

"They lock that place up at night, don't they? If he doesn't show up by the end of the day you can cover it with just a few men until they open again in the morning."

"Sure, but what do I do then? If this guy doesn't show by tomorrow night we're going to have to work out something else."

He leaned back in his chair, but he didn't take his eyes from the warehouse door down below.

"Look, Art, let me take over for a while. What's the signal?"

He looked up, doubtful about turning over to anyone else.

"Go ahead. If you wear yourself out now you won't be fit for the tough part later on."

That convinced him and I took his seat as he left. A minute later I saw him go into the warehouse. Coming out after a moment, he walked up the street toward his local office. All I had to do was sit there, and if I saw Henriques take the monkeys, pull the shade down halfway to start the works in motion.

If that sounds easy, just try it for an hour or two. I was afraid to take my eyes from the place for a second. With all the people moving around, fork-lifts and trucks and dollies cutting in and out, I didn't dare move. First I started to get thirsty and then a little groggy, and just before Ross got back I began looking for an empty bottle or can, anything that would serve to satisfy the cry for help that was coming from my GU tract.

Ross took over, and after taking care of first things first, I came back for a last word.

"Art, if you can keep this effort going until tomorrow night, then I don't think we ought to take it any further. If the FLP want their monkeys they'll have that much time to come for them. If they don't come by tomorrow night we can figure they're not coming at all and call this off and work out something else. Okay?"

He nodded grimly, not liking the idea but unable to come up with anything better.

When I got down stairs I remembered I'd left the field station without taking time for breakfast. I walked a few blocks along the shady streets looking for a likely place to get some lunch before going back to work. There seemed to be a number of good places, but when I saw a small sports car parked in front of one spot I went in with nothing but hope that I'd find what I was looking for inside.

Only a few tables were occupied, and when my eyes got used to the dimness of the place I saw her sitting at the back. If she saw me approaching she gave no sign, not even looking up from her plate when I sat down at the other side of the small table. For a moment I thought she might put down her knife and fork, get up and walk out; if she had, I was fully prepared to make a real scene out of it.

Maybe she realized that and just continued to eat, her eyes on her plate and her face set in stone. The waiter came up with a menu, but I just waved him away, telling him I'd have the same as Felisa. When he'd gone I spoke to her for the first time, keeping my voice low.

"Felisa, if you act this way every time we have a misunderstanding then we're going to have a hell of a life together."

She didn't look up, but I saw color come to her cheeks.

"The very least you could have done the other night was give me a chance to explain. I think that's what I would have done had it been the other way round."

Still no answer, but I could see that she was breathing just a bit faster.

"And if you'd said that you couldn't explain what it was, then I'd have taken that on faith."

I thought she was going to say something, but right at that moment the old waiter appeared and set my plate in front of me. Automatically I reached for knife and fork, then I looked at her again.

She was gazing right into my eyes. "Eat your turtle stew, Mike. It's too good to waste."

She'd driven down to Colón to arrange for the delivery of some new equipment from the Free Zone. She'd be back at the field station for dinner. I took her out to her car and kissed her right in front of the world. She went off to take care of her business and I walked back to see how Ross was doing.

No changes there. I got the car and started back for Gamboa. I saw what Ross had meant about covering the approaches to Colón. If you're heading for the Republic there are just two ways to go and they come together a couple of miles out of Colón. With radio control he could have cut his team in half. As it was, he'd have to keep his man in sight just about all the way. It wasn't the best setup in the world, but it was the only one he had.

I made good time getting back, heading directly for the station and not taking time to hunt for the others out in the boondocks. They knew what they were doing without me to fuss over them.

Herbert was there, of course. It was almost time for his regular two hours of sleep, but he was up and working at the big table in the center of the room. He had the same chart I'd looked at the night before, embellished now with colored ink, plus several sheets of what looked like mathematical equations. I'd forgotten all about him, but there was no reason I couldn't take time to listen right now.

"I've been working on the makeup of the FLP," he said. "Putting together all the data we have and matching it against a reasonable estimate of the time frame as we know it."

"Okay, what have you got?"

He hunted around among his papers and came up with a calendar.

"Now, which one of the FLP do we know of first?"

"I guess that would be the one who planted the smoke bomb in the lock mechanism."

"No, that's not what I mean. He was the first we heard of, but which one do we know about first, speaking chronologically?"

I thought for a moment. "I suppose that would be Benitez, the lab technician who took the virus. The one with blue eyes."

Herbert pointed to the calendar. "And we have a witness who puts Benitez in southern New Jersey from this date to this one and another who says he left there a day later. Now, who do we know of appearing next?"

"Charles Davis, the American who bought three monkeys in Boston."

Herbert pointed to his calendar. The date that Davis had been reported was the day following Benitez's departure. "Next?"

"That would be Ernesto Fernandez, the one who shipped the first three from Providence."

"How far from Boston to Providence?"

"Not much. Maybe an hour or so."

He pointed again to the calendar. It was the same date.

"Let's keep going. Who's next?"

"The one Ross is waiting for now, German Henriques, the man who picked up the first three rhesuses. No. Wait a minute. We heard of him next, but he didn't appear until the ship arrived in Colón."

"That's right. Before then, after about a week or so, the next one to turn up was another American, the hippie with long blond hair. Irwin Jones, the one the dealers didn't trust to take good care of the animals. That was in New York." Herbert ticked off the date on the calendar. "Next?"

"The nervous one in Baltimore, Luis Martínez."

His finger pointed to the next day, plenty of time to get from New York to the dockside in Baltimore.

"Now let's do a little educated thinking. Martínez goes to the airport in New York or Washington and takes a plane to Tocumen, here in Panama. Say the next day. Now, what was the date of the first FLP 'demonstration' here?"

I didn't have to look anymore. It had come a couple of days later.

"Now, the date of the arrival of the first shipment and the first report of a rhesus running around free?"

That fit right in. So did the sabotage at the magazines, followed by the blowing up of the chopper.

"Last we have the planting of the *Haemagogus* larvae, right here."

That was just two nights before. The rhesus arrival was in the time frame for the FLP to infect and release them. Freighters don't run on timetables, but this one had docked within a day or so of when the monkeys would be needed. The timing of the whole operation was almost uncanny.

"Herbert, you've done a hell of a good piece of work, at least as good as these people from the FLP."

"Captain, how many of them do you really think there are?"

"I've thought about it. There's the medical specialist, the one we know as Benitez. There's the explosives man, who we don't have a name for. One of them is a hell of a good shot. He nicked that chopper in just the right spot, according to Hutto. Now, stateside there were the two Americans, Davis and Jones, the blond hippie and the other leg man, who made the buys. I'd say there must be between six and ten in the whole FLP, including the top man, the one who does the planning. What's your estimate?"

"Just as it's always been. The whole FLP may be just one man," he said calmly.

I didn't know what the hell to say. My head just wasn't set to accept any idea like that. The mere thought that one lone man had the whole might and majesty of the United States by the short hairs and was twisting was more than you could grasp when it was tossed at you like that. The whole thing was ridiculous, of course, and I said so.

Herbert pointed to another part of his chart.

"What's the one special physical characteristic we've got for Benitez?"

"Wait a minute. I remember. He's got blue eyes."

"And that's fairly unusual for a Latin. Unusual enough for people to remember it. He couldn't go around wearing sunglasses while he was working in the lab, so your witnesses noticed them. Now, when he made his next appearance, he used an Anglo-Saxon name, Davis, and changed his accent so nobody thought anything about the color of his eyes. A few hours later he was being a Latin again and, as Fernandez, he wore sunglasses. He went back to the Anglo-Saxon as Irwin Jones and added a blond wig that would go with blue eyes. It was normal enough so that the witnesses didn't even notice it. Next he returned to Latin again as Martínez, the man who didn't want to touch anything. No report on his eyes, but I think that if there had, it would have been that Martínez's eyes were blue."

"Well, Herbert, it's an interesting idea, but I wouldn't want to gamble on it."

"To be frank, it took me some time to reach the conclusion. Maybe that's because I've been putting myself in his place. That's dangerous, because while he may be at my intelligence level, he's still another person, with a different personality makeup. For example, he enjoys a joke and wants to share it."

"What does that mean?" I asked.

"The humor of the situation is right there for anyone who wants to take the trouble to find it."

"I don't see any joke."

"Can't you see it? He's told us."

"What do you mean, he's told us?"

"Just look at the names he's used. Alejandro Benitez, Charles Davis, Ernesto Fernandez, German Henriques, Irwin Jones, Luis Martínez. He's just followed the alphabet."

He'd written the names down and he passed the list over.

"Wait a minute, Herbert. He broke the pattern between *J* and *L.* What happened to *K?*"

"*K* is not a letter used in Spanish, except for foreign words they've adopted, like *kilogramo* or *kerosena.* Our man is Spanish-speaking, so he just left it out. If he'd needed another name he'd have used something like Noriberto Osmena, followed by, say, Pablo Quiñones and Raul Salazar."

"Maybe all those names were picked by one man, but he didn't necessarily have to be the one to use them."

"Look at it the other way, Captain. From all we know, this is a most unusual man. He has the capacity to learn, and learn quickly, all the technical matters that ordinary men, even those with talent and intelligence, like your Sergeant Hutto, take half a lifetime to master. From his actions we know he is willing to inflict losses to achieve his goal, but not one more than is absolutely necessary. With his own ability, he doesn't need others to take any major part in the affairs of his FLP. He may make use of outsiders, but only when there is no better or more efficient way to do it on his own."

"Herbert, I don't know whether to pray that you're right or wrong. If you've worked this out to the right solution, then we've only got one man to catch. The trouble is that he's going to be pretty tough to find. We've got to outthink him and I'm not sure that we've got what it takes. Not you, mind you. It's the rest of us poor mortals, who just got average brains dealt out to them."

Herbert began gathering up his notes and calculations. He'd made his point and that was that. He'd taken the evidence he had to work with and put it through the mill and he'd come up with a projection he could live with.

That didn't mean I could, though. I knew that there were anthropologists who could start out with a bone chip, and with nothing else to go on, put together the whole picture of the creature it belonged to. That was okay as far as anatomy went, but it didn't give the slightest inkling about what the thing had in its brain. The kind of man who could think up a stunt like Paradox might be a genius, but he had to have some limitations. He'd be as prone to worry and self-doubt as anyone and when he did hit a low spot he would need to have some support, some other human he could talk to about his fears. I put that thought to Herbert.

He shrugged and then nodded, like a man who doesn't want to argue and is willing to concede a minor point just to end the discussion.

"Yes, I took that factor into account. Without actually knowing the man, it's hard to give it the proper weight, but it still doesn't materially alter the basic equation. Taken as a whole and without further testing, the hypothesis will compute."

Holding his papers and the chart, he went to his room. A couple of minutes later I heard the shower. Herbert was right on schedule.

Maybe I should have given Herbert's idea more thought, but when I heard a car door slam outside I was on my feet and ready to hear what the others had found. The moment they came in the door I knew it was trouble.

Garcés spoke first. "We found more larvae, some planted the other night and some that were dropped off last night."

"Last night? That's impossible. Nobody got past us. Right, John?"

Garcés shook his head wearily. "These were new ones, a bunch in a puddle under a road culvert and more in some wild banana plants and a couple of others."

Potter nodded. "That's right, Captain. They had to be new tracks. A couple of times they were right on top of the ones I'd made. They were back last night."

It didn't make sense. The only road was the one in from the south. There was no other way for a car to get into the area.

"Which way were the new tracks heading, John?"

"They were heading south. He'd swing left or right every so often, but there's no way he could be going any way but south. I checked him all the way and far as I can tell, he stayed in the jungle until he was past where we were waiting. Then he got on the hardtop road and that's where I lost him."

Maybe he'd walked right past us on his way back north to get his car and we'd just plain missed him. That didn't sound right, though. He'd have to have covered his route and made the trip back at a dead run to travel that far. Unless.

Unless there was somebody else, somebody waiting with a car to pick him up and get him clear. If so, that shot the hell out of Herbert's one-man-gang theory. Our guy just had to have help to manage what had been done. One man had driven the other in just before dark, let him out and then picked him up before daylight. That had to be the way they did it. So much for Herbert.

There was a long silence. Garcés and Nagy were just sitting, all too obviously happy to be off their feet and resting. Only Potter looked as if he had something to say.

"What is it, John?"

He looked down at his big hands and it was clear he was trying to find the right words. Finally he began and it was pretty obvious he didn't like what he had to say.

"Sir, we've been figuring that these people used a car to get in, right?"

"That's the only way, isn't it?"

He shook his head. "Maybe they took the train. It stops right up here at Gamboa."

"No way, John. The Canal Zone police have a man to meet every train. If they see someone who doesn't belong they ask questions."

The answer had slid right off my tongue, but I wasn't willing to really put my weight on it. Not with the FLP. I went to the phone and dialed Ross. It only took him about five minutes to get me an answer.

"That's right about the Canal Zone cops meeting every train. They always have. Nobody got off at Gamboa last night who didn't belong there."

"So that's out?"

"Not really. The Panama Railroad is one track. Last night's train was sidetracked north of the town to let the northbound go past. It does that every night."

That had to be the right answer. Our guy had taken the train southbound from the Atlantic side. He'd known about the regular sidetrack and all he had to do was drop off the train and wait. When the train cleared and the Zone cop had gone off about his business, all that was left was a few minutes' walking along the track, across the bridge, and he was in the target area. He had all the rest of the night to travel down the line and board the first train or bus in the morning. He could go either way, north or south, as he chose.

The thing was it was something that one man alone could do. He'd use help if he had it, but it would work if he didn't.

In Herbert's theory, it would compute.

• • •

17

I waited at the guesthouse long enough to take a call from Ross. The docks had shut down for the night and the monkeys were safe and sound inside the warehouse. He'd left just enough men there to keep up the surveillance. There wasn't any chance that our man could get in and then walk off with a cageful of monkeys under each arm and not be seen. He'd need a vehicle if he wanted to move them. They were safe enough until morning.

As far as I could see, I'd done everything possible to cover the situation. Now I was entitled to a little time for myself. From the living room window I could see Felisa's quarters, the sports car parked in the carport. I went out and cut straight across the clipped lawn to her front door. I didn't even bother to look at Doc Calder's place. If he saw me I didn't really care.

I still wasn't sure what had hit me. For instance, why had I made that remark to Felisa about the life we were going to spend together? If I'd had any thoughts about that, they'd been way down deep in my subconscious, bursting out without my awareness that they even existed. My one experience, back in college, when I had to act like a well-trained domestic animal had been a catastrophe. I'd been shanghaied into being a loving husband and father long before I was ready. I had no way of knowing if I was ready now.

In my line of work, I knew that I wasn't going to get a chance to be a nine-to-five, time-and-a-half-for-overtime, two-weeks-vacation-with-pay kind of breadwinner. If I had any plans to get Felisa involved on a permanent basis in my life, I owed her a chance to match all that against her own expectations and to call everything off before any serious damage was done.

Whatever I had in my mind vanished when she opened the door. I went in and she got me a cold beer to drink while she finished changing for dinner. She left her bedroom door open so we could talk and I could see her slim figure moving around as she did the things women will do only in front of a man with whom they have a firm relationship.

The living room was filled with all kinds of native work that Felisa said she'd either bought or been given by the villagers she'd met on collecting trips. There were some really fine *molas,* the appliqué work that the Cuna women do over on the San Blas Islands, a carved wooden *santo* and some beautifully displayed shells. Her drapes were a kind of rough homespun that she'd had specially made for the room, as she had the grass mats scattered on the floor. There were books and records, and if ever a room reflected the occupant, this was it.

It was already getting dark when we went to the dining hall. She picked the same table we'd used the last time we'd eaten there together. Over at the big table Doc Calder was eating with Garcés and Nagy, but his face gave no sign that he had any thoughts about us. We ate quickly and then took care of the babies at the animal house.

When Felisa locked up she drew me along after her, away from the living area and down toward the lake. There was a little stretch of sandy beach and we sat and looked out over the water. If I was going to tell Felisa anything at all about the guy she was getting involved with, this was the time, before things went too far. There was just so much I could tell her, and Paradox wasn't part of it. I'd often wondered how men like Art Ross tell their wives what they do for a living. Do they just make up a cover story and hope to hell it doesn't get blown? Do they say nothing and let the poor woman wonder what she's married?

The way it worked out, I didn't get a chance to say a word. Much as I wanted to, good as my intentions were, Felisa had other things in mind. Later, when I took her to her door, the time wasn't right. Not the way she was acting. Not on what the slick magazines call "the most wonderful night of a woman's life."

When I got back to the guesthouse Calder was there. For a moment I thought he'd come to talk about Felisa, but it turned out to be a lot different.

"There's been some trouble in Balboa."

I felt my stomach drop about two floors. If it was the FLP, it had to be bad news.

"About an hour ago someone attacked the flagpole in front of Balboa High School, the one where the American flag is flown. There was an explosion and the pole came down."

That didn't sound like much and I said so.

"It's not the property loss," he said, "so much as the fact of that particular pole being attacked."

"So they put up a new one. One pole is like another."

He shook his head. "You don't understand. That pole means a great deal to both the Panamanians and the people who live in the Zone. It was a demonstration there that set off the riots back in sixty-four, the worst they've ever had down here. There were deaths on both sides, property damage in the millions and the Zone under siege for days. Each side blamed the other for starting things and there's plenty of evidence to support them both. An attack right there is going to be taken all over the country and the Zone as a direct slap in the face of the U.S.

authorities. By now the news has spread and anything might happen. The boiling point is pretty low and something like this might be all that some people might need to get ugly."

He was right, of course. Both camps had their wild men just spoiling for trouble. There was a good chance that the FLP hadn't been involved at all. That's what I held on to until the phone rang.

"I thought you'd want to hear about what happened," Hutto told me. "Remember those three missing thermite grenades? Well, it took just one to take that steel pole down. Only took him a minute to tape one to the base of the pole with a pull wire on the ring. He waited for the right moment to blow it, too."

"What do you mean?"

"Well, the Canal Zone cops that are usually in the area had all been pulled away to guard the canal itself. The guy waited until the movie let out a few blocks away. The streets were full of cars—people going home after the first show and others coming for the second. He yanked his pull wire and probably just drove away in the crowd. Anyway, there were a couple of hundred people around when the grenade went off. It burned right through the base of the pole and down she came without hurting a soul."

"Wait a minute, Sergeant. Has anybody called the papers or the radio stations to take credit for it?"

"Not so far, sir. Nobody seems to know who did it."

That sounded like the FLP. Showy property damage and nobody hurt. This time it had a political slant, propaganda value, and no chance to cover up what had happened. One more twist on the canal authorities. How could they claim to be able to protect the waterway when they couldn't even guard a flagpole?

"Did you notify Major Ross?"

"One of the other men did that. Do you want me to stay here, Captain?"

"You might as well. Of the five stunts they've pulled, four have been at the Pacific end."

He rang off and I thought about that idea for a minute. Did it mean the FLP was trying to make us keep looking in the one area while they were getting ready for a big bang somewhere else?

I put that out of my mind. The thing at the moment was to try to work up a response to the flagpole incident. There was one sure thing. The Panamanians who wanted to chase the Yankees clear out of their country and take over the canal themselves were going to get a big morale boost. On the other side of the line, it was going to make the Zonians dig in their heels even harder and demand that their paradise be surrounded with a Chinese wall armed with nuclear weapons.

Calder thought so, too. "There's been some progress, but most of it has come too late. Installations like ours have tried hard to hire Panamanian scientists, like Dr. Wagner, for our staff and the old double scale of wages was abolished years ago. A Panamanian gets the same pay as any U.S. citizen. Their flag is flown in the Zone, but that hasn't shut up the extremists on either side."

It was a bad scene all around and it didn't look any better in the morning. For one thing, it was getting harder and harder to keep up our cover story. We were still stuck with it, and if we were going to keep up the pretense that we didn't know anything about the final stage in Paradox, I was going to have to begin looking more like a man making a film.

Felisa would be spending the morning with us and she came in for breakfast dressed accordingly. She was wearing a faded blue work shirt, a pair of jeans and heavy work shoes. She sat down with the rest of us and tore into a lumberjack breakfast. She ate European style, without all the fork switching we do, her slim fingers gripping knife and fork without waste motion.

Her hands fascinated me, the nails well-kept but short and

unpolished, the whole effect being of a set of fine tools that the owner has complete mastery over. When we finished she piled into the car with us and I drove out to the location. While Sam and Potter were setting up the camera and loading it, she went off with Nagy in search of material to film. When they'd found what they were looking for we moved along and she stood back and watched the work.

Sam framed up on the first specimen and I let Felisa take a look through the eyepiece. There wasn't a doubt that she was interested not only in the subject, but in the whole business of nature photography. Her questions were direct and to the point and I could see that it was work she hoped someday to do herself. She had the knack that few people show, the ability to look at an object and visualize how it will appear on a screen.

By noon we had some nice footage in the can and when the crew stopped for lunch I drove Felisa back to the field station. She went in to eat and I got to the phone.

"The goddamn monkeys are still there," Ross told me. "What do we do now?"

"Nobody paying any attention to them?"

"Just some guy who's been feeding them. I went down and looked at them myself. It's a damn shame keeping them penned up like that. Most of them are still shaky from the trip and in those small cages they must be getting on each other's nerves."

"Look, Art, do you mind if I come down there myself? It's just possible he's waiting for the last minute to pick them up. Maybe I can be of some help."

"Sure, if you want," he said, adding bitterly, "You know where I'll be."

I was there in a hour. I gave him a little time off, taking his place so he could get some rest and something different to look at. When he came back it was past three in the afternoon.

"Okay, Mike, what do we do now?"

"It comes down to one of two things. We can leave them

there with a couple of men to keep an eye on them or we can just go ahead and seize them."

"I don't care much for either one. Two men can't hope to tail this Henriques without being spotted. It would be a waste of time. Still, we can't just sweep them up and walk off."

"Why not, Art? We'll do it legally enough. It's a case of cruelty to animals, for one thing. Left in those cages, they're a health menace as well. If you want, we can even get a court order just to keep everything kosher. If the guy shows up and wants his monkeys, we can take it from there."

"What do we do with them then?"

"Well, what would they do if it was just an ordinary case?"

"Probably turn them over to the vets for care, and if they weren't claimed, then they'd be sold or something."

"Okay. Here's what we'll do. Suppose we handle it like a regular case but we ship the rhesuses to the field station. They've got facilities for them—I've seen them myself—and they'll be under lock and key. If Henriques comes looking for them, just have him referred to Gamboa. He can come up and claim them and we'll have something set up. I'll clear it with Doc Calder. How does that sound?"

"I guess so, but how can you watch them around the clock at the field station?"

"If you can give me just three men, we'll handle the rest. Is it a deal?"

"Okay. You take over here and I'll go set it up with the dockmaster. He'll probably be glad to see them go."

I took over the watch and in a little while I saw Ross go into the warehouse with a gray-haired man in a white shirt. Just before five a white Canal Company truck backed up to the door and the driver and his helper loaded on the two cages. A minute later they pulled away, followed shortly behind by a car I recognized as Ross's. He was taking no chances on the monkeys getting out of his sight until they were under lock and key.

I got my car and tagged along behind Ross, finally turning into the field station gate right after them. They stopped at the administration building and I saw Calder come out with a bunch of keys and climb into the car with Ross, and then we all paraded down to the animal house.

One of the big outdoor-indoor cages had been prepared, but when the rhesuses were let out of their traveling cages they showed no interest in their new quarters. Instead they huddled together in two or three tight little groups in the corners, making no attempt to use all the space they had. Calder got a banana and held it out to the nearest one, but while the animal looked at it, he made no attempt to reach out and take it. When Calder held it closer I saw the monkey's lips curl back as he showed his teeth. Calder stepped back, leaving the banana on the floor of the cage.

"That's rather strange," he said. "As a rule the rhesus is a good traveler and they rarely show fear of man, even the ones that are wild-caught."

They looked okay to me, just your regular run-of-the-mill organ grinder's monkey, but Calder was disturbed.

"You know, I'd feel a lot better if the Army vet came up and took a look at these animals."

Ross was out of the place like a shot. He was back five minutes later with a scrap of paper he handed to Calder.

"Putney will be here as fast as he can make it. He asked if you could have these things ready for him—a microscope and some other stuff."

Calder looked at it and said, "I'll have a room set up for him in the next lab."

He left to get things arranged and Ross and I sat down and looked at the monkeys. He knew damn well what I had in my mind and finally he burst right out with it.

"Mike, there's no way in hell that anyone could have gotten to those monkeys after they were landed. If they're sick they got the bug while they were still on the *Pineda.*"

"Take it easy, Art. Nobody's suggesting anything. Wait for Putney and we'll know a lot more. It's only about fifteen miles from Fort Clayton and he'll be here any minute."

He got up and went to the door of the animal house and he was still there when Putney arrived. I got away from the cage door to give the vet room and watched him go to work.

He put on a pair of heavy gloves and then picked one monkey out and made a grab for him. The rhesus saw him coming, but he just didn't seem to have the strength to get away. Putney lifted him out and closed the cage door before putting his patient on the table in the aisle.

From what I could see, he did everything a people doctor does except ask questions. He took the temperature, pulse and respiration, and drew a blood sample, and after he'd put the monkey back, he got a specimen of droppings from one of the traveling cages. When he finished he looked at the two of us.

"This will take a little while. Suppose you go back to your quarters and I'll see you there when I've finished."

Calder locked up and he and Putney went off while Ross and I walked over to the guesthouse. Nagy and Garcés were there and I told them what the situation was. Garcés wasn't happy a bit.

"How many stops did that ship make on the trip down?"

Ross told him and he thought about that for a minute. "They could have picked up an infection anywhere along the way. Packed in like that, it would go right through the whole bunch. Could even be nothing but a common cold. Let's not go looking for trouble."

That seemed to make Ross feel a little better. Potter got him a drink and he settled back in his chair. "Let's not say anything to the vet about Paradox. I think it's best if we just let him make his diagnosis on what he finds and not give him any preconceived notion."

That made sense. If we started talking about yellow jack, it might affect Putney's thinking or his judgment. We didn't have long to wait.

The two of them came in, Putney carrying a plastic bag with the samples he'd collected.

"I've asked Dr. Calder to have the whole animal building sprayed immediately. We won't move any of the animals, but I'd prefer if no one went in there who didn't absolutely have a need to enter. The rhesus cage is to be kept covered with netting and they are not to be let into the outside cage under any circumstances."

Ross said, "Have you any idea what's wrong with them?"

The vet shook his head. "I won't have anything before morning. Don't like to make guesses. What do you know about these animals?"

I told him what we knew.

"Most likely something they picked up on their trip. No reputable supply house would sell animals in that condition."

"What kind of diseases can these things get?"

"Just about anything a human can. That's what makes the rhesus such a valuable research animal. All sorts of things to consider. Could have picked it up from a sailor or a longshoreman at a port where they stopped. Could be they've got malaria."

"The rhesus monkey gets malaria?"

He nodded and then, almost as an afterthought, he added, "Could even be yellow fever."

18

With the rhesuses there at the field station and only the three men that Ross could spare to watch them, we were going to have to take part of the guard job ourselves. That meant doing our cover work right in the station grounds, where we could keep the animal house under our eyes. Luckily there was a way to do that.

Purists may call it nature-faking, but it's the only way you can work with agile animals and birds and get anything like usable results. I asked Calder about it and he said he'd help.

Sam and I picked out one of the outdoor cages and while Potter went off to collect some leafy branches and other props, the station carpenter fitted one end of the cage with a pane of glass. When everything was set we could put an animal or bird into the setup and film it without its getting camera-shy and deciding to make a rapid departure. While the others were getting everything ready, I took a call from Ross.

"Putney just called. Whatever those monkeys have, it's worse than just a cold."

"What do we do now?"

"First I've got to tell the commander. I'm not looking forward to it, but he's got a right to know."

"I think we'd better call The Rock, too. We're getting to the place where the decisions are going to have to come from higher up. I'll leave now and you might call Tiny and tell her to get her people together. I'll bring Garcés with me."

"Okay. I don't think I'll be at Quarry Heights very long."

He was right about that. I don't think he'd enjoyed his chat with his boss and I wasn't looking forward to mine. The call was all set and when Ross hooked up his phone to an amplifier, everyone could speak or listen as he chose. On the other end were Tiny, Colonel Simpson, the Army medic, and Murfree. I led off, telling about the monkeys and what we'd done with them.

Tiny asked, "Any idea about how they were infected?"

"Could have been anywhere on the trip. They weren't under guard on the *Pineda.*"

"You're sure they weren't reached after they'd been landed?"

"I don't know how. They were under surveillance every second of the day and night."

Simpson broke in. "Wait a minute, Keefe. From the preliminary report it looks as though the rhesuses are in the early stages of the disease. Yellow fever has a very short incubation. Obviously these things can't be pinpointed, but my own guess is that they had to be exposed less than three days ago."

"Colonel, they were ashore and in the warehouse two days ago and at sea for several days before that."

Tiny said, "Wait a minute. I thought you said they were under direct observation?"

"Well, the door to the warehouse was. Major Ross had the whole area staked out and . . ."

"And what?"

Ross spoke up. Guarding the monkeys had been his job.

"What Keefe means is that we weren't actually sitting beside the shipping cages. We didn't dare get that close and take a chance of scaring our man away."

Simpson said, "So it's perfectly possible that someone got at the rhesuses without your seeing a thing and infected them while your men were on guard outside."

"I guess so. He'd have to be a hell of a cool customer to do it, though. If he'd been spotted, the whole plan would have gone down the pipe. Paradox might have ended right there."

"I don't think so," Tiny said. "If Mike's cover has been blown, and the FLP suspect that we know what they have in mind, they'd have to assume we'd have those rhesuses staked out just waiting for Henriques to come calling for them. As long as no one was seen actually leaving with them, the man was safe enough."

Garcés hadn't said a word so far, but I saw he was waiting for a chance to get into the conversation. I waved to him and he spoke up.

"I think we'd better have those monkeys destroyed. Each one is a time bomb just waiting to go off."

"What do you think, Mike?" That was Tiny.

"If you do, we're right back where we started. As of now, the only bait we have to draw the FLP is right there at the field station. As long as they know the monkeys are there, it stands to reason they'll make a try at releasing them. Ross has his men staked out in the next building with direct observation on a locked gate and a locked door. We'll be working right there ourselves. If the FLP is going to make a try, they'll be seen before they even get into the yard."

Simpson's voice broke in. "I'm sorry, Keefe. We just don't dare take the chance. Suppose you destroy the monkeys as quietly as you can and guard the building as if you hadn't. After all, the important thing is that the FLP think the rhesuses are in there, isn't it?"

"I can't take that chance. There are too many people who are entitled to go in. If the FLP has an informant on the station staff they'll know what we're doing. They'll have their laugh and go off and set up something else."

Ross didn't like it. "I've got to go along with Major Garcés. We don't dare let those monkeys live. I say destroy them and be done with it and the sooner the better."

"No." Tiny's voice was like a shot. "If you want that as an order, I'll put it that way."

She was making it tough for Ross. By the book he reported only to the local commander and took his orders from him, but after he'd finished this tour, he'd still be in the same service with Tiny.

"Look, Art," she said, "you'll be covered. Now, what I want all of you to do is stick with the program. Mike, you and Major Garcés get back into position and carry on. Art, I want to talk to your vet and let Colonel Simpson hear his report. We'll decide in the next few hours what we're going to do."

There was a click and Ross put the phone back on its cradle.

"What do you suppose she wants with Putney?" I asked.

Ross just shook his head.

"We'll stop by his place and ask him to come over here to make his report."

He didn't even look up when Garcés and I left.

We'd had to wait a couple of minutes for Captain Putney. He was in his working outfit—long white coat, the pockets stuffed with instruments. Anyone could see that he knew what he was doing, but that didn't make it any easier to talk with him. He was more than just a laconic Yankee, letting each word go as if he were spending from capital. He wasn't about to commit himself until he had hard facts to work with. Finally I asked him to give us his best guess.

First he told me what they didn't have. "Rule out malaria, dengue and yellow fever."

"They don't have yellow fever?"

"Not regular urban yellow fever."

"Well, do they have the jungle form, then?"

"Too early to tell. Culture isn't ready yet."

"All right, Doc. From what you know now, what's your opinion?"

"Mostly they'll recover. Might lose a few."

"Believe me, I'm not worried about that. Are they infectious right now? Can they pass the disease?"

"Yep. Infectious as they can be."

It was like spearing olives in a narrow bottle.

"How long will they remain that way?"

"Those that don't die, probably three or four days more. Don't know much about the subject. Not much literature."

I asked him to get over to see Ross, and Garcés and I left. Garcés didn't say much on the way until I had a question.

"How long before the mosquitoes incubate the virus and turn into lethal weapons?"

"I don't know, Mike. It's just as Putney says. There's very little known, but if the cycle works on the jungle mosquito the way it does with the *Aedes,* then I'd guess between ten days and two weeks. From that point on they can infect any susceptible creature."

"What are you getting in the trap count? Any changes in the bug population?"

"No. I've got every man I can spare on it, but so far there's been no change."

We rode along in silence until just before we got to the field station, when Garcés asked, "Do you think I can get some time off this weekend? If anything breaks I can get back right away."

I'd forgotten all about the way the days were passing. It was Friday and everything would be shutting down. We wouldn't have to do anything but keep an eye on the animal house. I could even let the others take some time off as long as we arranged shifts.

It also meant that Felisa would be leaving before supper for her mother's place, to stay until Monday morning. It looked as if I was going to be in for a couple of real quiet days.

It was almost lunchtime when we got back, and the special photo cage was ready for the first actor. When we broke I passed the word about taking time off. Everyone had something he wanted to take care of, except Herbert, of course, and we worked out a roster so that each man could have some time and still keep the monkeys covered. When we went back to work they all seemed a lot happier.

Nagy and Felisa picked out the subjects we'd use from the cages inside. I kept everyone else out of the place. I tried to get a look at the rhesuses through one of the barred windows, but all I could see was the netting that draped their cage.

We worked right up to about four and then I called for a wrap. I had a drink with Felisa while she changed and then saw her leave for the city. I walked over to the guesthouse and was just about to shower before dinner when Putney drove up.

"Like to take a look at those monkeys," he said.

There wasn't any need for me to go along, so I sent him over to Calder's quarters for the key. I saw them walk down the slope together and by the time I was dressed Putney was back.

"How are the patients?"

"Not too good. I've got a bigger, mosquito-proof cage down at the lab. I'll bring that up in the morning for them. Want to burn the cages they traveled in, too. Probably have the culture report then."

He didn't take me up on my offer of a drink and I told him I'd be around when he came back in the morning. After he drove away I got ready to go to the dining hall with Nagy. He'd been carrying most of the load on the film project while I'd been charging around doing my imitation of a pup trying to catch its tail. It was a hell of a way to treat anyone as talented as Nagy, but it hadn't seemed to bother him. We were on our way to dinner when Doc Calder caught up with us.

"I think you'd better come down to the office before you eat," he said.

What he had wasn't very good and it was all in the stack of newspapers piled on his desk. He handed the top one to me.

"That's one of the English-language sheets. You read that and I'll give you the gist of the others, but they're all about the same."

**A NEW ZONIAN TRICK?
U.S. NOW USING PROVOCATEURS
TO CREATE NEW CANAL
"INCIDENTS"**

Faced with the strong determination of the Panamanian government and people to remain calm and to refrain from all acts of violence that might be used as excuses for the American authorities to implement new and stricter repressive measures, the imperialists have now begun to create "incidents" of their own. All have been planned to generate still more resentment among the canal community without causing any real damage, either personal or property, and pass the blame to patriots here in the Republic. New and more stringent measures have been put in force for the "security" of the canal, which are, in fact, bald attempts to harass and annoy the loyal Panamanian employees, who are the men who really make the canal operate.

There was a lot more of the same, ending with this in big, bold type:

THIS NEWSPAPER HAS INVESTIGATED CAREFULLY AND FULLY AND CAN FIND NO EVIDENCE THAT ANY OF THESE ACTS WERE COMMITTED BY ONE OF THE KNOWN PATRIOTIC GROUPS.

What it amounted to was that while the Panamanian authorities didn't know any more than we did about the FLP, they were beginning to get a strong odor on their side of the Zone border. If we had any idea about sitting on the lid and keeping Paradox strictly our own business, it wouldn't be long before we'd have to let the rest of the world in on our troubles.

By the time we'd got through the papers it was too late to eat at the station. Calder knew a place along the highway and he drove us over in his car. The food was good and another time I would have enjoyed the change.

On the way back I couldn't keep down the yawns and when we got to the field station I turned down Calder's offer of a drink in his quarters and headed for bed. John and Sam Wynn were watching TV. They'd checked the guard and there was nothing to report.

Herbert was busy with something and seeing him reminded me that I'd been keeping his one-man theory to myself. There wasn't any flaw I could see in his reasoning, but it somehow didn't ring right. Probably I was just too tired to think it through. I put the whole thing out of my mind and went to bed.

You'd think that tired as I was, I'd have slept until noon at the very least, but I was up at six and one of the first in for breakfast. Most of the staff people were gone for the weekend, living it up in the fleshpots of Panama City or whatever scientists do for kicks in their time off. Calder was there, but he'd leave after Putney had been let into the animal house with the monkeys' new, mosquito-proof cage.

"Will you want to go inside for any reason?" Calder asked.

"Not that I can think of."

"Then I won't leave a set of keys with you."

"Who all have keys?"

"Dr. Wagner has one, I have mine and a third is kept by the station duty officer, one of the staff. If anyone has to get in, he has to sign the keys in and out. Not that we're afraid of theft, mind you. It's just that very often experiments are in progress with some of the animals and we have to be sure that the controls are observed."

"So nobody goes in except the staff?"

"There's a caretaker. He keeps the place clean and feeds the animals not on special controlled diets. He signs for the keys like everyone else."

It sounded secure enough. With Felisa and Calder away, the only keys would be in the administration building, controlled by the duty officer. One of us would keep the gate and the animal building door under constant direct observation, so I felt the monkeys would be safe.

Putney arrived while I was on watch. He was driving his own car, and a small GI van tailed along behind, with a couple of his men. I saw them unload the new cage and move it inside the building. It was a lot bigger than the one the rhesuses were in and a lot heavier, judging by the way Putney's men hefted it through the gate. They must have been sweating freely by the time they got it in place and removed its traveling cover.

It seemed to take quite a while, but it couldn't have been easy to get the beasts moved even if they were sick. The men brought out the two traveling cages wrapped in heavy plastic, and sliding them into the van, they took off. Putney locked the building door and then snapped the padlock on the gate in the outer fence, tugging at it to make sure it was secure. Then he came up the hill to where I was sitting in front of the guest-house.

"That diagnosis I made on your monkeys has been confirmed," he announced.

"Did you pass the word to Colonel Eriksen?"

He nodded. "Yep. Told her they ought to be destroyed right away. Don't waste a minute."

"And what did she say?"

"Told me not to. Had some ideas of her own." He pulled on his lower lip. "Strong-minded woman, that. Like to meet her."

"Strong-minded" I already knew, but I'd never figured Tiny to be stupid; in fact, her not wanting to put those animals away was downright crazy. If she had made that kind of decision on her own, I just hoped she wasn't going to have to answer some tough questions later on. She'd always played close to the vest, but this was something she should have checked out with higher authority. I hoped she had.

But that was her problem. Mine was that I was going to have to tell her that I was going to marry a foreign national and lose most of my clearance for her kind of work.

When Putney drove off, I got a magazine and settled down under a tree. Sam Wynn and Nagy left for the city, leaving Potter with me. From some source of his own John had got some fishline and hooks, and taking a fresh-cut bamboo pole, he went down to the lakeshore to see what he could catch.

For the next hour or so everything was quiet and then I heard a bumping and rattling from behind the dining hall. In a minute I saw a man in white coveralls with the field station initials on the back, pulling a two-wheeled cart. There was a pair of big plastic garbage cans in it, probably fresh greens and vegetables for the animals. The man's head was bent down under a wide-brimmed straw hat and when the road sloped downhill I saw his feet, in clean white sneakers, dig in to brake the heavy cart. As he passed he looked up and smiled and nodded to me, but when I called out to him he didn't answer.

When he got to the animal house he opened up and lugged

the heavy cans inside, and even at that distance I could hear him sloshing and rattling around in there. A half hour later he came out, reloaded the cans, locked up and left, pulling the cart uphill with a funny sort of hitching gait that favored one leg. He went out of sight and I returned to my magazine, taking an occasional look at the empty carport beside Felisa's bungalow.

Somehow I filled the time. I tried a chess game with Herbert, but even when he handicapped himself with all but a few pieces he whipped me handily. Sam Wynn came back and gave his camera its weekly cleaning and then started a long letter to his wife in Honolulu. John took off for a while and went out with his own camera and a long lens to get some bird shots. I drove to Gamboa and got a couple of paperbacks, a case of beer and a quart of vanilla ice cream for Potter.

Sunday morning I did manage to sleep a little later. I went down to Gamboa again and got some news magazines, then settled down under my tree and tried to catch up with the rest of the world.

The big news seemed to be about people making loud noises and killing bystanders. That went for Northern Ireland, London, Israel, Cyprus, Cambodia, Africa and New York. I finally tossed it aside and wondered why the FLP couldn't act like all the rest of the lunatics, who just murder people by the dozen.

The animal attendant came by just as he had the day before, hitching along with that funny step of his, and went down to the animal house. I called to him, but either he didn't hear or he was too busy trying to keep the cart from getting away on the downgrade. When he finished up and left, we all went to the dining hall for a regular Sunday dinner. They'd be closed for supper that night, but we could always get something from the commissary in Gamboa.

About two, Nagy got back. He'd stayed overnight at the big hotel, El Panama, having met up with some ladies from a tourist party and spent the evening in the casino and the nightclub. He looked just a trifle singed around the edges and headed for his room with little more than a grunt after his hike from the train station.

I had just refigured the hours that I'd have to wait before Felisa got back when there was a flash of color and her little car pulled into the carport. I was down there in record time, not even waiting for her to get inside the house before I kissed her.

She had a wicker hamper on the seat beside her and I carried it into her little kitchen.

"Put it down gently, Mike. There's a bottle of wine, a roast chicken and a few other things inside."

"What did you have in mind?"

"First I thought we might eat here, but I think I have a better plan. There is a place not far away where I go when I want to be alone. Now I think I'd like to share it with you. It's a little cove right beside the lake where we can sit or even swim."

"I don't think I've got anything to wear for swimming."

She smiled. "That's all right, Mike. Neither do I."

She took a moment to change into slacks and a shirt and we were back in the car. It was a pleasure to watch her drive. She handled the little car as if it were a violin, never giving it more than it needed and using its power with utmost control.

We went only a short way back down the highway and then turned to the left on a dirt track that ran for a mile or so before it came to a dead end. We covered the last few hundred yards on foot and there we were.

The place was a tiny Eden, a little cove with a gently sloping sandy bottom, the water clear and inviting. When the sky began to flame it was a real effort to leave and go back to the station. Felisa drove right to the animal house to check on her children. She had her keys on the same ring with those for her car and we went in together. The animals and birds rustled around as usual, and while Felisa prepared the bottle and the pan of mash,

I went over to look at the rhesuses.

The new cage was a lot bigger than the first, swathed in heavy nylon netting. I tried to see through it, but the rear was in shadow. Finally I pulled back the netting and crouched down to see how the poor monkeys were making out. I still didn't see a thing inside the cage.

The monkeys were gone.

• • •

19

"All right, Mike, take it easy." Tiny's voice had that snap-crackle-pop tone she used when she really went into action. "Now, what do you need?"

I had my answer ready. "First of all, I need some numbers. It's going to take a hell of a lot more men to interdict that area than the local command can begin to supply. It's got to be sealed off tighter than Fort Knox."

"No sweat. There's a standby company of MPs at Fort Bragg. They'll be on their way in an hour. What's next?"

"We've got to get those sick monkeys. There's a dozen of them out there somewhere and we don't dare leave one."

There was a pause while she talked to someone with her at the command center in The Rock. "There's a company of Special Forces in Florida. A lot of them are Latins and most have had the jungle operations course in Panama. They'll be there by morning."

"They're going to need some weapons for this kind of thing. Can you scare up some light shotguns?"

"Okay. Both companies will bring everything they need, tentage and all. The only thing the command down there will have to supply will be rations and fuel."

"Who's going to command all these troops? He better be somebody who knows what he's doing."

"As of right now you're in command. We haven't got time to get another man filled in."

"Look, I'm only a Signal Corps captain, and reserve at that."

"Just do as you're told. You're the man in command no matter what. If I had time I'd get you promoted, but there are other things I've got to do first. Now get a pencil and take some notes."

"Okay. Shoot."

"I'll have all this on its way down in official form, but you alert the command. First, the whole Canal Zone between the Atlantic and Pacific locks—that's Gatun Lake and Gaillard Cut—is designated as operational for Paradox. Coordinate with the local people as you think best, but the center of the isthmus is all yours.

"Advise the command surgeon that we've requisitioned enough vaccine to take care of his people and it's on its way. There will be additional shipments to cover the local population across the line in a day or so.

"Request that the commander review his evacuation plan, set priorities and be ready to move all but the essential minimum personnel to guard and operate the canal. Both Airlift and Sealift commands have been alerted and are ready to move.

"Four mobile general hospital units are standing by on red alert and plans must be ready to deploy them wherever they'll be needed most. Colonel Simpson up here will coordinate that with the command surgeon.

"Naval elements from Guantánamo and San Diego are already at sea and will move into the area to land marines if there is any sign of civil disorder. Your local Navy commander is to contact Captain Murfree here if he needs help.

"Now, I want you to get this next absolutely straight and pass the word to all concerned down there. Operation Paradox is still

Top Secret and that classification will only be lifted on direct written orders from here."

"How are we supposed to do that? You're going to fill up the jungle with armed troops, seal off a whole section of the Zone, and you expect us to keep it quiet?"

She didn't get to answer that. Another voice broke in, one that was used to a lot of authority and instant obedience.

"The information officer down there is to create a small leak. The operation is a field exercise designed to test the integrity of the canal defense against some new hardware. Everything going on in your operational area is to be explained as preparation for the exercise. The two assigned companies are the kind of troops who would normally be involved in a deal of that kind. Everything else is to be kept under wraps until the situation is fully developed."

"I'm sorry, sir. I don't get that."

"It's simple enough. All preparations will be made under full security until we can't afford to wait longer."

"And when will that be?"

"When you find your first active case of yellow fever that can be attributed to the activities of the FLP. That's when we go public, and not before. When you pass the word that you've got a bona fide case, we'll clear you to come out in the open. Then and not before."

There wasn't any point in arguing with the general. He'd got his orders and I had mine. Until it was fully apparent that the FLP plan was paying off for them, it was going to be business as usual for the canal and all that was connected with it. They were doing everything possible to get ready, but up to the last moment we had to gamble on a miracle. The way it looked to me, that was what it was going to take.

Tiny took over. "When do you meet with the local command?"

"In about a half hour. The Chief of Staff is getting his people together right now."

"Okay. Keep us posted."

The line went dead and I got ready to go into the lion's den.

The MP at the tunnel entrance checked my ID and when he found my name on his roster I was allowed into the big conference room. I saw Ross sitting with the G-2 and took a seat with them. Most of the military were already in their seats and when the Zone governor and his chief of police arrived we got down to business. The Chief of Staff opened it up.

"The matters discussed at this meeting are Top Secret. As far as your own staffs are concerned, the "need to know" rule is suspended. The operation we are about to discuss will be protected by a cover and you are directed to receive approval directly from me before you expand the number of persons cleared for knowledge of the situation."

He turned over to the old man, who immediately received everyone's full attention. He had me read the notes I'd taken on the phone call to The Rock and then they got down to work.

Plans were made to receive, transport and supply my two companies. The provost marshal huddled with Ross and me to set the exact lines where the company from Bragg would operate. I'd expected that his nose might be out of joint at having an outsider, and a captain at that, walk in and take over a big piece of his territory, but he was so happy at the news that he'd be getting his own men back from the controlled area that it didn't bother him a bit. He went out to pass the word to his operations officer and I settled back to listen to the planning.

The medics would assign their people for the immunization program if things got that far, establishing stations at schools and firehouses to give shots to everyone who might have been exposed.

The leper hospital at Palo Seco would be staffed and equipped to serve as a quarantine station. They wouldn't need any fancy equipment for that. There's not much you can do for a victim of yellow jack, no wonder drug that is more effective than aspirin. He wins or loses the battle on his own; you can only do your best to keep him comfortable.

Priorities were set up for the evacuation; those who would be left were only a handful to keep an eye on things. The canal would close down, of course, and naval units would move in to supervise the blockade.

Effective right away, every precaution would be taken to make sure that the cordon around the target area would be observed. The Panama Railroad trains would continue to run, but steps would be taken to ensure that no one left the cars between Gatun and Pedro Miguel except those authorized to do so. The Madden highway would stay open for traffic between the canal terminals.

Summit Gardens would be closed "for extensive repairs." A story would be leaked that a pair of jaguars had escaped from the zoo, in hopes that the news might discourage the iguana-hunters.

There was lots more that didn't concern me and I just sat until the chief of staff called a two-hour recess to let everyone get his people busy on their part of the plan. They went streaming out of the place, but I wasn't off the hook yet. Ross tapped me on the arm and I tagged along behind him and the G-2 into the old man's office.

He had a visitor, a civilian, with State Department written all over him. He appeared about sixty, with the pouchy eyes and bilious look of someone who's had to eat too many formal dinners and cocktail party hors d'oeuvres. I didn't feel that he was going to do much to cheer us up.

"Briefly, what are we supposed to tell the Panamanians? They've already begun to notice your activities around Gamboa. Now they're certain to ask questions. Do we tell them anything about this FLP of yours or do we just let them get hit with an epidemic?"

He wasn't asking the general. The questions were coming straight at me. I didn't know who this guy was and I wasn't going to say a thing until I was told to by the old man.

"Go ahead, Keefe. What do you think?"

"Sir, with all due respect, I'm not supposed to think. I'm a captain and I'm paid to do as I'm told. The book says you have to be a lieutenant colonel before you can make decisions."

The faintest hint of a smile showed for just a moment before the old man spoke. After all, he'd had to spend some time as a captain himself before he got to be a three-star general.

"All right. Let's just stick to facts. What are your chances of stopping this FLP as of right now? Finding them, that is, before they get this plan of theirs too far along to be stopped?"

"Not very good, sir. Not any better than they were when we started. We've been going along waiting for a mistake that we can exploit. So far there hasn't been any sign that one has been made or ever will be."

"What do you think, Ross?"

"I've got to agree. Keefe and his group have done everything they possibly could. This is his kind of job and he's had plenty of experience at it. He's got good people with him, every man a specialist in his field. I can't think of a thing I'd have done differently."

It was nice to hear some kind words, but they only served to soothe my feelings. Beyond that they weren't much help. I was the one who was supposed to come up with the answers. The general still wanted facts.

"Now, according to the best estimate you can make, when will the FLP pass the point of no return?"

"It's got to be pretty soon. Given the time the disease needs to incubate and the target date we think the leader is aiming for, we're down to days at most. Even that's only a guess. This man has a talent for doing what we least expect him to. All we've been able to do so far is react. By that time he's on his way to set up something else. The conventional way to deal with a situation like that is to pour in manpower, but with this man it wouldn't help even if we had a trooper standing on every square foot of the whole damn zone. Believe me, I don't like to admit it, but this man is a hell of a lot smarter than we are."

The civilian broke in. "Wait a minute. You're talking about the FLP as though it were only the one man. No matter how smart he is, it stands to reason that one of the others, not as smart as the leader, will do something you can exploit with all the resources you've got."

Both the general and Ross were staring at me. I was trying to be damn careful in what I said, but somehow I'd let it slip. Now I had to measure my words one by one. They'd be around to haunt me for a hell of a long time.

"We have been dealing with the possibility that the FLP may consist of just one man working alone. He may get some technical help from others, but according to our analysis, it is well within the bounds of possibility that the conception and execution of everything we know that the FLP's done lies within this man's capability."

The civilian began to splutter. "Somehow I can't accept that. One man just couldn't create all this havoc all by himself. I don't believe it."

If it hadn't all been so serious, I could have told him that it didn't mean a continental damn what he thought or believed. I took a softer line.

"Sir, in our line of work we rarely deal in absolutes. What I'm trying to say is that we've got to deal with the one-man possibility along with anything else we can work out from the facts we've got. We can't afford the luxury of disbelief. If our facts add up to a conclusion, then we've got to consider it along with everything else. So far I'll say that in my opinion the FLP is a very small outfit."

The general leaned forward. "Have you any kind of line on who this man is?"

"No, sir. We have a minimal description, but it's not much help. This man is able to put on a whole new identity the way I change my shirt."

"Or where his base of operations is?"

"Common sense says that it's somewhere east of the canal and probably across the line in the Republic. Basically that means he can operate along a fifty-mile open border wherever he chooses and when. So far we don't think he is aware of our suspicions about the true nature of Paradox or that we have the slightest idea of what his end game will be."

The civilian said, "Well, at least that's something."

"Sorry. It won't be much longer before we have to let him see that we suspect. When the troops arrive and move in he'll know. Now we'll begin to act and he has to react. That means he's going to make his plans taking into account a whole new set of factors. Every time we make a move he's going to have to revise his setup if he wants to stick to his timetable. He's not going to be able to call every shot and be sure he scores a clean hit. One miss and he's in trouble. If we can exploit it, we'll have gone a long way to solving the problem." I took a deep breath. "I hope to God that's right."

The man from the embassy still wasn't buying it. "Just tell me this. What do I advise the ambassador to say if he gets a direct question from the local government?"

He had to know the answer to that one already, but I guess he wanted to pass the buck to the general. The old man gave him a funny look and then laid it on the line.

"You tell him to lie. We're running a special test of the canal defenses which is going to affect traffic in the Zone for a short time. That's as good a story as any."

The man began to sputter but the general chopped him off. "Keefe's orders are to proceed with Operation Paradox until the situation is resolved. We are still Top Secret and we stay that way unless we have a confirmed case of yellow fever that can be attributed to this FLP. When that happens we go public. The local authorities will be alerted immediately and assured of our full cooperation with everything we have to give."

There was an awkward silence for a moment as the other man fought down his anger. People from his side of the government aren't used to having the military horse them.

"General, I've got to protest, and you may consider it official. Perhaps my point of view is altered by what I know is going on over there, but I can tell you this. If there is the slightest leak and the local government finds out that we knew about the FLP and what your Paradox is all about, you can kiss the whole works goodbye. There won't be any arbitration and you can start packing. I can't permit that."

The general reached for the red phone and pushed it over. "If you want to go over my head . . ."

He nodded to Ross and me and we took the hint and left the room. When we were called back the civilian had his hat on and his face was flaming.

The general gave us the word. "You will proceed as directed. That's official."

I guess my eyebrows must have shot up and he saw it.

"I don't want you to think I don't agree with the decision, if that makes any difference to you. My own views have nothing to do with it anyway. All I know is that we have yet to see our first confirmed case of yellow fever. We may have a lot of evidence that someone is trying to start an epidemic, but that doesn't mean they are going to get away with it. We'll do everything we can with established methods to prevent it. If this FLP outfit fails for one reason or another, then we'll have done our job and the American position will be no better or worse for it.

If they succeed in spite of us, then we'll be ready to cope with that problem, but we can't just give up and let them go through with this thing. Not if we're going to go on claiming to be civilized."

I'd guess that was both for my benefit and for that of his civilian visitor. The Army would handle this deal the best way it could in following the orders that had come down from on high. They might not like it, but they'd shut their mouths and get down to work.

The general continued. "You'll use your MPs to seal off the entire area which is identified with the FLP attempt. No one in or out who isn't authorized. The other troops will fine-tooth-comb the area inside the cordon and remove any animal that might transmit the disease."

That made sense. It also meant that we were telling the FLP we were fully aware of what they were trying to do. Anyone trying to penetrate the area would be stopped and if they managed to slip in anyway they'd be found by the troops inside. Maybe it wasn't the way Herbert would set it up, but it was the way the Army was equipped to handle the problem, the way they knew best. Maybe someday there would be a Standard Operating Procedure for this kind of exercise and we could follow that. Until then we'd just have to do it by the book we had.

I got up to go, but the Old Man had one more thought.

"Let's hope there is something in this one man theory."

"Why is that, sir?"

"You catch him and that will put an end to the whole affair."

Tiny heard me out right to the end. Then she asked, "Do you really go along with Herbert on this?"

"I don't know. He's made a hell of a case, and with what we've got right now, it all checks out."

"What does that mean?"

"God damn it, Tiny, it means that Herbert could be right. Maybe there's just one man out there who's a hell of a lot smarter than us poor mortals and who can call his own shots and pull them off."

I didn't say anything about her decision to leave those sick monkeys alive and the fact that they'd been slid out right from under my own nose. She did.

"How do you think he got those rhesuses out of there?"

"It beats the hell out of me. I was sitting there myself, and as far as I saw, they didn't go past me. If we left them there as bait, I only know that the bait is gone and all I've got to show for it is a bare hook."

I hadn't gone so far as to believe in magic. There had to be some explanation of how the monkeys got out of the animal house, and for whatever good it would do, someday we'd find out. For whatever good it would do. Maybe if Putney had made a stronger case, Tiny would have been convinced that the animals should have been taken care of. Maybe I should have. It didn't make any difference now. They were gone.

If Tiny knew what was going through my mind, she didn't say anything about it.

"You'd better get out to the air base, Mike. If they're on time, your private army is due in anytime now."

When I finally got to the air base, the big transports were already on the ground and were off-loading at the ramp. The MPs from Bragg had been first to land and most of their tentage and heavy gear was now loaded in the waiting trucks. They'd brought their own jeeps, which had been gassed and had taken their places at the end of the convoy. The MP motor sergeant had assigned drivers to the cargo vehicles, and as soon as the Green Berets were ready we'd pull out. I found the MP company commander, a red-headed bantam of a captain named Dunphy, and together we hunted up the other CO.

He was a big first lieutenant named Polansky, taller than my own six one and carrying lots of muscle. He was standing to one side, letting his NCOs do their work without getting in their way. His own calm must have been contagious because everything was moving smoothly and quietly, a good sign. I asked them to ride up to the bivouac area in my car and I'd fill them in on what was expected.

The only thing bothering them was the problem of rations, and when I told them that their issue was in the first truck they seemed just a bit more impressed at the support they were getting.

In the few minutes we still had to wait, I called the field station. The one man I wanted right away was Potter and I told him to meet me at the new camp with some things I'd be needing. Everyone else was to hang loose until I had time to think of what to do with them.

When the troops were loaded I led them through the darkness out to the highway and headed north, the two COs in my sedan.

"There's no time for any kind of written orders and what I'm going to do is just give you the general mission and let you handle most of it your own way. One thing we've got to prevent, and that is any confusion from the fact that the men don't know each other. If you can manage it, I'd like to set up the camp so everyone gets to know the men in the other outfit. Maybe having a single mess might help. Put your command posts together, if you can, make the men mix. I don't know how long this will take, but plan on a good long stretch."

Dunphy asked, "How do we draw rations and supplies?"

"Detail your own men to make the supply run. I don't want anyone coming into this area and taking stories home with him. The only people to be inside the cordon are those who belong to you.

"Dunphy, the perimeter is your job. My sergeant is on his way with the maps right now. That means roadblocks and walking patrols. Your men are to convoy anyone going to or coming from Gamboa while they're in our sector. Anyone they suspect may be trying to enter is to be detained until he's cleared. If somebody asks questions, the story is that there's a super-spooky test going on.

"Polansky, your men are going on a monkey hunt. That's why you brought the light shotguns."

If they thought I'd gone bananas they were too well-mannered to say so.

"You're going to have to take it on faith that the exercise is important and deadly serious. If I could I'd tell you why, but I guess you're smart enough to figure it out for yourselves. There's one kind of monkey in particular that we're looking for. It's not one of the local types, but the Indian rhesus monkey."

"How do we know which are which?"

"For one thing, only the ones that belong here prefer to live in trees and have the ability to hang by their tails. The rhesus may sleep in a tree, but during the day it feeds on the ground."

"What do we do when we get one?"

"Good question. Those monkeys are sick and what they're sick with is very likely catching. Sergeant Potter is bringing pictures of the rhesus. If anyone even suspects he's got one—or gets any other kind of monkey—send it back to the CP. We'll take it from there. If I'm away, Potter will know what to do. Any other animal on his list is to be brought in, checked and released outside the area.

"The sector has been broken down into search areas already. Move your men out as soon as there's light enough and start sweeping. If anyone finds any intruders, radio in at once. Don't try to move them or take any chances. Just sit on them until somebody comes out to take the men off your hands. Consider anyone you find to be extremely dangerous. Any questions?"

Dunphy spoke up. "Just how much force can we use?"

It was a question that had to be asked, and I had to come up with the answer.

"I don't want any corpses. Not for a lot of reasons, but mostly because they can't answer questions. Your men can take life only to save life. I'll give you that in writing if that's what you want."

"That's okay. I'm outside stopping anybody who tries to get in or out and Polansky is inside catching monkeys."

Polansky didn't say anything and when I looked at him he just nodded. He had every right to think that the assignment sounded crazy and I couldn't deny it.

"As soon as you can, get your radios netted together and agree on a password and countersign. Change them every time you send out another relief. One thing more," I added. "From now on your men are deaf, dumb and blind to anyone who asks what we are doing. They don't even know their own names."

When we got to the bivouac area I led the way in along a trail off the paved road. Potter was waiting with the things I'd asked for and together we watched the camp being erected. The tall, dry grass was tramped down, and with no more than truck headlights for illumination, the tents began to rise. In a way it was almost like a circus coming to town. There wasn't a man who didn't know what he was supposed to do and the dark stillness was broken only by the quiet orders of the NCOs. These were picked troops, ready to set up shop anywhere. The little camp was laid out and tents started to go up. I heard the generators cough into life and the cooks went to work on breakfast. By full daylight the food was being served and the first MPs were heading out to take over the sealing of the area. When the Green Berets moved out, I took the chance to go up to the field station to get into fatigues and make some phone calls. Also I wanted a talk with Calder.

"To be perfectly frank, Captain, I don't have the remotest idea of how those monkeys were removed."

"Well, let's take it step by step. They were there Saturday morning when Captain Putney brought up their new cage. Did anyone else sign a key out after that?"

"Yes, the attendant signed out a set when he fed the animals and cleaned up at his regular time. His name is the only one in the book."

"What about this attendant? Is he okay?"

"Méndez has been here at the field station for years, long before I took over. He's Panamanian, originally employed as a blaster's helper on the Third Lock project. There was a premature blast and Méndez turned out to be something of a hero. He saved the lives of the others around the charge and was rather badly injured in the process. He was permanently deafened, one leg was smashed and there was a certain amount of brain damage. He's perfectly capable of doing his work here but not much more. Originally he was taken on at the request of the canal authorities, but there's nothing charitable about it. He earns his salary and the use of the house assigned to him here on the station grounds. Méndez has a sort of instinctive feel for small animals and birds and we've all learned from him. He's good with children, too. He and his wife always have a couple of their grandchildren visiting."

"Can you see him being involved with anything political like the FLP?"

Calder was positive. "Not by any stretch of the imagination. As I said before, he's had brain damage. He's not an idiot, but when it comes to anything more than animals or children, he's just not equipped to cope with it."

"He could be faking that, couldn't he?"

"For thirty years?"

"Still, if he was the only one in there on Saturday and Sunday, it's pretty hard to explain how the monkeys were taken."

He looked puzzled. "You mean Saturday, don't you?"

"No, I mean Saturday and Sunday, too. I saw him myself."

When Calder spoke next he measured his words carefully. "Captain, I can tell you for a fact that Méndez was not here on Sunday. I drove him and his wife to the station at Gamboa after he finished his work on Saturday. They were going to a christening in the city and he had every right to go if he wished. They came back on the first train this morning and walked over here from the railroad station."

He looked at me closely. "If you saw someone on Sunday, it wasn't Manuel Méndez." He paused for a moment. "If he had a key, whoever he was, he didn't sign it out."

I wasn't really listening. Instead I was trying to remember what I'd seen of Méndez from my seat under the tree. He'd looked up and smiled at me, but he hadn't shown any sign that he'd heard what I said. The deafness explained that. Now, that's what I saw on Saturday. I thought about Sunday next. He hadn't looked up as he went past that day, keeping his head down as he tried to manage his cart. The brim of his straw hat had covered his face, but he looked right, hitching along with his funny kind of walk.

If that wasn't Manuel Méndez, it could only have been one other person. He'd done his regular parlor trick, putting on a whole new identity. The one thing he couldn't change, his face, he'd kept hidden under the hat brim. Once inside the animal house, he'd taken the sick monkeys and immobilized them with anesthetic or tranquilizers, packed them into the big plastic garbage cans and trundled away with them.

All the time we'd been watching for him to turn up he'd been doing some watching himself, learning the field station routine and working out his plan. When the right moment had come, he'd walked right past me and the other men on guard.

He'd had almost twenty-four hours to release the monkeys, timed to the hatching of the larvae he'd set out so carefully.

We no longer had days to work with. We were down to hours and minutes.

• • •

20

The north checkpoint had been set up just below the Canal Zone prison at Gamboa and when I pulled up, the MPs on duty were checking out a carload of Panamanians. The MPs were on their best behavior, doing their job and smiling without comment at the cracks that were being passed around. When they signaled that their search was over and waved to the driver to move out, I pulled up and stopped. The sergeant, a big man named Phipps, according to his name tag, gave me a neat salute and when I asked him how things were going he smiled wryly and shrugged.

"There's been some bitching, sir, but most of them just figure it's only some kind of Army Mickey Mouse. Nothing to make a big thing out of."

I drove on without saying any more. The men knew their job and would do it until they were told to quit. I drove about a mile and then had to slow down again.

I'd bumped into the left wing of Polansky's southbound sweep, the men who filed down the highway making sure that the animals scared up by the main group couldn't cross the road without being seen. They'd seen a lot of wild life—squirrels, some coatis, a small group of deer—but nothing in the way of monkeys, rhesus or the local types. I made the run and crossed the railroad tracks and in a few minutes I swung into the camp.

There'd been a lot done even in the short time I'd been away. Just inside the entrance to the area the medics had set up their aid station, the corpsmen from both companies joining forces to handle the steady stream of minor injuries. Most were cuts and deep scratches the men were picking up as they drove through the stands of saw grass, which slashed like a razor. A couple had been gashed pretty badly by the long, cruel thorns of black palm, the kind that acts as if it can't wait for you to touch it but has to reach right out and grab you no matter how wide a berth you try to give it.

A few yards farther on the Special Forces men were building a big *bohio,* a palm-thatched, open-sided kind of pavilion that was to serve as a mess hall and general gathering place. One detail was stringing lights and another was busy making tables and benches out of the materials right at hand. There was no way of knowing how long the little camp would be occupied, but even if it was only for a day or two the troops were going to make it as livable as they could with the resources they could draw on and their own ingenuity.

Off beyond the kitchen tents were the two orderly tents and the quarters for officers and men. Trampled grass showed where the natural paths were being stamped out by the traffic. Elsewhere it still stood, tall and dry, and I saw that the men who smoked were carefully grinding out their cigarettes under their heels.

As much as possible they had taken advantage of what shade there was under the trees, leaving the big open area beyond as a place to park the vehicles not in use. Off to one side, marked with big "No Smoking" signs, was a gasoline tanker for servicing the trucks and jeeps, while back under the trees a couple of mechanics were getting set up to deal with the casualties in the automotive line. Just beyond them was a mosquito trap with its tenant.

I was looking around at the way the camp was taking shape —aerials erected, latrines already doing business and even a clothesline flapping in the steady breeze from the north—when I heard the angry buzz of a light helicopter. It circled the open field while the pilot leaned out for a close look and then it hovered for a moment and landed, flattening the tall grass.

The big main blade was still spinning when I saw Ross slide out and run, shoulders hunched down, toward the tents. When he straightened up and saw me, he headed my way, and together we went over to Polansky's orderly tent.

The big Green Beret lieutenant was huddled over a map table with his operations sergeant, shaking his head and looking both baffled and frustrated.

"It's worse than anything we ever saw in 'Nam," he muttered. "Those guys can't walk a straight line for more than a couple of feet in that stuff. The place is full of little dry channels and broken rocks, and tangled the way it is, an elephant could hide in there."

"How about monkeys? Any sign of the rhesuses?"

He shook his head in disgust. "They think maybe they've seen some traces, but nothing you can go on. My guess is that they're up in the canopy sitting it out until we leave. It's either climb up for them or start chopping down a couple of thousand trees." He turned away from the map and stared out the open doorway of the tent.

I went over and looked down at the map and it was pretty obvious what the problem was. It was a big-scale survey and the contour lines showed clearly just how broken up the terrain was. I noticed Potter outside, waiting quietly for me to have a moment for him.

"You have any ideas, John?"

"Maybe, Captain. If we could get a couple of choppers to sweep the area just above treetop level, they'd shake loose just about anything up there. Then the men on the ground could follow along and police up what came down."

It was worth a try and we made a quick test with the chopper that had brought Ross. It hadn't been at work for twenty minutes when we got the first call from the men out in the field. One rhesus had landed almost at their feet. It had had its wind knocked out, but it was in pretty good shape otherwise. In less than an hour three more ships were on their way and we began to get some results.

The men started coming in from the jungle in shifts for their noon meal and a short break and the first elements brought in four dead rhesuses, plus the first one, still alive and mad as hell at being stuffed into a plastic bag with only his head sticking out, and four local howlers, also madder than you could believe.

I bundled up the whole batch and headed for the veterinary lab.

Putney was waiting for me and he helped me bring the patients inside.

"How long will it take you to check these things out?"

"What do you want to know?"

"If they're sick, I guess, and if they are, just what it is they have. How long will that take?"

He gave me a funny look and said, "Long enough for you to go and get something to eat. PX cafeteria right down the way."

I took the hint and got out of his way. I knew that with his kind there was no use trying to hurry things up. When he gave his opinion he was going to be damn sure of his facts. Putney's type doesn't go off half-cocked.

It didn't take long to eat and when I got back to his office I could see him through the glass door of the lab, bent over a microscope, and a couple of his technicians busy with the animals. I used the time to call Garcés. His report didn't do a thing to cheer me up.

"I've got every man I have working the traps and checking the mosquito figures. The weather people have been working up the wind picture and they say it's going to hold at a steady four to eight miles an hour out of the north and northeast. That's the regular setup for the trade winds at this time of year."

"What does that mean in terms I can understand?"

"It means that somebody has been seeding the terrain just to the northeast of the target area with live bugs. There's been a steady rise at every trap site and it's not just one or two species. Right now we're getting the biggest increase just north of your roadblock and across the Gaillard Highway."

"Any of them the ones that spread yellow fever?"

"They're all suspected or known vectors, but that takes in a lot of territory. What you've got to realize is that we don't know much about this form of the disease. It's all new territory as far as we're concerned."

"How long will it take for them to get into the danger area?"

"Some came in this morning. Probably won't be much of a rise during the afternoon. The wind tends to drop off until after dark. The night-flying types will be coming in tonight."

"Isn't there some way you can pinpoint where they're being planted and get out there and spray or something?"

"Let me put it this way: how many rhesuses have you found?"

"We've got five so far. With any luck we ought to get the rest before too long."

"Okay. You've been hunting a fair-sized animal—big enough to be seen at a good distance—in a limited area. You're asking me to find thousands of bugs in a couple of hundred square miles of dense jungle. Have a heart."

He was right, of course, but there was just one thing I couldn't forget.

"If there's just one sick rhesus left for those bugs to make a meal from, then we've had it."

I rang off and tried to sit still until Putney had his report.

"Rhesus number one died of a massive internal hemorrhage after a severe fall. Numbers two and three must have landed on their heads. Number four died of snake bite and must have been stiff when he hit the ground. The one you brought in alive has a mild concussion and will recover. The howler monkeys are all okay."

"How many of the rhesuses had yellow fever in them? The whole bunch?"

"Not a one. Checked the whole bunch and there's not a trace."

"Don't be silly, Doc. We know that at least three of them had to be sicker'n hell."

"Not these monkeys. Checked them all and if they hadn't fallen they'd all be out there jumping around and doing their thing."

I shook my head, trying to clear out the confusion. I knew I was tired, but even so I couldn't believe what Putney was saying.

"These are rhesuses, aren't they?"

He nodded.

"And a couple of days ago weren't you the one that said those rhesus monkeys all had jungle yellow fever?"

"You're talking about the first batch. They're mostly dead, but I've still got a few that may pull through. The ones you just brought down must be from the second batch."

I didn't know which of us had gone crazy. "What second batch?"

"The one your Colonel Eriksen sent down Friday night from Miami. Same ones I put in the place of the first batch. Didn't she tell you?"

I drove back to the bivouac feeling better than I had in days. I was so happy, in fact, I couldn't even work up a mad at Tiny for pulling the stunt without telling me. Still, she probably had a point. As long as I thought there were twelve sick monkeys or any part of them out on the loose, I'd act like it, chasing around just the way I had all night and morning, giving a performance of a man scared to death for all the world to see.

Putney had played it pretty cool, too.

"Gave each one an immunization shot. Probably made them just sick enough to look like the real thing."

He'd used the new cage to hide the healthy rhesuses and then taken the sick bunch out in the traveling crates and straight to his place. The "sick" ones that had been turned out in the jungle got over their reaction, and if the Green Berets happened to miss a few, it wouldn't mean a thing. They'd live to a great old age, frustrated without female companions, but healthy.

Meanwhile our FLP buddy was beating around in the jungle building up the mosquito population like a man all dressed up with no place to go. Outside of some pretty itchy mosquito bites, it wasn't going to mean a thing if there was no diseased animal for them to visit first.

He'd made his first big mistake.

My job now was to make sure he didn't find out.

It was about four when they finished the first sweep, too late to start another and get much done before dark. The choppers went home and the men began to come into camp. The big thatched hut was finished, complete with a small bar that the supply truck had stocked with soda, beer and ice. About a hundred yards up the road a small stream was crossed by a culvert, making a fairish pool, and it didn't take long for it to fill up with naked soldiers trying to get rid of the dirt and sweat of the day.

I lined up for a beer, then took a seat to unwind a little. One of the Green Berets—a medic sergeant first class named Benavides—came over and reminded me that we'd met in 'Nam. I recalled working with him, and he told me there were a couple of other Puerto Ricans in the outfit who'd been on the same film. Almost every man and all the officers in the two companies had pulled at least one tour in the garden spot of Southeast Asia and it didn't take long for a fair bull session to start.

Shortly before dark, I headed for the new latrine. Somebody had located it just beyond the horse stall and when I came back a trooper asked me what the horse was there for.

When I'd explained, he looked at the poor nag.

"Sir, that's the sorriest-lookin' animal I ever saw."

"Look, lad, for the kind of work he does, you don't have to get Secretariat. All this thing has to do is smell bad."

"And he doesn't get bit?"

"Nope. All he has to do is stand there and think."

When I left, the trooper was trying to figure out how he could give the poor thing an apple, but the big padlock had him stopped.

Potter and I stayed and ate with the troops. There must have been some things on the planes that weren't listed in the book, because after we'd eaten, a couple of floodlights were set up and when the generator went on a pickup game of volleyball began. Dunphy and Polansky captained the first two teams and I saw that they had taken pains to mix the men up, half MPs and half Green Berets on each side of the net.

I watched for a while and then got Potter and headed for the field station. The patrols were out and there wasn't a thing I could do that would be more useful than try to make up some lost sleep.

Things went pretty well the second day. The men knew the drill, and while they didn't like the work, they went right at it. A couple more rhesuses were brought down and I got them off to Putney, keeping up the gag that they were dangerous.

Garcés had been right about the mosquitoes. They'd built up during the night and by morning they'd become a real nuisance. The camp began to reek of mosquito repellent and a couple of men had to go over to the medics. When the supply truck got ready to leave I heard the supply sergeant from the MP company tell the driver to pick up an additional supply of the liquid and some spray cans as well.

The night patrols didn't have much to report. They'd had to put up with some bitching from people who couldn't see why they had to be convoyed home to Gamboa. They'd flushed out a few iguana-hunters and a carload of kids from Balboa High School who'd come up to the Gardens to admire the moon.

The soldier who'd been so interested in the old horse turned up during the morning with a badly gashed left hand where he'd tangled with a black palm. He came back from the aid tent with his hand heavily bandaged and went down to look at his friend. He stood there a few minutes and then he came over to me.

"Captain, I hate to bother you, but I think there's something wrong with that horse."

"Trooper, what's wrong with that horse is what we're all going to get if we live long enough. It's called old age."

"Sir, I've been around horses all my life until I came into the MPs and I think it's pretty sick."

More to humor him than for any other reason, I got up and walked over to the trap. When I got closer I saw that you didn't have to be a vet to know that the nag was down with something. Its head hung low and a long, ropy string of mucus from its nostrils almost reached the ground. I went up for a closer look and then suddenly the animal gave a convulsive shudder and a flood of blackish vomit came gushing from its mouth.

"Get that horse out of there."

"There's a padlock, sir."

"Then shoot it off."

I stepped back as the man drew his pistol and aimed carefully at the wood beside the hasp. There was a report and I reached up and yanked the door open. I tried to edge my way into the stall to reach the halter and get the creature out, but before I could he gave another tremendous shudder and dropped to his knees.

"Give me your gun, soldier."

"Let me, sir. I know how."

The kid sighted through the screening and squeezed the trigger. The horse never knew what hit him. He dropped, making the stall rock and setting the water in his trough sloshing. I stepped over the horse and looked down into the water.

It was swarming with wrigglers and I could see that the screening had been cut away so that once she had paid her respects to the sick horse, each hatched mosquito should have no trouble finding her way out.

There wasn't any doubt that while we'd all been looking up in the treetops, our friend had been insuring his bet. Sick as that horse had been, he must have been infected long before we'd set up the bivouac. It had just been by the fluke of our locating right there and a kid who'd used his eyes that we'd found out.

I didn't know if any of the wrigglers had hatched, but I wasn't going to take chances. Before I sent for Putney and Garcés, I had a party out checking every horse, with orders to destroy those who were even barely suspect and dump the contents of the water troughs.

When the vet got there he took a quick look and allowed as how I'd done the right thing. He took over the job of getting rid of the dead horse and I got busy with Garcés.

He looked over the wrigglers we'd found, but when I asked if he thought any had already hatched he just shrugged.

"We'll know in ten or twelve days."

I didn't have to ask what he meant. That would be when the bugs would be ripe with the fever virus. A couple of days after that the first cases would appear.

When I finally got back to the guesthouse I called the others together. There was no longer any reason to keep up our fancy cover story. Someday they might actually make a film on the subject, but with my luck it would go to somebody else while I got to do a picture about crossing the polar ice cap with a dog team.

Stanley Nagy could go back to his researches at the Columbian Institution without even being able to talk about what he'd done on Operation Paradox. I promised to look him up if ever I got to Washington long enough to send out laundry.

Sam Wynn would pack the camera gear and head back to Hawaii and his family. We hadn't even had the night on the town I'd been hoping for, the kind of party we could talk about when next we met.

John Potter would stay with me until Paradox wound up one way or another. Not only is John a cool hand to have on a job, but he's got what Napoleon always liked in a general—luck—and I was going to need that in wholesale lots.

That left Herbert.

"I'd like to stay on," he announced.

"That's okay with me," I said, "but may I ask why?"

He shrugged. "It's hard to explain. I suppose you can put it down to curiosity. I still want to meet the man."

It wasn't until later, after Nagy and Sam Wynn had left for the airport at Tocumen, that I got to ask him about it.

"Do you think we're really going to find him?"

His answer was firm. "Yes, both logically and statistically."

"What does that mean?"

He put down his book and swiveled around in his favorite wicker chair to look directly at me.

"Up until now he's been able to control his variables. He has eliminated anything that might have subjected him to the laws of chance to what he considered an excessive degree. He's avoided any kind of situation he could not manipulate. Now you've narrowed his field of action. You've cut down on his options, if you want to put it that way. What it amounts to is that now he's going to have to take chances at odds he formerly would have considered too great. He's got to take risks and hope that he's guessing right. The game has come full circle. Now he has to guess what you're doing."

"Okay, Herbert. What am I going to do?"

"Look at it this way. If you strip away the things that are not essential, the 'demonstrations,' for example, what is left? His plan is based on the final gambit. At the start of the game he had three essential pieces. He had a virus, a host animal to start things going, and an available supply of the vector. The only problem, really, was in scheduling the plan so that everything would fall into place at the right moment. His biggest asset was that only he knew what the end game would be. When he lost that, his position had to be constantly reassessed and adapted to a series of changing conditions. Now what does he have left? We can assume he has kept his virus culture alive. From what Major Garcés reports, the whole area is alive with mosquitoes. What is missing is a host animal, even one, to culture the disease in its body and be there for the mosquitoes to bite."

"Look, Herbert, I've got over a hundred men in the area right now. They have orders to capture any host mammal they find. In another day there won't be anything left to bite."

"Then he'll have to introduce it."

"How, for God's sake?"

"I can only assume that it will be ingenious. It will also fail, most likely. You are fully alert now and he doesn't have time to create something infallible."

"Then what?"

"If I am right in my conclusion, he will be forced to take the final step, the one most likely to succeed."

"And what will that be?"

"He'll need a host for the disease more intelligent than a monkey or a horse. One that can think and keep thinking while you and your men are combing the area."

"Okay, what animal is that?"

"Himself."

"You mean commit suicide to make sure his plan works? That's going pretty far, Herbert, farther than even this man would take things. I can't buy that. It seems to me he'd be a lot more likely to give up the Paradox plan and wait for something else."

He didn't answer that directly. "Captain, in 1900 a young doctor from Baltimore named Jesse Lazear was serving with Walter Reed in the Yellow Fever Commission in Cuba after the Spanish-American War. Lazear knew yellow jack. It had already struck in his home city. The theory that the vector of the disease was a mosquito had been advanced but never proved. Lazear allowed a mosquito that had bitten a known yellow fever victim to bite him next. He contracted the disease and he died of it but"—he paused for a moment—"by that act he proved the mosquito vector theory. Thousands of lives have been saved by the simple fact that Jesse Lazear gave his life to prove. He was only thirty-four when he died, but his name will live as long as there are medical researchers to pass the story along.

"That's what made it possible for the Americans to build that ditch out there when the French had failed. Every schoolkid in the Zone and in Panama knows the names of Reed and Carroll and Agramonte and Jesse Lazear, the ones who made it possible. Our friend of the FLP knows the story, too. In the end he will do the same thing to accomplish the great good he thinks he's got to do."

"You mean he wants to die?"

"Of course not. He's got everything to live for. Even if he contracts yellow jack it's not a certainty that it will kill him. With proper care and treatment he has a chance of recovery."

"Sure, with proper care, but he's going to have to stay out where the greatest number of mosquitoes will bite him."

"Then it's more likely that he'll die."

"Statistically?"

He nodded his head sadly. "Yes. Statistically."

"And you still think that the whole FLP is just the one man?"

He turned and gave me a steady look. "All the evidence we have points to that assumption. Everything we know about the FLP is consonant with that. There's nothing that can't be compatible with it."

"So you're positive?"

When he answered, it was said so slowly that I felt almost like a stupid kid.

" 'Positive' is a word used only in a situation where there is a one hundred percent probability. This hypothesis has not yet reached that degree. I can say only that the odds are high and all the new input serves only to raise them."

"So we can assume there's only the one man? If we eliminate him we solve the problem." I stopped for a moment and then added, "Statistically."

"Statistically."

21

Maybe we had the statistics on our side, but only as long as we could keep up the full effort. That wasn't as easy as it sounds. Ross came to talk about it.

"The old man is getting pretty antsy. The ambassador is giving him a hell of a lot of static, asking questions that don't have any answers. The Pentagon has him boxed in, without any elbow room in his orders. On top of that, he's got to deal with the governor."

"What's his problem?"

"Same old thing. Money. With all the civilians and cops on double shifts, he's got to find the extra cash for overtime pay, extra gas and maintenance, plus all the rest of his increased costs. There's no use telling him that it's still cheaper than an epidemic, not when he's the one who has to cope."

Maybe I should have pointed out that problems like those were what the brass got their big salaries to handle. It's easy enough when things are moving along well and right with the program. When you get down to where the hairs are short it's another matter.

"Garcés is getting to be a problem, too," Ross continued.

"What's his trouble? I thought he was all wrapped up in getting rid of mosquitoes."

"He says he's not making any headway and that the harder he works his crews and those from the Zone government, the faster more bugs turn up."

"What does he propose to do about it?"

"That's the problem. He wants to start aerial spraying before the rains begin and the whole situation gets out of hand."

"Well, that doesn't sound like such a bad idea."

"It is when you think that the only thing that will really work is DDT."

"Jesus, I didn't think anyone used that anymore. Not with what they know about its long-range effects."

"You're right. There's no way to use it without the whole world starting to scream, but Garcés says that's the only thing that will do the trick. All the things that make DDT so bad are what he says he needs. High toxicity for the immediate effect and persistence to make sure that the area will stay insect-free."

"They're never going to let him use it. That would be playing right into the FLP's plan. The whole Paradox story would have to come out to explain why DDT was being used. Even if the epidemic plan was scotched and nobody got sick from yellow jack, we'd still have to take the responsibility for what we do to the environment."

"Don't be too sure, Mike. Right now they're still saying no, but if the situation gets any worse they're bound to weaken. The longer it takes to find the man who's responsible for all this and put him out of action, the more likely it is they'll have to let Garcés go ahead with the spraying. It's just a matter of choosing the lesser of two evils, but if they do or they don't, they're still going to make poor old Uncle Sam look like the incompetent imperialist the local cartoonists like to draw."

"Have you talked to Tiny?"

He nodded and I could see that the thought didn't do much to cheer him up. He seemed pretty resigned about it, though.

"I've known Tiny Eriksen ever since she was a captain and I was a second lieutenant. Over the years I've had her tooth marks all over me. A few more won't make much difference."

He got up, but before he went to his car he had one more item.

"We've had some beefs about your MPs moving out some iguana-hunters. They claimed they were roughed up, but nobody had any bruises to show so maybe they just added that to give their story a little more color. Better pass the word to Dunphy to have his men use the soft approach."

That was all we needed. It didn't mean a thing that the MPs had been doing their job properly. What counted was what the alleged victims claimed had been done. I looked up Dunphy and gave him the message. He became a little uptight at the implied criticism of his troops, but I smoothed things over and he said he'd make sure everyone got the word.

Now, to look at an iguana you'd think that the only possible use for the beast might be for making pocketbooks out of its hide. Still, to the Panamanians the iguana is as beautiful as a peacock and a hell of a lot tastier. It's a lizard, of course, a reptile, about the size of a cocker spaniel, and it resembles a small, leftover dinosaur. The people who've tasted it swear up and down that it's delicious and better than turkey or steak or Maine lobster. Best of all, it's free.

The people of the isthmus have been hunting and eating them since long before Balboa and the other real estate developers arrived, and they hunt and eat them to this day even though it's strictly illegal. All it takes is a machete and a mixed pack of dogs trained for the work. The method is simple enough.

You take the dogs for a stroll in the jungle. They hunt up the iguana and the chase is on. The iguana is pretty damn fast and he takes off, with the smaller dogs in hot pursuit. All they do is keep up at first, but the lizard is strictly a sprinter and not much on the long course. He begins to tire and that's when the middleweights and heavyweights move in, keeping the iguana engaged for the hunter to do his thing. They have a trick way of securing the animal's legs up over its back to immobilize its long claws, and once that's been taken care of they pick up the iguana by the tail and trot him along home. A few days of fattening on table scraps and he's all set for star billing on the Sunday dinner table. It's a nice clean sport with fun and profit for all, except of course the iguana.

There are plenty of them in the jungle areas in the Zone and lots of good roads for the hunters to use. They know the back trails, too, and they'd been trying to work their way around our MPs. Dodging them just added to the sport, making the gringos look stupid. It kept our men on their toes.

By the third day the routine was pretty well set. Dunphy kept rotating his guards around the area while Polansky's men cruised inside the perimeter. The cooks from the two companies kept trying to outdo each other and the chow was damn good even by garrison standards.

With no outsiders, even military, allowed in the sector, supplies had to be drawn by our own people. Each company detailed a man to drive to Balboa for rations and mail and any other supplies the camp needed. They'd pick up a new film to run after dark and Special Service came through with more athletic gear and some books and magazines.

Out in the search area we'd reduced ourselves to one helicopter and it didn't bring down very much. We'd accounted for all the rhesuses but one and I figured that one had made dinner for some jungle cat or maybe a boa. Everything else in the way of wild life had long since been chased out, except a few hardy birds.

I stuck pretty close to the bivouac. Our FLP friend had to

know that we'd aced him on the monkeys. He was running out of time, and as Herbert would put it, statistically he had to come up with something new or cancel the whole deal.

I wanted to be right on hand when the new game was called.

I tried to keep from thinking about what might happen if our guy got the brass ring. It wasn't just the yellow jack. People would die, but in the end it would be brought under control and things would go back to normal.

The DDT was another matter.

You couldn't pick a better place for it to do its worst than the Canal Zone. A lot of the spray would land directly in the lake and from there it wouldn't take long to make its way out through the locks and into the shallow bay. The spray that settled on the land was just as bad. It would be absorbed into the plants and the soil and for years it would leach out and work down to the sea. With the local population getting most of its protein from the ocean, those at the top of the food chain would be getting a concentrated dosage every day to add to what they'd already stored in their bodies. There wasn't going to be the slightest question about who was to blame. Not the FLP, something nobody had ever heard of and wouldn't believe anyway. Every warped body would be a constant accusation and a guarantee that relations between the two countries wouldn't stand a chance of improvement.

Late afternoon of the fourth day, I was sitting with Dunphy, the MP captain. We each had a can of beer and the smell of steak was drifting over from the kitchen tent. It was shift-change time and trucks and jeeps were rolling in with the men who had just been relieved. One by one the NCOs gave their reports. It was all pretty routine until one young sergeant came up with a funny one.

"It was one of those iguana-hunters, a little guy, pretty ragged, and he only had one dog. He must have seen us coming and he took off across the road and headed away from us. That didn't mean anything, but what was funny was the little dog."

"What do you mean, funny. What was wrong with it?" I asked.

"I guess it was the way it looked. The owner had shaved the poor thing. Every hair on it except its head and the tip of its tail. Looked like hell."

This was getting interesting. "What happened then? Did the dog take off, too?"

"No, and that was funny. I heard the guy yelling for it, but the mutt just started turning around and kind of whimpering."

"What did you do then?"

"Well, sir, we had a try at catching it, but it wouldn't let us get close enough. It would run off a way and then sit down and lick at a place on its left leg. It finally took off and by that time our relief was there. I told the other guys about the dog and they said they'd keep an eye out for it."

If he had any more to say, I didn't give him a chance. I grabbed him by the arm and dragged him to the nearest jeep, yelling orders all the way.

It was after dark when Potter finally found it, standing in a brook and doing its best to shake off the mosquitoes that were trying to feast on its shaven back. It was pretty badly bitten already, its bare skin studded with red welts, some of them bleeding where he'd tried to scratch. I wrapped him in my fatigue jacket and got him back to camp, where Putney was standing by. He had everything he needed and went to work on the poor pup. I stood there and waited for his verdict.

"Found the place where he was injected. I guess your man is right-handed. Held the dog's head under his left arm and then used the hypo on its left leg."

"Is it sick?"

"Not yet, but it's going to be. Takes a day or so. Judging by what I see, he was infected this afternoon and turned out pretty soon after. This time tomorrow would be a lot different."

"Then the mosquitoes that bit him are okay? Is that what you mean?"

All the talk had run him dry and he just nodded.

He went off with the dog and I called Ross and Garcés. We couldn't wait much longer, and I wanted to talk to Tiny.

"Okay, before I go in to see the boss I want an expression from each one of you," Tiny said. "Garcés, I think we know where you stand."

"I'm for starting to spray as fast as we can get it going. No more delays. We don't dare."

"That's pretty clear. Art, what do you think?"

"I've checked with my commander. He's against it until we have no other alternative. He's looking at it from his point of view, of course. If you spray this whole area with DDT, you'll wreck any hope of getting a settlement with the local people."

"How about you, Mike?"

"Before I say anything, let me ask a question. How long will it take to set the operation up?"

"The equipment will have to be taken out of storage and mounted and then we'll have to make up the solution. The Chemical Corps here say they need that much time plus the time it takes to fly down there. Say about twenty-four hours."

Ross broke in. "Mike, if you're going to suggest that we get everything set up down here and then wait till the very last minute, I can tell you the general won't buy it. That's not the kind of thing you can keep under wraps. Not in Panama anyway. Thirty minutes after those planes arrive, the presidential palace across the line is going to light up and yell 'Tilt.' That idea is out."

"Wait a minute, Art," I said. "There's still some middle ground. What if we stage the planes in Puerto Rico? They can plan the whole deal right there and not even have to land in the Zone."

Tiny asked, "Would your commander buy that, Art?"

"As long as the planes are not actually here, I think I can get him to okay that."

"Garcés? That okay with you?"

"No. I still say we spray and put a stop to this Paradox thing. Just remember, Colonel, the last big outbreak was in 1948. The disease traveled about thirteen miles every month. The longer we wait, the bigger the job is going to be. We may even wind up having to spray everything from Mexico to Colombia."

"All right, Garcés. You've made your point. Now stay on the line for a minute or so."

We sat there looking at each other. My stomach growled and I kicked myself for not having eaten my steak at the first serving. Ross and Garcés said nothing. Finally Tiny came back on the line.

"We're going to go with Mike's idea. Art, you'll be notified as soon as the planes are ready to deploy, but you will not act until your commander has cleared with the Headshed."

The mighty had spoken. I drove back to the field station.

While I'd been on the phone, Potter had picked up some sandwiches, and I ate mine while he drove. Felisa's quarters were dark and there was no sign of her car. Apart from a few quick words spoken while others were standing nearby, I'd hardly seen her since I'd left her in the animal house. Much as I wanted to be with her there just hadn't been time and I knew she must be both puzzled and hurt.

Herbert was the only one left in the guesthouse besides Potter and myself, and after I'd showered I told him what had happened with the little dog. "God only knows what he'll do next."

"Maybe I can be of help?"

"I hope so, Herbert. I can use it."

"It's that he's established a certain pattern and it's worked so far. Let's assume he thinks so, too."

"If there's a pattern, I haven't seen it."

"You have but you didn't recognize it. Let me ask you this. When he wanted to get into the canal lock area, what did he do?"

"He dressed up like someone who belonged there."

"And when he wanted to get at the monkeys in the warehouse at Colón he did the same thing. He just acted like someone with a right to be there. The same thing when he wanted to get the monkeys from the animal house. He acted like the regular attendant and no one noticed him. Today he wanted to get that dog through your cordon, so he dressed himself up as an iguana-hunter and that's what your soldiers assumed he was and were content just to chase him away."

"Okay, that's all true, but it still doesn't give us a hint of what he'll do next."

"Bear with me a moment longer, Captain. Look at things from his point of view. He's filled the area with mosquitoes, but the one thing you've kept him from doing is introducing an infected animal. He's failed with the rhesuses, with the horses and with the dog. Now I think he'll play his last card."

"Herbert, are you still on the same kick, that he'll infect himself? Well, let's say, for the sake of the argument, that he does. He's still got to get where it will be of some use. The whole area is interdicted. Nothing moves in there but uniformed troops of the U.S. Army."

"Uniformed troops?"

"That's right, with helmets, uniforms, insignia and boots, plus berets for the Special Forces and brassards for the MPs."

"Captain, do you really think that a man capable of conceiving Paradox, of transporting a live virus for two thousand miles, of penetrating every defense you've set up, will have any trouble getting those things?"

"Oh, my God."

Dunphy and Polansky didn't say a word, but they knew what I meant. Effective immediately, every man would be required to carry proof of identity or have someone who knew him within hailing distance. Anyone in uniform who couldn't be vouched for was to be disarmed and brought in for immediate interrogation. Special attention was to be paid to anyone who tallied with the description we had of our man—slim, around five eight, a hundred fifty pounds, blue eyes.

It wasn't very good, but it would have to do.

22

Next morning we set up the new patrol system. They were to keep up the hunt for any animal disease carriers, but the main object was to make sure there was no man loose inside our net. Each team would carry a shotgun, and every man was to be armed with either pistol or rifle. The other orders remained the same. Challenge and detain, but fire only to halt and not to kill. There was one chance in a million that a perfectly innocent man might wander in and then panic if he was ordered to halt.

When the patrols rolled out, I got a cup of coffee and settled down in the big hut to worry. If they ever make that an Olympic event, I'm a cinch for at least a bronze.

All the normal daily chores were going on around me. The cooks and KPs were cleaning up from breakfast, the clatter of mess trays and pots rising above the music from someone's transistor radio.

Over in the motor pool the mechanics were servicing vehicles and filling them with fuel from the tank truck.

The MPs from the night shift were going down the road to the culvert pool with towels and soap, to take a dip before they turned in.

I saw Benavides, the big Green Beret medic, toss a mail sack into the back of a waiting truck and then leaf through a stack of requisitions and other forms on an aluminum clipboard. His helper, a young MP, joined him and they got ready to make the regular daily run to Balboa for rations and supplies.

He saw me watching him and came over to ask if there was anything I wanted him to bring back. I couldn't think of anything, but I wondered how he'd got the duty.

"We're taking turns, Captain. That way each man has a chance to get out of camp, even if it's only to ride down and come right back."

I could see his point. If we stayed much longer I was going to have to work out some way that the men could get passes into town for a few hours. Sunday we'd have to bring a chaplain and his assistant into the camp and there would be other problems.

The supply truck pulled out, the night shift came back from the pool and turned in, and for a while, things were quiet. I went over to where the radios had been set up and listened to the traffic for a while. It was all routine, just the regular small chatter that the troops pass back and forth.

As I strolled around I tried to put myself in the position of a man who wanted to hide out right in the camp. The way we were set up, with both companies mixed, he wouldn't want to move around much. If he did, it would only be a short time before either an MP or a Green Beret NCO stopped him, if only to ask why he wasn't on detail.

There was just a chance that he might hunt up an unused place to sleep in, but that was risky, too. The men in each tent knew each other and he'd be suspected right away.

He'd have trouble getting anything to eat. With cooks from both outfits serving the chow line, it would only take one of them to ask him who he was. Still, that might work and I went over to the kitchen tent and gave the word for everyone to keep his eyes open.

It wasn't until I got to the aid tent that I saw something that might work for him. With Benavides off on the supply run, the MP medic was taking sick call. He had his gear set up and there were four or five men lined up waiting to be seen.

Most of them were there to get a fresh dressing on a cut or bad scratch, sitting in the shade of the tent and talking quietly. I strolled over and gave them a closer look.

Hot as it was, they'd all discarded their fatigue jackets and headgear; their green undershirts were sweat-stained almost black.

The last man in line looked just plain sick. He was slumped over, his head almost between his knees. The other men paid no attention to him, letting him suffer in silence. I walked past them and got the MP medic.

"Those men waiting in line," I said quietly. "Are they all from your company?"

He stood up and looked at the waiting troopers.

"All but that last guy. He must be from the Special Forces outfit."

"Are you sure he belongs to them?"

"Not unless I can see his face. Most of them I've seen around."

"Okay. Now get up calmly, like you were going for some medicine or something, and get me a weapon."

He looked up, startled, but he did as he was told. He was back in a minute with a .45 for me and I saw he had one for himself. With the medic right behind me, I went over to the sick soldier. I stopped about five or six feet in front of him and waved to the other men in line to get out of the way and then cocked the pistol.

If the man sitting in front of me heard it, he didn't bother to look up. His head was propped on one forearm, which rested on his knees, the other hanging at his side.

"All right, soldier, look at me." I said it loud and clear, leaving no doubt about who I was talking to.

I saw him shake his head a little, as if to clear it, and then he looked up at me. When he saw the pistol his eyes widened.

They were brown.

His name was Arribal, he was a Spec 5 in the Green Berets and he came, originally, from Ponce. He also had an acute case of appendicitis, which got him an ambulance ride to the hospital and a stern warning not to talk about what he'd been doing in our area.

I got Ross on the radio and told him to keep an eye on the man, then listened to the latest bulletin. Since we were talking in the clear, he didn't give me much detail, but I got the gist of it.

"You know that doctor friend of Tiny's?" he asked.

That had to be Colonel Simpson.

"It seems he jumped the gun and he'd already alerted those people we were talking about the other day."

I guessed he meant Chemical Warfare.

"Another thing. Those Air Force guys have moved, so if you want to get in touch with them I've got their new address."

That was as far as he could go, but I got the message. The spray planes were in place in Puerto Rico. The question now was how long could we hold off putting them to work? They'd need an hour or so to make their flight and then time enough to lay down a curtain from Gamboa to Paraíso before dark.

We'd have to clear the whole area and close the highways, the railroad and the canal itself for long enough to let the chemicals settle out of the air. The whole camp would have to be picked up and moved in time to be well out before the planes arrived. It was going to take some tight planning.

Time came for lunch, but I didn't have much appetite. I was so full of GI coffee I was starting to get dizzy, my stomach protesting the constant stream of brown liquid without a bit of nourishment. The men had already begun to eat when the supply truck rolled in. Benavides swung it around behind the kitchen tent to get the perishables out of the heat as quickly as he could. When I saw him next, Polansky and Dunphy had joined me with their mess trays.

He'd taken the mail sack in and he came into the hut for a cold one before he ate. He had a newspaper for me and I opened it while he got his drink and sat down at the table with us.

"I scrounged up an old fuel drum," he said. "There's some angle iron I know I can get and if it's okay I'll get the motor sergeant to make up a couple of barbecues." He thought for a minute. "With any luck, I think I might even be able to get some little pigs if I can get out of camp for a while."

He sounded pretty hopeful, but when Polansky looked at me I shook my head. Though I like roast pig as well as the next man, if we were going to have any it would have to be after we'd secured from Paradox, and right then I wasn't taking bets on it.

If Benavides was disappointed he didn't say anything. He took a deep drink and then spoke to Dunphy.

"How's that sick MP doing, Captain?"

Dunphy said, "You mean Arribal? All I know is that he's in the hospital with appendicitis."

"No, sir, not that one. I mean the other. The one I picked up just a few minutes ago on my way back."

I put down the paper. "Let's get this straight. You just brought a man into camp? A sick MP?"

He looked at me, startled by my tone. "That's right. I saw him sitting by the road about a hundred yards inside the roadblock. He looked so sick I pulled up and asked him if he was okay."

"He was all alone?"

"Far as I could see. I guess the rest of his patrol had gone on without him."

"Did you know this man? Ever seen him before?"

"Not that I know of. He had a brassard and I knew he was an MP."

Dunphy broke in. "Where was the man you had from my company? Did he know this sick man?"

"Well, he was in the back of the truck. It's cooler back there than up in the cab. I don't know if he saw the sick guy or not."

With every eye on him, he was beginning to get a little rattled.

"Okay, Benavides," I said, "just take it easy. I want you to think hard and tell me exactly what happened."

He took a deep breath. "Well, I'd just gone past the checkpoint. There's a curve there and as I came around I still hadn't finished shifting gears. I saw the man on the right side of the road sitting on the bank. I pulled up and yelled at him and asked him what was wrong."

"Now, before you go on, how was he dressed?"

"Fatigues and helmet. He had his rifle, too. Wait a minute. He had his fatigue jacket off. It was on the ground beside him."

"What did he look like?"

"Like a Puerto Rican or some other kind of Latin. Anyway, he said he felt sick and he'd like a ride back to camp."

"What language did he use?"

His forehead creased as he tried to recall. "English, I think. Anyway, I told him to climb in. He kind of stumbled over and I opened the right-hand door from inside for him. For a second I thought he wasn't going to be able to climb in, but he made it and I put the truck in gear and started off."

"Okay. Now he's in the cab with you. What did he look like?"

He tried to remember. He really did, but finally he said, "I don't know. I was driving and he was kind of slumped down in his seat. I asked him what was wrong and he said he'd found a mango tree and eaten some. Wait a minute. Something else. I remember thinking he must have brought some with him because his jacket swung like he had something heavy in his pocket."

Out of the corner of my eye I saw Dunphy gesture to one of

his officers. I kept on with Benavides.

"Now, Sergeant, what happened when you got into camp?"

"I stopped at the aid tent and let him out there. I came on up and started unloading."

"Did you see the man actually go into the tent?"

He shook his head. "No. Even if I'd looked in my mirror the dust would have hidden him."

The MP officer was back with his medic. He had the sick book with him and it took just thirty seconds to get his answer. Apart from the cuts and scratches, Arribal was the only man who had reported to sick call. The last man had been seen more than two hours before. No one else had come in.

All my back hairs were up now. "All right, Benavides. You must have gotten one good look at the man when he got into the truck cab. Close your eyes and see if you can remember."

He closed his eyes, and in the moment it took him to bring up the image, I could see the sweat break out.

"He's about middle size, slim but not skinny, dark skin about like mine. He's got his dog tags and a small gold cross on a chain. He's maybe twenty-four or -five, hair needs cutting. He looks pale, like maybe he's got a fever coming on."

"That sound like any of your men, Dunphy?"

"Not really. We're checking everyone out right now, the patrols and the men in camp."

Benavides was still trying to get some more details.

"How about his eyes, Sergeant? What color?"

"Brown, I guess. He had those silvery wrap-around aviator glasses."

"Could he have had blue eyes?"

He opened his own. "I guess so."

He was inside the area.

I had to accept that. Herbert had been right and our man had used his favorite trick to come through the cordon.

He was inside, he was armed and he was sick. Whether he was

infectious at the moment didn't make much difference. He would be pretty soon, probably a matter, now, of hours. We had until dark to find him and put him under wraps.

No, that wasn't true either. If we didn't find him by dark he'd be a live bomb, a lethal meal for any stray mosquito to take and then get ready to pass the fever on. That meant that if we didn't have him by two, at the latest, I'd have to ask for the spray planes.

By three we'd have to start closing up shop and move back to the higher ground before the planes arrived.

From four o'clock on he'd have the place to himself when the DDT came raining out of the sky.

We were down to hours, but we weren't out yet. He'd been in the camp less than forty-five minutes ago and he couldn't travel far. The sleeping MPs were shaken awake and sent out to the perimeter. While Polansky got every available man ready to move out, I plotted the search area. There wasn't time for anything fancy, just as tight a ring as we could draw, sweeping the man in toward the camp, where Potter and I would be waiting for him.

It seemed to take hours to get everything organized. The hands on my watch were setting some kind of speed record while I used curses I thought I'd forgotten years before. The longer we waited, the bigger the distance he could cover on foot and the wider the zone we'd have to sweep.

He had the rifle and the ammunition he'd stolen from the magazine and he knew how to use it quickly and efficiently. Something else.

I didn't think that what he'd had in his fatigue jacket were mangoes any more than I thought they were salami sandwiches. He'd taken three thermite grenades from the magazine. Only one had been used.

Finally the men began to mount up. Polansky and his company officers were going out themselves, leaving Potter and me with only a radio operator. They were just about ready when the Green Beret motor sergeant came running in from his maintenance area.

"Sir, one of our jeeps is missing."

• • •

23

There wasn't a goddamn thing to do but bring everything to a screeching halt. With a jeep he could have got anywhere inside the sector. We didn't dare relax the MP cordon and that meant pulling together another search plan which took in everything inside the net.

We used another five precious minutes for that and then, finally, the men took off. They had to really sweep the area, checking every bridge and culvert, under and behind every fallen tree, the length of the railroad right of way, anyplace that would serve to hide a man.

I gave ten seconds' thought to calling for more men from the garrison and really flooding the place with bodies. I had to throw that idea away right off. Not only would it take too long, but we'd run the risk of our people beginning to shoot at each other if they knew that the man they were hunting was in uniform. This way I had men who knew each other and had had five days to get used to the terrain.

Just before noon they found the jeep. It had been driven up close to a caved-in piece of hillside, and vines and cut branches had been piled against it. I drew a new circle around the spot and started another sweep. This one allowed plenty of distance for travel after he'd left the vehicle, no matter how sick he was.

At one o'clock I radioed to Ross. The spray planes were to warm up, and if we had clearance from The Rock, they could take off at two, leaving us time to clear out before they started making their runs at low level.

I stood over the radioman's shoulder listening to the reports coming in, none of them good. Potter was with me and I could see he was scared as I was. He wasn't worried for himself. I knew that. What he knew as well as I was that if something didn't happen soon to bail me out, I could kiss goodbye my idea of staying in the Army long enough to get a pension. When John Potter worries he shows it.

It was close to two when the circle closed on the place where the jeep had been left. They hadn't found a thing. I got Polansky on the radio.

"Okay, we give it one more try. This time the whole thing. Move in on the camp and try to time it so you arrive before three to start evacuating."

I passed the handset back to the operator and went outside. To all intents and purposes, Operation Paradox was over. I'd ordered the last sweep, but I didn't have much faith that they'd find anything out there in the jungle besides the mosquitoes that were still drifting in on every breeze. I looked around the empty camp, wishing I were anywhere else in the solar system. Potter brought me back to earth.

"Captain, can I say something?"

"Sure, John. Anything you like."

"Well, if I was that FLP fellow I'd stay as far away from that search as I could get."

"I thought so, too, John. That's why I allowed the extra distance around the place where he left the jeep."

"You figure he got into camp, stole the jeep and then hid it out and took off, right?"

"That's it. I figured when he got it and how long it would take to get it there and hide it out."

"Captain, I hope I'm not out of line, but I think maybe that's not what he did."

"Well, what did he do? The jeep didn't drive itself there."

"No, sir, but suppose he stole the jeep first, hid it out at a place he knew and then hiked back to get picked up by Sergeant Benavides in the truck?"

"You mean the jeep is nothing but a red herring to get us to go charging off in the wrong direction. Jesus, John, you could be right. Wait a minute, though. If he's not out there, where the hell is he?"

"I thought about that some. I don't think he had any idea of waiting around outside the camp area. It's too easy to trail somebody out there. The grass is all dry and a man makes a trail a blind man could follow. Somehow I got to thinking about a fish. What does he do when he's inside a net?"

"Generally, he sees it, panics and tries to get away from it. When it gets in so close he can see it all around him, he panics and tries to break out or jump over. That's when he gets caught."

"Sure, Captain, but this man's no fish. He does what the fish should have done, and that's dive for the bottom and lay there while the net's gathered in over his head."

"It's a good idea, John, but I'm damned if I know what I can do anymore."

It was two and I went back and radioed Ross. He was standing by and I told him to go ahead and call Puerto Rico. He had his clearance and everything was set on that end.

"If anything goes wrong I've got an open line to the air controller and he'll be in contact with them as soon as they're in range."

I didn't know what he meant, but it didn't matter. I saw Potter nosing around, his heavy riot gun held lightly in one hand. Polansky was still out there making the last sweep and as his line grew shorter he started sending men in to begin striking camp.

The cooks packed up first, loading the big field ranges, the half-cooked evening meal and all their supplies on a cargo truck and then sending it over to be fueled and ready to roll.

Dunphy called in and asked if he could send a detail back to take care of their part of the camp. When the search parties started coming in just before three, most of the tents were down and waiting to be loaded.

Tired as they were, the men got to work, anxious to finish it. They'd move to a new location near the field station and set up again while we decided what to do next.

A couple of men trod the well-worn path through the dry grass that led to the latrine and started the work of filling it in and marking the place. One by one the trucks were loaded and sent over to be gassed at the tanker. The camp that had gone up so quickly came down a little more slowly, leaving bare patches of trampled earth and grass, the paths that had been used to go from place to place now leading nowhere.

Between the moving trucks and the heavy canvas tents dragging across the dry earth to be folded and tied, a cloud of dust began to cover the whole site. It rose up about eight or ten feet and then the breeze snatched at it, the same breeze that, in about an hour, would carry the DDT spray down the Cut and on to Miraflores and Balboa and the bay.

I sat in the homemade mess hall and watched the men at work. A couple of them came in and began to load the stock of beer and cold drinks from the bar on the bed of a truck, and when the last of it was transferred the driver climbed into the cab while the other man sprawled out on the stack of cases, a soda in his hand.

There was no reason to wait any longer. Potter and I got into our sedan, ready to lead the convoy toward Gamboa when they'd finished refueling. The truck with the beer and soda was the last in line for gas. As soon as it was ready the tanker could shut down, and when it was ready to roll, we'd leave. I drove over to the gas truck and got out to watch.

The last driver was a chatty type. He had the big nozzle thrust down into the tank beside his cab.

"How come we're pulling out, Captain?"

I was in no mood for any kind of talk, so I just gave him some sort of short answer.

"This is a pretty nice spot. Of course the bugs have bothered some of the guys, but they kind of leave me alone."

I saw him fish in his pocket and bring out a cigarette. Just as he was about to put it into his mouth, I stopped him.

"That isn't very smart, is it? Between the gas fumes and all this dry grass."

He smiled sheepishly and put the butt behind his ear.

"How about the other man? Does he smoke?"

"I don't know, sir."

"What do you mean? Aren't the two of you assigned to this truck?"

He shook his head. "No, sir. My regular man is on detail. I just grabbed this guy from the KPs. He asked if he could give me a hand and I said it was okay with me. He must be on light duty, he's so shaky, but he said he was okay."

"And you don't know him at all?"

"Not as far as I know. Like I said, he must be from the other outfit."

I stepped back as he finished what he was doing, signaling to Potter to get out of the sedan and move in on the other side of the truck. When the driver capped his tank and went to hang up the hose, I started moving down one side of the truck while Potter took the other, trying to synchronize our arrival at the rear. I waited for a moment to make sure he was in position and then yelled:

"Now, John."

I took the last few steps to the rear of the truck and saw Potter appear. He was just raising the riot gun when a slim figure shot out of the back of the truck and sprawled on the ground. I got a glimpse of black hair and wraparound glasses in the split second before he shot to his feet. He took off like a terrier, tearing around to the far side of the tanker, the open fatigue jacket he wore flying behind him. I heard the unmistakable sound of the riot gun being cocked and I knew Potter was raising it, ready to fire. He was right at my side, but I yelled as loudly as I could.

"Hold fire, John. The tanker's still got gas in it."

A charge of double-O buckshot at that range would tear right through the steel walls of the tank and the burning wadding would ignite it like a giant torch.

I didn't have a weapon and God only knows if the stupid driver did and there was no time to get one. We'd have to rely on the riot gun. The nearest troops were a hundred yards away; plenty of time for our man to make it to the tree line. Potter's weapon was great at short range, but at any distance the chances of hitting a target were pretty slim.

Potter was still using his head. Instead of playing ring-around-the-rosy, he just dropped to his knees and started working his way under the tank truck. The guy couldn't look every way at once. If John could get close enough, he could drop his gun and go for a straight open field tackle.

It might have worked except for Blabbermouth. It had finally dawned on him that something funny was happening and he just had to get in on it.

"Hey, Sarge, what're you doing under there?"

That was all it took. With Potter still under the truck, our man took off. John scrambled the rest of the way and as I came around the rear, he raised the gun and roared out the command to halt.

The man was about out of range, but I suppose he didn't know that. He slowed and came to a halt before he reached the tree line. It must have taken his last bit of strength because he just stood there, his shoulders hunched forward, his breath coming in great, shuddering gasps, and then, slowly, he sank to his knees. We started forward, Potter with his riot gun still up. The man we'd been searching for so long was just about in our hands.

He knelt there, motionless, as if at prayer, but if he was praying it wasn't for long. Still on his knees, he swung around, his right arm back, and even though I couldn't read the label, I knew what it was that he flung straight at us. It arched through the air and I was sure he must have pulled the pin and waited for the last possible minute before he sent it on its way.

The grenade landed with a thud between us; there was a loud report and a searing wave of heat and chemical smoke, and I flung myself desperately away from it, rolling over and over to get clear. Potter must have done the same thing, unable to even fire his weapon into the dense cloud of white smoke that gushed from the grenade, enveloping everything for yards around.

I heard the dry crackle of burning grass and in a moment it had reached me. I struggled to my feet and backed away, holding my arm across my nose to shut out the smoke and ash flying around me. It wouldn't take more than a second to reach the tanker and I turned and ran toward where I thought the troops were waiting before the whole damn shebang blew. I had almost reached them when there was a sickening kind of wrenching sound and then an ear-shattering report as the tank truck was ripped apart, sending a shower of burning gasoline over the area, igniting the rest of the grass and the dry tops of the smaller trees.

I turned around, looking wildly for some sign of Potter, unaware of the men who were trying to slap out the parts of my uniform that had caught fire. The blast had blown away a good bit of the white cloud from the grenade and even with the smoke from the burning grass I could see that the field held nothing but the charred hulk of the tank truck and the truck at its side, both still burning and giving off the bitter stench of flaming rubber and insulation. There was no sign of Potter and no sign of the man who had started it all.

I guess that's when I lost control. I suppose I started to scream as the men came swarming out of the trucks to try to stop the grass fire with blankets and boughs and fire extinguishers. There was nothing to do for the trucks or what was left of my sedan and all they could do was try to keep the flames from spreading.

There were a couple of men holding me on the ground and I can remember Benavides dabbing at me with some kind of ointment and then I felt myself dropping and the lights went out.

It couldn't have been very long before I came to. The fires were out and the men were coming back to the waiting trucks, their feet stirring up the charred remains of the grass and the powdery ash. Benavides was putting a small bandage on my arm and he held it firmly with one hand when I tried to shake him away.

"Did they find Potter?"

"I don't know, Captain. I've been here with you."

He finished with the dressing and when I tried to get up he helped me to my feet. He didn't attempt to follow when I walked past him, heading away from the smoldering trucks toward all that remained of the camp, the thatch-roofed hut, which now seemed so different. It had been only minutes since Potter and I had been sitting there. There was something in my hand and I looked down stupidly to see what it was.

Someone had handed me a canteen and I drank deeply and then twisted on the cap and went up to the hut. I tried to make myself go in and sit down, but I couldn't get my feet to take me any farther. Instead I dropped to the ground, propping my back against one of the poles and drawing my knees as close to my chest as I could bring them. I folded my arms and let my head drop, trying to blot out the scene around me.

I couldn't seem to get what had happened deep down to the real me. Potter was indestructible, elemental like rocks and mountains, not subject to the same mortality as ordinary people. I had always been the one who had to be taken care of, Potter the one with the head and heart to yank us out of anything, no matter how bad it got.

For a man who could always get along with anyone, Potter had always been careful about giving his real friendship. Men don't talk much about that kind of thing and maybe Army men less than most, but that's the way I'd always looked at him.

I'm not talking about loyalty. If you've got good men with you that comes without question, just as you give it to them, taking care to keep the two-way bond solid and secure.

That's what I thought of, sitting there on the ground. I could hear the men moving around and I knew I had to do something about getting out of there. I opened my eyes and there on the ground in front of me I saw a dusty pair of size fourteen GI field boots. My head shot up and I found myself looking into the smiling face of John Potter.

His fatigues were charred and streaked with ash, there wasn't a hair left on his head, but he still had his toothpick held tightly in his even white teeth. His riot gun was in his right hand and over his left shoulder a limp figure had been slung.

"Where do you want him, Captain?"

24

It was a long night. Fast as the hands of my watch had spun the afternoon before, that's how slowly they crept through the hours of darkness. I probably could have got undressed and into my bed, but something kept me dressed and ready in case I was needed. I did take a few cat naps, but all they did was give me a bad taste in my mouth. Maybe it was the booster shot of vaccine we'd all been given that made me so logy, but more likely, it was the inevitable letdown.

A couple of times I opened the door and looked at the man in the bed. He'd barely been able to keep his head up while Benavides had stripped and bathed him the afternoon before and then laid him in bed. By the time the doctor got there from Gorgas Hospital and started the intravenous feeding, he was almost comatose, making no sound or movement when the needle went into his arm. Even with only the one shaded light in the room, I could already see the yellowish cast of jaundice, sure sign that the virus had reached his liver. The chart on the table showed a steep, steady climb on the temperature record, but so far there had been no sign of the black vomit signaling the internal bleeding that comes just before the end.

There hadn't been a lot of choices for taking care of him. I wasn't going to take him all the way to the main hospital, with the risk of contagion what it was. What little the hospital could do for him didn't require any fancy equipment. Whatever he'd need could more easily be brought to him. The field station was the logical choice. There was plenty of room in the guesthouse and we could set it up as a quarantine area as easily as any other.

First thing, of course, had been to reach Ross on the radio. I didn't take time to explain and he didn't waste time asking questions. If he was going to make it at all it would be a near thing. He signed right off and got busy trying to abort the spray mission. I went back to our prisoner.

Potter and Benavides had strapped him to a litter and hoisted it into the back of a truck. The three of us climbed in and the driver took off for Gamboa. I couldn't hear much over the noise of the engine, but I leaned out to see if the planes were approaching. Ross must have made it because when we got to the guesthouse and the engine was killed, there was no sound from the sky. What we had to do now was get our patient inside and protected.

By the time we arrived, the regular Friday-afternoon exodus was over and unless they were looking out a window, I don't think anyone saw us bring the litter inside. While Benavides and Potter got busy on the man, I hit the phone.

I called Doc Calder first. I knew he wouldn't object to what we were doing and he didn't. Instead he just said that the things we'd need would be brought to our back door and if we thought he could be of use he'd come in and share the quarantine. I couldn't see any need, so I thanked him and got Ross on the line.

Thanks to some kind of delay in Puerto Rico that had held up their takeoff, the planes had been caught just as they came in sight of the isthmus and they'd been turned back.

"I suppose we can close down on Paradox, can't we?" Ross asked.

"I hope so. There may be something we don't yet know

about, so I wouldn't just tell everyone to go home right away. The security can shift to an easier condition, but I wouldn't let my guard down all the way just yet. We still need some more answers."

"Does that mean you aren't staying with the one-man-gang theory?"

"I don't know and that's the truth. Right now I've got a dying man on my hands. I've got to have a doctor and everything he thinks he'll need to take care of this guy."

"Do you want a couple of nurses?"

"No, we'll handle it. If you send any more people here it's going to make more trouble than it's worth. Just tell the doc to bring his toothbrush and a change of socks. Right now I've got work to do."

I hung up and tried to think of what to do first. I knew just enough about the situation to figure out what was required. I turned to get up and there was Herbert. I'd forgotten him.

"I'm sorry, Herbert, but you should have left when you had the chance. I'm afraid you've got to stay in here with us for the duration."

"Don't be sorry, Captain. Even if I could leave I'd prefer to stay and see it through." He looked through the open door of the sickroom. "Perhaps I can help out to pay my way."

He did, too. I heard the two-wheeled cart that Méndez used come rattling up to the back door, Calder pulling at the shafts. He brought it as close as he could and then walked quickly away. I called to Potter and the three of us ran everything inside and got to work.

First we draped the sickbed with two mosquito nets and sprayed as much insecticide as we dared along the walls and in the corners. Calder had sent some rolls of wide tape and we got busy sealing every screen to its frame, slapping tape on any hole that looked big enough to let a bug in.

We did that all through the guesthouse, with the exception

of the door in the rear. That we draped with another net, which anyone coming in would have to enter before he could close the door and be sprayed. The first one in was the doctor.

He took a quick look around at what we'd done and I guess it was okay because all he did was grunt and head right for his patient. I suppose he approved of what Benavides had done as well, because he just opened up the boxes he'd brought and the two of them got to work.

It wasn't until he'd finished up and come out to take a look at Potter that I got a chance to talk with him.

"How does he look?"

"Like a man with a galloping case of yellow jack. Do you have any idea when he was exposed?"

"Not really, except that he meant to be infectious when he finally got into the area. How does he look to you?"

"I'm not a specialist. The only ones who are in a position to talk with any knowledge are the research men, and they know more about how the fever affects monkeys than men. If you want a guess, I'd say that he's just about ripe."

I looked on as the doc examined Potter. He was a little guy with wiry hair that stuck straight up. His name was Polikoff, and specialist or not, he knew his business. Potter had a few burns on his arms and the backs of his hands and after the doc took care of them and looked at me, he went to work on a booster shot for each of the four of us. I saw him give one to himself and then go back to the sickroom.

Herbert went with him and in a minute Benavides came out. We got cleaned up and then I switched on the radio and called the new camp. Polansky and Dunphy said they were set up, and aside from a delay in serving supper, they were as well organized as they'd been in the old spot.

I gave Dunphy the word to discontinue his roadblocks and to let traffic move everywhere except right around the old camp. In the morning I wanted patrols out to make sure no one was doing anything funny, but no more maximum effort. Over the weekend they could give the men passes, though not more than half of them were to be away from camp at any time. The new camp was off limits to all outsiders and the men on pass were not to wear unit insignia or talk about the mission. I left it to them to make sure of that.

Dunphy asked, "Have you got any food over there?"

"Now that you mention it, no, we don't."

"You're going to have to get fed by someone. Why not let us handle that part?"

It was damn nice of him to think of that and make the offer. Ten minutes later a truck pulled up, and when it drove off I found a hot meal right on our doorstep. Considering what the food had been through, it looked fine.

I set it up on the worktable in the big living room, using the stock of dishes and stuff in the guesthouse kitchen, and when Potter and Benavides were finished showering, we all sat down and ate. If it hadn't been for the man in the next room, it would have been pretty nice.

Potter kept looking at him through the open door. It was beginning to look as if, having captured him, John was taking an extra interest. Without a hair on his face or head, he looked like something carved in ebony and I realized that he was a hell of a good-looking guy. How he'd managed to stay true to his marriage with the Army was just one more remarkable thing about him.

After we'd eaten, the doc and Benavides went back to the sickroom and John, Herbert and I got things cleaned up. Following Polikoff's instructions, we set the food containers outside the door and then poured boiling water over them. A little later I heard the truck return and when it left I looked out. The things were gone and in their place was a case of cold beer.

When the first daylight began streaking in, I got out of my chair and went in to look at our friend. His eyes were open as Benavides gently sponged his body with alcohol, but when I raised my eyebrows to the doc he just shrugged and went back to the book he was reading.

Breakfast came and some newspapers. There was nothing to show that any notice had been taken, officially at least, of what had been going on in the Zone. That didn't mean that there hadn't been bits and pieces of rumors floating around. Not in a country as small as Panama.

Potter took over the nursing duties and Benavides turned in while Herbert and I cleaned up from breakfast. Through the window over the sink I could see Felisa's place, the shades drawn and the carport empty. I had a lot of things to think about, but when we finished up I poured a couple of cups of coffee and Herbert and I took them back to the living room.

"Last night you said you wanted to stay, Herbert. Why?"

"Selfishness, I suppose. That and pure curiosity."

"What does that mean?"

"It's only a piece of self-indulgence, but if I can, I want to know this man, talk with him if that's possible."

I didn't say anything, preferring to let him tell it his own way.

"This may sound pretentious, or conceited if you choose, but it's not often I get to meet a man of my own age and intelligence. I hope you understand that I don't think either of us can take credit for what we've been given any more than the man who's been dealt a perfect hand at bridge. Statistically, sooner or later, these things happen. We were put among those at the very top of the graph, a very tiny fraction of the species.

"Don't think that we don't have our problems. In school, for example. The endless wait for the others to solve an equation that you completed while it was being written on the blackboard. The sense of frustration when you see someone take a mass of data and arrive at a totally wrong conclusion, one that cannot possibly fit the facts.

"For a child it's not an enviable position. Before your emotions have had a chance to mature you realize that there are things you can accomplish that your elders will never achieve. My parents are people of some intelligence and education, but they were so awed at what they'd produced that I was never allowed to be a kid.

"The man in the next room knows all that. From what I see, our abilities are different. His are scientific, mine more philosophical, but he's someone I can communicate with."

He stopped and looked up and I saw that Polikoff had been standing in the sickroom doorway, listening to our talk.

"What do you think, Doctor? Will I have a chance to talk to him?"

"That's also a matter of statistics. The people here seem to have a certain degree of inherited resistance to the fever. Had I reached him when the fever first took hold, the supportive measures might have helped carry him through. As it is, just about all he has to fight with is his own strength, the resources he has and his own will to live. Still, the disease has to run its course. His fever will mount as his body tries to reject the virus until it reaches the crisis level. It will probably moderate then."

"And he'll pull through?"

"He may if he has the remaining strength."

"But if he doesn't?"

"Then he'll begin to hemorrhage, we'll see the characteristic black vomit, and he'll die."

Saturday was a long day and a longer night. Just after daylight on Sunday the fever broke. He was conscious and awake, the strange blue eyes in his dark-skinned face bright and alert. He didn't try to talk, but contented himself with watching the men who were trying to help him fight. When Herbert came in to take over the watch and sat in the chair at the head of the bed, I thought he was trying to turn and face him.

"May I talk to him, Doctor?"

"Yes, a little, but don't let him try to answer."

Our breakfast had been delivered and while we ate I could hear Herbert's voice, too soft to make out the words, as he leaned over the sick man, bringing his face as close as the netting would allow.

When we finished eating Polikoff brought Herbert away from the bedside. He wanted his patient to sleep and try to build a little strength. While Herbert ate I asked what he'd learned.

"He's really remarkable."

"In what way?"

"Well, for one thing he's got what I've always known I lack. A real sense of humor."

"You mean you let him speak?"

"No, that wasn't really necessary. He's quite capable of communicating almost without words."

"What did he let you know about the FLP? Is he really the whole thing, all by himself?"

"Of course. What he wanted to know was the line of reasoning I'd followed to reach that conclusion."

"He knew you were the one that figured it out? Or did you tell him yourself?"

"That wasn't necessary. He recognized me from the first."

"That's pretty steep, Herbert. Just how did he recognize you?"

"Let's put it this way. If you were told to go to a crowded hotel lobby to meet another captain, with both of you in civilian clothes, would you be able to pick him out?"

He was right. Every beast knows its own breed. It takes one to know one.

"Still, are you sure that he was telling you the truth about the FLP?"

"Captain, a man like that doesn't lie. He doesn't have to."

It looked as if Herbert had closed the statistical gap. His "probability quotient," or whatever he called it, was now 100 percent.

"You didn't think to ask him his name, did you?"

"Why, no. Is that important?"

"No. Not really."

When the man in the bed awakened, the doctor let Herbert go in again. He didn't stay long and when he came out I started to speak and then caught sight of his face Suddenly I knew why Herbert had been so determined to stick with Paradox right to the bitter end. It didn't take any special genius to figure out that to him the other man was the closest he would ever come to a human being whom he might call brother. There was a mind there that his own could contend with, an intellect that would not yield to the force of his own. The stricken look on Herbert's face told the whole story. He'd found his brother just in time to see him snatched away forever. The battle of the intellects would never be fought. Herbert would never know which was the better mind—which could outthink the other.

It was just a little later that the vomiting began. Polikoff, with Potter and Benavides, worked over him, supporting him and trying to ease the convulsions that racked the frail body. There was nothing for me to do but wait.

About five or so it was over. Polikoff came out and as he dialed the phone to call for an ambulance I saw Potter bend over the bed and close those strange blue eyes and cover the face with the sheet. Then we just sat, the room darkening, until we heard the sound of the ambulance outside. Polikoff helped load the stretcher into the vehicle and then climbed in for the ride to the morgue and to supervise the autopsy. The door to Herbert's room stayed closed and there was no sound from inside.

The sickroom door had been locked and would stay that way

until the place had been cleaned and fumigated. All that remained of the FLP was in a little heap on the living room table. Idly I poked through it.

There had been a couple of dollars in small bills and change, a gold cross on a thin chain and a bunch of keys. The dog tags that he'd worn had been traced to a GI who'd reported them lost or stolen. The cross I'd given to the ambulance driver, with word to have it put around the owner's neck when they'd finished the post-mortem and before he was buried. The money I'd drop in the first church poor box I'd find. Idly I jingled the keys in my palm.

Probably we'd never know what he'd done with the virus culture or the flares he stolen and the third incendiary grenade. More than likely we'd never know his name. There was no one we could tell who might mourn him. There was only Herbert, silent now behind the closed door.

I'd keep the keys. That was about all that remained, now, of the Frente Liberación de Panama. I held them in my hand as I went to the window and looked out at Felisa's cottage across the way. Then I went to bed.

25

Most of the next day I spent with Ross and at Quarry Heights. Benavides had gone back to the Green Beret company and Potter was catching up on his sleep. He didn't say anything, but I could see he was pretty broken up at what had happened. There was still no sign of Herbert, his door remaining closed, his food uneaten.

I drove down alone in the remaining sedan of the two Ross had assigned to me, taking the route past the burned-over bivouac to see what was being done. The remains of the destroyed vehicles were being hauled away, stirring up swirling bits of ash from the incinerated grass. The sanitary crews were moving in fresh stalls to replace those that had been damaged and new horses for the ones we'd had to shoot.

Just before I got to the underpass I had to slow down and stop while a troop of coatis crossed the road, heading for the area we'd cordoned. I guessed it wouldn't take long for the other animals to move in and restore the normal population.

Ross was waiting for me and together we went in to see the old man. He'd get a copy of the written report in time, but there was no reason to keep him hanging, not with all he'd had at stake. If the FLP plan had worked, he would have been the one with the bag. It didn't matter where the real fault lay. The man at the top collects for his whole command whether they're handing out roses or manure.

He heard us in silence, nodding now and then to indicate that he was getting it all. When I finished he made no comment one way or the other. His opinion of how I'd handled or messed up Operation Paradox would be made through channels. Someday I might even see it.

When we were dismissed we got Tiny on the phone. We scrambled and I heard the click of her recorder. I kept my report brief.

"You'll have the full report on the high-speed printer in a little while," I told her.

"So there's no reason for you to stay any longer, is there? I'll have orders cut for you and Potter and you can report back here as soon as you can get transportation."

"Are you sure you can hear me okay, Colonel?"

I knew perfectly well she could hear me. That was my way of letting her know that I didn't want what I was going to say recorded. I heard another click as she switched it off.

"Okay, Mike. What's on your mind?"

"I'm not sure. If I could put my finger on it I'd tell you."

"What does that mean?"

"I don't know why, but it just doesn't seem to add up right. There must be something we don't know about. I can't give you the kind of step-by-step analysis that Herbert would assemble, but I can't get over a feeling that it's still out of balance."

"What do you want to do?"

"I'm not even sure of that."

"Look, Mike, maybe you're just tired. You've been living with Paradox so long and so hard, it's understandable that you can't let down all at once. Get a good night's sleep and see how you feel."

"Damn it, Tiny, I've had a good night's sleep and it didn't

change a thing. If I have to, I'll ask for some leave and stay here on my own, and I know Potter will, too."

There was a pause and then she asked, "How much longer do you think you'll need? Couple of days be okay?"

That was fair enough. Maybe two days would do it—if I got even the tiniest idea of what to do with them.

When I arrived back at the field station the guesthouse was empty. Herbert's door stood open and so did Potter's. There was no sign of the mosquito-proofing we'd added, but there was still more than a hint of the smell of the fumigant. In the sick-room there was no trace of the bed, spring, mattress and frame, all hauled away to be burned. I washed up and walked to the dining hall.

Herbert and Potter were at a small table, just finishing up, but at the big table Calder and Felisa were still being served. Calder waved to me and gestured to a vacant chair across the table from them.

For the first few minutes he chatted about something, but I don't think that either Felisa or I really paid any attention. She kept her eyes fixed on her plate while I kept putting food into my mouth without really being aware of what it was.

She seemed to be trying to draw herself in, to occupy the smallest possible space, her shoulders drawn forward, her elbows held tight to her sides. She was still sitting like that when Calder finished and excused himself. Herbert and Potter had left and we were alone in the room. If I was going to do anything, this was the time.

She had laid down her fork and put her napkin on the table. Just as she was about to slide her chair back, I found the words.

"You think I've behaved badly, don't you? Perhaps you're right, but don't you think I'm entitled to a hearing?"

Without looking at me, she said, "If you have something to say, there's no reason why you shouldn't."

"You're not making it easier."

She didn't say anything, but I did see her shoulders relax.

"Look, Felisa, you're too intelligent not to realize that something has been going on and that I've been involved. I could probably come up with some sort of barely plausible story and you'd have to decide if you wanted to accept what you knew was really less than the truth. I'll save you the trouble of making that kind of decision. I'll just have to say that there was no way for me to tell you what I was doing and that there is no way for me to tell you now. I can only tell you that there has been no change in the way I feel about you. Like the rest, you're going to have to take that on faith alone."

For the first time she looked straight at me. "And you could not say that much to me until now?"

I shook my head.

Slowly she leaned back in her chair. I swallowed the last mouthful on my plate and stood up. As I turned to go, she slipped out of her chair and with a few quick strides she was beside me. Together we went out into the night.

Without speaking, we started down the path to the animal house. Once inside, she quickly got to work. The fawn's cast had been removed and it wobbled toward her on unsteady legs when she held out the bottle. The piglet was gone, its place taken by a baby tapir. When she'd fed it we locked up and climbed the hill to her bungalow. I wasn't aware if anyone saw us go in. I just didn't care.

I don't know what it was that awakened me. She was making no sound, but in the dim light I could see her shoulders move with her sobbing. I knew I should just close my eyes and let her go on, but if I was ever going to ask, it had to be now. If I was ever going to find peace of mind I had to know.

"What was he to you?"

"Then he is dead?"

"Yes. It happened yesterday afternoon. Just before dark."

"I saw the ambulance come and go. I was still hoping, though."

A new wave of sobbing seized her, great soundless, tortured gasps. I waited for her to answer my question. Finally her breathing returned to normal.

"He was my brother."

"And you were the rest of the FLP?"

"Not at first. He did everything he could to make you believe that he was alone. Instead of hiding the fact, he left clues he said a really intelligent man would interpret that way."

He'd done it damn well, too. He'd worked backward from the solution, the "X", filling the equation so that our "really intelligent man," Herbert, had arrived at the right answer. I was the clown who had been hard to convince. Herbert used all the facts he'd collected and his equation balanced perfectly. You couldn't blame him. The data had been dropped like the clues in a paper chase, to lead him where it had been planned for him to arrive. He could prove his was the right answer while all I had to go on was only a funny feeling that it was all too pat.

Almost as if she were reading my mind, Felisa went on.

"At first he would let me do very little. He made use later on of the fact that I was here at the field station, close to the place he'd picked. When the monkeys were brought here he needed more from me, but he waited until I was away to use what I had told him."

"And you think that what he tried to do was right?"

Her voice dropped. "I don't know. He said it was and that was sufficient for me. I didn't question him."

I felt her move her arm, extending her hand to where it almost touched mine, waiting for some small sign of reassurance.

I fought down the impulse to take her in my arms and lay without moving.

"You knew about me, didn't you?" she asked.

"Not at first. After a while I began to think that while he was working alone, someone had to be giving him some help and information. There were too many things that couldn't be explained any other way. He made no inquiries in Colón, but still he knew the monkeys were here and how they were secured. Somehow he'd learned the station routine, that Méndez would be away on Sunday, where to find the cart and the right clothing. He needed the right keys and I knew he didn't get them from Calder or the duty officer. That left your set, even if you weren't here at the time. Then, just to confirm it, there were things he didn't know. Like the fact that healthy monkeys had been substituted for his infected ones. He didn't know because you didn't know. It took only one more piece to fill the puzzle."

"Yes?"

"We found a bunch of keys in his pocket. One was a car key, but we hadn't found any car that we could connect with him. When I tried the key in your little sports car, it fit."

"So tonight at dinner you knew for sure. Still you said nothing. Why, Mike?"

I didn't answer, not wanting to put it into words. She knew, though, and she curled herself beside me.

"You thought that he might be something else? Not my brother?"

I put my arms around her and for a minute she just lay quietly. Her crying stopped and her breathing slowed. At last, in a voice so low I could barely make out the words, she went on.

"It's only in the last week that I've really known what he was planning. When he realized that you knew what it was, he came to me for help. At first I was horribly frightened by the whole terrible idea. He explained it as he saw it. He said it was the only way for our country to gain its real freedom. When I asked about the people who would die if he went through with his plan, he said that even your own nation when it gained its independence had its share of death and suffering. His plan was the only way a small nation could defeat a great and powerful one. He made it sound right, so good and noble and patriotic. These are things I know very little about and if he felt what he was doing was the right thing, then I had to accept his judgment."

"What did he want you to do?"

"Only the things you spoke of. I was ready to do much more, but he wouldn't permit that. Maybe it was because, brilliant though he was, he had oddly old-fashioned ideas about women. If there were risks, he would take them alone. All he would permit me to do was give him the information he needed and my second set of car keys."

"When was this?"

"Last Sunday at my mother's house. He was very worried because you seemed to be anticipating what he might do. He said only a man with intelligence equal to his own could do that. He asked about each of you, but the one he was most interested in was Herbert Klingman."

She was quiet again and then she asked, "What will happen to me now that you know?"

"Nothing, as far as I know."

"You will not report what I've told you?"

"Yes, I'll report it. I have to if I'm going to do the job they pay me for. They're entitled to everything I know."

"And about us? You'll tell them that, too?"

"As much as they need to know."

"What will they do if you tell them we will remain together?"

"I'll be given new duties. Work that is not connected with security."

"You would not like that, would you?"

"It doesn't really matter. You do a job. You draw your pay.

After twenty years you retire, if you like, on half pay."

She fell quiet again and this time I hoped she would sleep.

What woke me next was the breeze that comes just before morning, cool against my side. I knew without reaching out that she wasn't there. I opened my eyes and saw a dim light in her living room. I put my bare feet on the cold floor and went out to look for her.

She was sitting at the table, her back to me, wearing her work clothes and boots. She had rolled her left sleeve back to the shoulder and when I got to her side I saw why.

On the table was a heavy metal canister, its padlock and lid removed, and nested in the padding inside was a single egg. A strip of clear tape hung down from a half-inch hole in the shell. Lying beside the canister was a hypodermic syringe, empty now, a last drop of fluid still clinging to its tip.

I reached down and picked up the needle. She saw me but didn't raise her head. In the crook of her arm was a single bright drop of drying blood.

"If you had slept another minute I would have been gone."

"But why? The FLP, or whatever you want to call it, is dead. It vomited its life into an enamel pan. Is that what you want for yourself?"

"You have to try to understand, Mike. I never knew our father. There have been only two men in my life. Now one is dead and the other I cannot have. Right now you are willing to sacrifice the life you have made for yourself for my sake, but it wouldn't be long before you began to hate me for it. This, at least, is something I can do for him. Finish what he wanted to do."

She stood up and faced me. "Let me go, Mike. Even if I fail, it will not be because I was not willing to try."

"No. It wouldn't work anyway. Even if you had gone before

I woke up I would have assembled the men and gone out to hunt you down. It takes a day or two before you'd become infectious and we'd have found you before then."

I put the lid back on the canister and snapped the padlock.

"Now I'm going in there and get my clothes on. Then we're getting into my car and I'm driving you to Gorgas Hospital. I'll cook up some story about how you came to inject yourself. When you leave the hospital we'll talk about what we're going to do next."

I didn't give her a chance to object or say a word. I went into the bedroom and pulled on my clothes. I had just slid on my shoes when I heard her car engine start. I was up to full running speed when I came through the door, but she had already backed out, and with a crashing of gears, she shot off up the drive.

My car was behind the guesthouse and by the time I reached it hers was already out of sight. I had the keys in my hand and by luck I hit the ignition on the first stab. The car started and I swung out and jammed my foot down on the gas. The dust she'd raised was still thick as I hit top speed, my foot to the floor, braking only for the turn onto the paved road. Far ahead I could see the flash of her headlights on the hillsides and then she hit the long straightaway that would take us past Summit to the junction with the Madden Road.

At the speed I was going, it didn't take long for my heavier car to begin closing the gap. As I went past the entrance to the Gardens I got my first glimpse of her taillights a couple of hundred yards ahead. There was a flash of brighter red as she hit the brakes at the intersection, then swung right toward the downgrade.

I braked, taking longer than she had with my bigger car. It careened as I fought it around the turn and floorboarded again, sure now that on the long straight stretch I could overtake the smaller car. I caught a quick flash of red as she approached the underpass. Her headlights blazed against the solid masonry, stark against the dark green vines. There was a moment of wild careening as her car left the road and hurtled into the embankment with a rending crash of metal. I rammed my foot on the brake, bearing down with all my strength to stop the sedan, yanking on the hand brake to add every last bit of force. The brakes fought against the force of the wheels, producing a piercing scream, the car slewing and careening as it shot through the underpass and came to a halt fifty yards beyond. A cloud of bitter smoke from the seared brakes gushed out in the car's wake. I tore open the door and reached for the extinguisher attached to the fire wall.

My lungs almost bursting, I ran back through the underpass, the extinguisher ready to use before it was too late. The little car must still have had plenty of speed left after it climbed the bank. The oil in the crankcase and the gas in the tank were already ablaze at either end of the wreck, but it was what I saw in the passenger space that stopped me. The blaze there was almost pure white, in contrast with the angry red of the burning oil and gasoline. A thousand extinguishers couldn't have put it out. The last thermite grenade was accounted for.

Potter drove. I sat beside him, with Herbert in the back seat. It had been cloudy when we packed up to leave the field station and now the overcast was building up, the ceiling dropping lower and lower as we traveled the road we'd covered so many times. When Potter slowed for the intersection and turned south I closed my eyes, but it didn't help.

I could still see the underpass, the seared trees and the mangled remains of the little car. It would have been hauled away, and in a few months the burned underbrush and vines would grow and cover the last traces of the twin gouges the wheels had torn into the soft earth of the bank. It would take a little longer for the side of the viaduct to weather away the marks of fire and steel that scored its sides.

Instead I tried to call up the look of her face in the dimness of her bedroom, the white flash of her body as she knifed through the water of the little cove, the soft tone of her voice when we spoke in the night.

I kept my eyes closed until I heard Potter's deep, rich voice. "Look, Captain. It's beginning to rain."

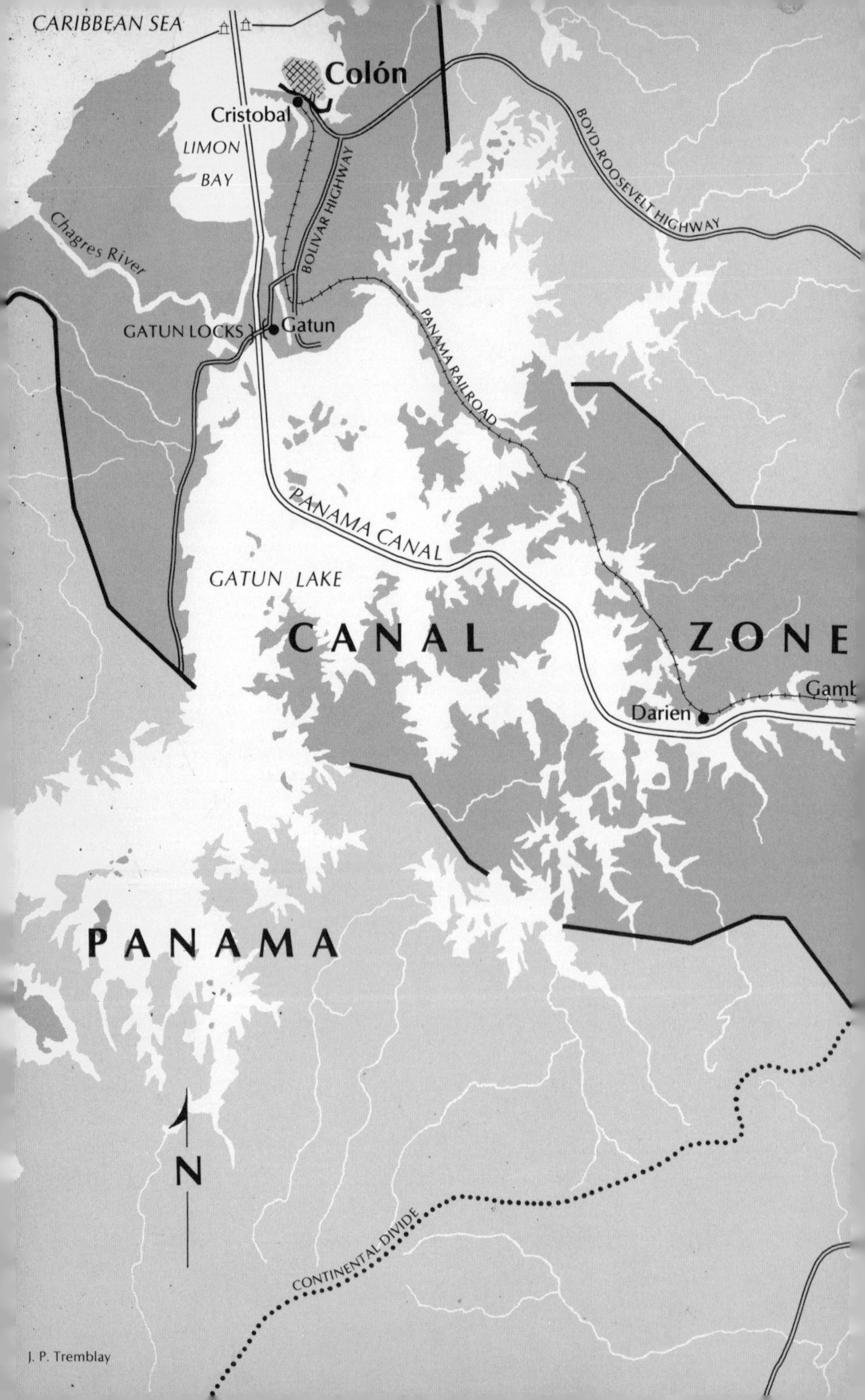
CARIBBEAN SEA
Colón
Cristobal
LIMON
BAY
Chagres River
BOLIVAR HIGHWAY
BOYD-ROOSEVELT HIGHWAY
GATUN LOCKS
Gatun
PANAMA RAILROAD
PANAMA CANAL
GATUN LAKE
CANAL
ZONE
Gamb
Darien
PANAMA
N
CONTINENTAL DIVIDE

J. P. Tremblay